Carol Arens delights in t
characters into hot water,
and then giving them a ha
she's not writing she enjoys spending time with
her family, beach-camping or lounging about in
a mountain cabin. At home, she enjoys playing
with her grandchildren and gardening. During rare
spare moments you will find her snuggled up with
a good book. Carol enjoys hearing from readers at
carolarens@yahoo.com or on Facebook.

THE TRUTH BEHIND THE GOVERNESS

Carol Arens

MILLS & BOON

First published in Great Britain 2024
by Mills & Boon, an imprint of HarperCollins*Publishers* Ltd,
1 London Bridge Street, London, SE1 9GF

www.harpercollins.co.uk

HarperCollins*Publishers*, Macken House, 39/40 Mayor Street Upper, Dublin 1, D01 C9W8, Ireland

The Truth Behind the Governess © 2024 Carol Arens

ISBN: 978-0-263-32091-6

09/24

This book contains FSC™ certified paper
and other controlled sources to ensure responsible forest management.

For more information visit www.harpercollins.co.uk/green.

Printed and Bound in the UK using 100% Renewable Electricity
at CPI Group (UK) Ltd, Croydon, CR0 4YY

This book is dedicated to my dear friends
Sue Bruecker and Teri Feski.

Prologue

Liverpool—
March 1863

An insect, barely seen in the midnight shadow of the porch, skittered across the toe of Clement Marston's boot. He gave it no notice.

It was all he could do to find his next breath. To hold together when all he wanted to do was shatter.

The woman walking behind him was not holding together. Her soft weeping sounded as mournful as the ship's horn wailing in the harbour.

He glanced back over his shoulder at the house they'd walked away from. Saw the light in his sister's chamber window go out.

A fist grabbed his soul, squeezed with no mercy.

Alice Jayne would no longer need the lamp. His sister was dead.

'She is with her husband now,' he murmured, seeking to give and take what comfort was to be had in the thought. Alice Jayne had loved the man against society's approval. Three years past she had run away with her sailor, giving up the title that might have been hers except for love.

'Sir, let me take one of the babies,' the woman sniffled.

'Not yet, Miss Logan.'

His sister's girls were protected from the biting cold and rain under the coat draped over his shoulders. No need to expose them to the elements while walking to the carriage. He could not protect them from the tragedy of losing their mother, but he could protect them from the weather.

Miss Logan climbed into the carriage first, assisted by the driver. Once the nurse was settled he handed her one baby, then the other. The lady cooed over the infants while he settled on the other side of the carriage.

'Oh, Mr Marston.' The nurse, who only days ago had simply been the neighbour across the hallway from Alice Jayne, blinked wet eyes at him. 'What shall become of these sweet children?'

Clement was not certain.

At twenty-one years old he was ill equipped to be a father. But his brothers were even more ill equipped than he was. Duncan, having only recently inherited the title of Baron Granville, lived the loose life of a very wealthy society bachelor. So did his youngest brother, Eldon. Neither of them cared for anything beyond their next secret liaison.

'Your sister was my dearest friend, Sir.' Miss Logan patted the bottom of one blanket, her fingers trembling. 'I would like to ask…may I stay on as their nursemaid?'

He stared blankly at her. The woman was asking him to make a decision about the future of his sister's children as if he was the one in charge. As if he had some sort of plan.

As of two days ago, his plan had been to go to the Isle of Wight and search for insects. It was what entomologists did, discovered interesting things about unusual insects and then published their findings. Their names then became respected by their peers.

A nip of self-pity made him wonder if the ship's wail, mournfully pressing against the windows while the carriage bumped over dock stones, belonged to the ship he had purchased passage on.

It would be at the harbour already, he knew, having planned every detail of the trip with great eagerness. It was to be the first step towards becoming a renowned entomologist. He had long dreamed of finding an insect which was the rarest of the rare.

One of his nieces whimpered. Miss Logan murmured to the baby which seemed to be the signal for the other one to whimper.

He reached across. Miss Logan handed one of the babies over to him.

Feeling sorry for himself was quite unworthy in this moment. It was, however, an easier emotion to cope with than crushing grief.

He had spent several days with his sister while she fought her battle against childbed fever. During it all he had not given a great deal of attention to the infants. Noticing how Miss Logan had cared for them with such devotion, he had asked if she would take the position of nurse until Alice Jayne recovered.

She had not recovered, though, and here the lady sat, waiting for his answer.

'Touch her cheek, she will suck on the tip of your finger, Sir. It helps sometimes.'

For a moment, perhaps. But at some point the girls would need to feed. He assumed Miss Logan had somehow taken care of it during the week since their birth. He had not heard them crying.

Clement touched the soft curve of the baby's cheek. She turned and latched on to his finger with more force than he'd guessed a tiny infant would have. Of course, when it came to infants, guesses were all that he had.

'How did you manage this past week, keeping them fed?'

Miss Logan closed her eyes, biting her lip while she shook her head. 'I do not dare say. If I do, you will send me away and I...' Hugging the baby close to her heart, she rocked it. 'It will break my heart, Sir.'

'Have you recently lost a child, then? Fed these in its place?' It seemed a logical conclusion.

'It is something of the truth, Mr Marston.' It seemed for a moment as if she would not go on, but then she did. 'I did lose a child, but not in the way you think. I was not wed, so...so I could not keep him, not if I wished for him to have a decent life.'

The only sound was of jingling tack and surf breaking against the sea wall while he gathered his wits in the face of her confession.

'I appreciate your forthrightness, Miss Logan. Do not fear that I will judge you. Truly, I am grateful you helped my sister and her children.'

'She was a dear friend to me, your sister. I see her in you, Sir. Both of you the very souls of compassion. But it broke her when her husband's ship went down with all hands lost...only five miles from the harbour, too. A wicked tragedy. All of Liverpool grieved. I wonder if it is why Alice Jayne did not find the strength to rally.'

'If you wish to feed the babies now, I shall look away.'

'Thank you. They are getting restless.'

He looked out of the window, watching the rain streaking through the light of a streetlamp and the dark, vague shapes of masts bobbing in the harbour.

Fabric rustled. 'Here you are, my sweet little dove.'

After a short moment Miss Logan said, 'We are covered up, now.'

All he could see of the child were her booties peeking out from under the blanket draped over Miss Logan's shoulders. She sounded utterly content.

The baby girl in his arms grew ever restless.

Never in his life had he felt as helpless as he did now. 'Did my sister name them?'

He ought to have known a thing like that.

'She would have, but the labour was long and when she was finished, she could not speak much. She held each of her girls, though, kissed them, but then, well… she did not know much after that.'

Such was her state when he arrived. He hoped his sister had felt him at her bedside, but could not be certain. The doctor had encouraged him to speak to her as if she might rally and answer. Still, they had both understood there was little hope she would survive.

'We shall call this one Alice, then.' He bent his head, kissed Alice on her smooth forehead. 'And her sister shall be Jayne.'

'Oh, Sir! Named for their mother! That is lovely.' Miss Logan began a new bout of sniffling.

He would join her in it, but he had decisions to make.

The first was leaving Liverpool for the family home in London…and then shortly after that, leaving London.

They exchanged babies so Alice could feed.

With neither him nor Miss Logan having anything further to say, the echo of his sister's last breath consumed him.

But, no...he must think ahead. Looking back only dragged one down into a pit of grief which was difficult to climb out of. He knew that well since it had been little more than two years since he and his brothers had lost their parents.

'I shall purchase a home in the country. Will you come and help me care for the children?'

'Oh, yes! You are a saint to take them...and me.'

He was not. Only a grieving brother. And a man without the future he had dreamed of.

Then he heard a sound, one he had never heard before. Contented coos and sighs issued from under the blanket draped over Miss Logan. Somehow it managed to poke a pinhole in his grief. As small as it was, it allowed a frizzle of hope in.

Life would be different than he'd pictured it, but it would be a life, just the same.

'Perhaps, Miss Logan, we will manage.'

Chapter One

Whisper Glen, Cheshire—
June 1873

Lady Vivienne Curtis tucked this week's publication of *Whispering Times* under her arm, then set her camera on top of a waist-high tree stump. There was a particularly lovely bird who had perched in this very spot for three days in a row.

Sadly, photographing birds was ever so much more difficult than she'd thought it would be. Birds were quick, her camera was not. Perhaps she should develop a passion for photographing fruit baskets.

So far all she had managed to capture on the camera's glass plates was a blur which no one would guess had been a bird.

Still, the odds of capturing an image would be better here at her Great-Aunt Anne's estate than at home in London. The woods surrounding the manor house were alive with flitting feathered creatures.

Hopefully by the end of the family's week-long visit she'd have managed to take a few photographs.

There was a bush growing beside the stump which would make an adequate hiding place, being large and dense. She did not mind that it was somewhat scratchy because one expected a bit of discomfort while lying in wait.

Vivienne had a dream for her future, not that it mattered. She was as likely to obtain it as she was to get a bird to remain still for long enough while she took its photo. She might take a hundred of the most beautiful avian images anyone had ever seen and, still, no dream would come true for her.

Lady Vivienne Louise Curtis, daughter of the Marquess of Helmond, was destined for a prestigious marriage. Never, ever, in a million years, not for all her hoping and wishing, would she ever be the proprietress of a quaint little shop where she would sell her photos to admiring patrons.

Once she wed, her husband might forbid her to even go exploring with her camera. The day she wed, she would be chained to her new title. She could nearly hear the links clanking while huddling here in the shrubbery.

The very reason she and her parents were visiting Cheshire was to make a betrothal arrangement with Everett Parker, Marquess of Winterfeld, Great-Aunt Anne's stepson from her second marriage.

He was acceptable in every way...her father's equal in society, a widower with no children and a gentleman in behaviour as well as title.

Vivienne knew all this since she had been acquainted with Everett all of her life. She could not recall a time when he was not nearly a part of the family. She recalled being a small girl and chasing her puppy about the skirts of Lady Winterfeld's elegant wedding gown.

Everett had loved his wife deeply. The whole family had grieved when she'd died three years ago.

And now Vivienne was being pressed to wed him.

'Oh, feathers,' she mumbled, then opened *Whispering Times*, seeking a distraction from her thoughts while she waited for the bird. 'I must marry someone.'

If she did not choose Everett Parker, she might end up with a stranger who turned out to be a wastrel who would leave her in poverty. Or a cad who would crush her soul.

It wasn't as if she had not seen that happen to a friend or two. What she'd learned was that it was best to put off marriage for as long as one could. Knowing a man for a long time before committing one's future to him was wise.

She had known the Marquess for ever. If she agreed to wed him, it would make her parents happy.

In the past it had been Grace, her obedient sister, making them proud. Vivienne had been the one causing problems with her uncommon opinion on what made a lady content. She wouldn't mind being their angelic child for a time.

She yawned, read for a moment and then gazed through the branches at a pond glittering in sunlight. There were benches placed at the water's edge which looked quite inviting.

Since there was no chance of getting the image of a bird from the comfort of a bench, she sighed and settled in for a long prickly sit and returned her attention to the news of Whisper Glen.

This was a quiet village, though, and there was nothing overly dramatic to read about. There was a man seeking a governess, one who was willing to travel to bucolic areas and care for a pair of ten-year-old girls.

Bucolic? It sounded charming.

'Lucky woman...' she mumbled. To be paid to travel? And all the lady needed to do in return was play with ten-year-old girls? 'I would do it in a moment, if only...'

A whir of wings stirred the branches overhead. Apparently her bird had arrived, but now her attention was diverted because...why couldn't she be a governess who was willing to travel?

While she had never been a governess, she and her sister had bedevilled several of them while growing up. Indeed, having been a ten-year-old girl and having had governesses, she felt strongly that she would be qualified for the position. She could speak French. Sing in it, too, while plunking at piano keys. She was better at the harp and could teach her charges if the need arose.

While the bird chirruped Vivienne imagined herself on a great adventure, taking photos of all manner of fascinating things. Looked at in the right light, she had more to offer the children than merely instruction in ladylike behaviour. Wouldn't it be grand if she introduced them to the joy of capturing a moment in time on a glass plate?

A sudden movement made the bird take flight. Someone walked by at the edge of the pond. He sat on a bench. Ah, it was the widowed Marquess, Everett Parker.

He gazed at the water for a moment, then bent his head, folded his arms across his chest and crossed his long legs at the ankle. The poor man looked lonely. Would she make him happier if she allowed him to offer for her? Or would he recognise her reluctance to wed and feel bad for it?

Great-Aunt Anne, whom they both adored, had convinced Everett that he must find love again…and that he could find it with Vivienne if he looked hard enough. Seeing him now, Vivienne thought he had little hope of finding love again. Having loved his first wife so deeply, would he even be able to love another?

If he did propose to her, it would only be to make

his stepmother happy. The same as her reason for accepting him, to make her parents happy. She must marry someone. He must marry someone. A man of his station was rather obliged to wed again. He was her father's age, yes, but not ancient. There was still time for him to produce an heir.

Being stabbed with an idea, she stood suddenly from the bush, picked up her camera and tucked it under her arm along with the newspaper.

'Good day, Mr Parker.' She called him Mr Parker because it was what she had always called him.

Ordinarily she would not sit on a bench with a man and begin a conversation—however, they were not strangers and there were things which must be said between them.

'Good day, Vivienne.' He called her that because he had done so since she was a child when he used to pat her on the head. 'Did you just pop up out of that bush?'

'Indeed, yes, I was...trying to get a photograph of a bird.'

'Rather quick creatures to be preserved on a glass plate, I would imagine.'

She sat down, putting the camera next to her, but pressing the newspaper to her bosom.

'It is incredibly discouraging.'

Small talk would not get them to the point of her sitting here so she pressed on. 'I assume you know why my family has come to visit your stepmother at the very same time you are also visiting her?'

If he was surprised by the blunt question, it did not show in his expression. He continued to smile at her.

'I do, of course. Tell me, though...do you not consider me too old for you?

She looked at him in a way she had never done before. As a friend of her father's, she had not paid a great deal of attention to him in the light of marriage.

Lord Winterfeld had deep lines etched at the corners of his eyes, put there by sadness, she supposed. The hair at his temples was beginning to turn grey, the same as Father's was.

'You do not seem so terribly old,' she said, trying to put him at ease over the great difference in their ages. 'But you must still see me running about in pigtails.'

'I will admit, I barely recall you from that time, Vivienne. When you were in pigtails I was a newly-wed and my attention was only on my bride.'

'I am truly sorry for your loss. I cannot imagine how awful it must have been.'

A butterfly flitted about their heads. Everett reached a finger towards it, smiling.

'Pretty thing,' he said.

'The wings are pretty, but the rest of it is just an insect. I dislike insects.' Wicked nasty creatures which managed to creep into spaces they had no business creeping into and then springing out to startle one.

'Do you dislike me?' he asked.

Although the question seemed quite sudden, if there was ever a time to be forthright it was now.

'You mean as a husband, I assume?'

He nodded, gazing at the rippling surface of the pond. 'I would rather know it now if you do.'

'I do not dislike you in the least. But to be honest, if I had my way, I would not marry at all. I would open a little shop and...but never mind. As you know, I must wed for the good of the family name. Same as you must do. My parents will be happy at least, you know that. And Great-Aunt will be delirious with joy. She has strongly hinted at a union between us for some time now.'

He took a deep breath. 'May I speak with your father, then?'

With the briefest hesitation she answered, 'I believe it is for the best...only, before you do, may I ask that you indulge me in one small matter?'

'But of course, my dear.' His tone felt very much as if, once again, he was reaching out of the past and patting her on the head.

'My sister and her husband are going on holiday to the Continent for the summer. I would like to go with them. I ask that we make the announcement of our engagement after I return.'

'Naturally a young woman like you will want a bit of freedom before she settles down to the responsibility of having a household and a husband. I shall speak to your father, my dear, and suggest it is my idea to wait on the formal announcement. He will agree if it comes from me.'

Everett Parker was a good man, one who did not deserve being told a half-truth. A pang of guilt nipped her conscience. It was actually less of a half-truth and more of a complete lie.

'I do thank you.' She rose from the bench, picking up the camera. She had the silliest urge to give him a hug, the same as she would have given her father when he granted her a favour. 'I have business this afternoon in the village, but I shall see you at tea.'

Hurrying away, she clutched the now wrinkled copy of *Whispering Times* to her heart.

With half a stroke of luck, she was about to become a travelling governess for the summer.

Come the autumn, she would settle into her life as an engaged woman, honest in all her dealings.

'What sort of father...?'

Clement watched the latest applicant for governess rise ponderously from the chair across the desk from him, her lips pressed thin, her grimace flat. She shook her head, making her double chin waggle.

'What sort of father, I repeat, allows children to sneak insects into a lady's hat?'

The insect in question—a speckled bush cricket, female and green as clover—scurried across the floor to hide under a basket stuffed with periodicals.

Clement pushed back in his office chair with a resigned but silent sigh. He escorted the woman to the front door, then watched her march down the drive.

Ah well, she would never have suited them anyway. He needed a lady who was fit enough to keep up with Alice and Jayne while they travelled.

He had mentioned travel in his advertisement, but he was certain this candidate had misunderstood the nature of the trip. There would be no luxury accommodations.

Unfortunately she was his last applicant, too. He was starting to despair that his long-dreamed-of trip of exploration would ever happen.

With a sinking heart he pictured the tickets lying on his desk. Four train tickets, four tickets for passage to the Isle of Wight for him, his ten-year-old terrors and the governess he now had little hope of engaging.

No governess, no voyage of adventure.

There was no question of leaving the children behind while he travelled. For his sister's sake, he could not. A stranger, no matter how well intentioned, would not care for the girls with the love a mother would… or, in her place, an uncle.

A movement caught the corner of his eye, drawing his attention to the bridge spanning the stream.

Ah, there those little pixies were, skipping over the

bridge, then dashing off into the woods. Having foiled his attempts to hire a governess, they would be off to celebrate.

He called back the curse making his tongue itch. Fathers did not curse.

If only Miss Logan had not married and gone off to begin a family of her own. The girls had loved their nurse. Apparently they saw the progression of governesses into their lives as intruders. In the three years since Miss Logan had left them, four haggard women had come and gone.

Now, when he needed a governess most, it seemed he would not have her.

Each and every one of the ladies he'd interviewed had fallen victim to his girls' mischief. His daughters, which of course was what they were to him, were highly creative in their pranks. At times he overlooked their antics, admired their ingenuity, even.

This was not one of those times. He set out after the girls. A lecture was called for.

His future as an entomologist was at risk. He was already familiar with every sort of insect inhabiting his own grounds. If he wished to publish his findings and have his name known, he would need to broaden his exploration area.

Since he refused to leave the girls behind, he must have a woman to care for them.

'It is time you learned to behave as young ladies,' he grumbled.

He had one foot on the bridge when he spotted a fascinating spider. He bent to have a closer look, then he heard a voice.

Straightening, he saw a woman coming up the path towards the house in great haste. She pressed her bonnet in place with splayed fingers. Sunny yellow ribbons streamed behind her.

'Oh, please do not say I have come too late.'

Too late for what? he wondered. She was not dressed like any governess he had ever encountered.

But what other reason would there be for her to be dashing up his drive unless it was to apply for the position? While it would have been proper to make an appointment, he was grateful she had not observed the formality.

What a boon! It was as if good fortune had dropped her here at this particular moment when Alice and Jayne were off on their premature celebration. He felt a grin rising. They could not run off a potential governess when they didn't even know she was here. Perhaps he would get the best of those adorable mischief makers this time.

He met the lady halfway up the drive.

'Please say you have not hired another woman in my place,' she said, her breath coming in short gasps because of the run.

In her place? This was encouraging.

'As it happens, I am still interviewing. Please come inside.' They walked back to the house. He ushered her inside, then led her to his study, indicating the chair opposite his at the desk. 'I will send for tea while you catch your breath.'

He hurried to the kitchen and ordered tea to be delivered to his study.

Returning, he found the lady had removed her modest, yet cheerful, hat and placed it on her lap.

Her appearance set her apart from the other women he had interviewed. There was no hint of dowdiness about her. Her gown was sunny...downright cheerful, if perhaps with a few years of wear showing.

Craning her neck this way and that, she gazed at the paintings of rare and beautiful insects hanging on the walls.

'Aren't they marvellous?' he asked, although he was certain anyone would think so.

'Vivid,' she answered cautiously, 'In every detail.'

They were and yet he still had the feeling that she did not appreciate the full beauty of the images.

He sat across from her, settled into his chair and tried not to look desperate. But leaping locusts, just when all had seemed lost, here she was.

First off, he must know what she expected of travelling with him and the girls. If she thought it would be a luxurious excursion, he would lose yet another potential governess.

More than that, though, he would need to be forthcoming about what she would be facing with Alice and Jayne.

It wasn't as if the girls were bad at heart. They were simply sweet, loving children...who were determined not to have a governess.

He, as their father, was even more determined that they would.

Folding his hands on top of the desk, he considered his words while studying this surprising applicant.

She did not resemble a governess, being younger than most and far prettier. Prettier in an uncommon way. She was a moth, he decided, rather than a butterfly. While butterflies were lovely and easily admired, moths were equally beautiful, only in a less flashy way. As far as Clement was concerned, the rosy maple moth was a match for the painted lady butterfly any day...or night, as it were.

This woman, with her rich brown hair and eyes the shade of amber, was a lovely specimen...of woman naturally, not moth. He had to wonder why she was not already wed. She was too young to be considered on the shelf. Why would she be seeking a position and not a husband?

It was not his business, he knew that; it was only

that he was curious. But more than anything he was grateful she wished to apply for the post.

'I am Clement Marston,' he said, eager to get to the point of why she was sitting across from him. The sooner he hired her, the better. He could not be sure when Alice and Jayne would return so it would be prudent to keep the interview brief.

'A pleasure to meet you, Mr Marston. I am Vivienne Curtis.'

'It is lovely to meet you, Miss Curtis,' he replied. 'Thank you for your interest in the position.'

Chapter Two

Vivian hoped her aristocratic position did not show, having gone to some effort to disguise it. She had made sure to bring only older attire with her that she would normally only wear to go photographing birds. Nothing terribly drab, though. She had no wish to become depressed by wearing grey or brown, after all.

Her hair was done simply, without whirls and ribbons. If an acquaintance passed her on the street, she was certain they would not recognise her.

There was not much she could do about her well-bred manner of speech, however. But perhaps Mr Marston would not think much of it. Gently born ladies sometimes fell upon hard times, after all.

'The position sounds a most excellent opportunity.'

Luckily for Vivienne the flustered-looking woman who had charged past her on the road had clearly not thought so. She'd grumbled aloud about the children being a menace.

'Do you have experience with young girls?' Mr Marston asked.

She could hardly admit she had never had the care of a child, but... 'Yes, naturally, I was one myself... and I have a younger sister. I understand very well how their minds work.'

'What an unconventional answer. I've not heard it before.'

'No? I am surprised since it does seem an important aspect of performing the job well. Children must be understood if one is to relate to them. I believe it is important for them to be happy, but at the same time well behaved.' She emphasised that last bit because, according to the woman on the road, they were not. It was something she would need to deal with.

Mr Marston nodded his head ever so slightly.

'But how much actual experience do you have as governess?' he asked curiously. 'You seem rather young to have much.'

She had been raised by nannies and governesses all her life. What better experience could there be? However, once again, she could not tell him that.

'Not as old as some, I will admit. But it has been said that I have a particular affinity with children.'

Perhaps someone had said such a thing at one time. Just because she had never heard it did not mean no one had said it!

She gave him the most utterly charming smile she

knew how to give. No one had ever said she had an utterly charming smile, she would wager, but it could not hurt to try.

Although charming was surely not a qualification for the position, who objected to a dash of congeniality?

'I am well able to instruct the children in reading, writing and arithmetic. I will also teach them to sing songs *en français* if it will amuse them.'

'I wonder...' he murmured thoughtfully, then tapped his fingers on what appeared to be tickets for travel.

'If it is a matter of my letter of reference...' She dug about in the reticule she had put on the floor beside the chair. She handed him an envelope. 'Here you are.'

He opened it then set it on the desk atop the tickets. It seemed to take a lifetime for him to read it. The clock on the wall ticked louder with each long, tense moment.

At last he looked up, nodded. 'It is quite adequate.'

It was not merely adequate, it was positively glowing. She had spent hours writing it last night.

'As you will know from the advertisement, your charges would be my ten-year-old daughters, twins.'

'Yes, what a lovely age.' It would surely not be too difficult to keep them entertained.

She folded her hands primly in her lap so that her nervousness would not show. Getting the position was only one of the challenges she faced. She must also convince her sister and her husband to keep the secret. When they discovered she was not going to the Continent with them, they would likely object...with vigour.

However, her sister had already expressed concerns about her having to marry a man so much older than she was. Grace wished for Vivienne to have all the marital happiness she had found with George. That would go in her favour.

Yes, it was probable that Grace would support her summer of freedom. Her brother-in-law would be the harder one to convince.

'The girls are my late sister's children, but I have raised them since they were infants. I love them, naturally, but at the same time I feel I must advise you that they can get into mischief.'

'Oh, but I am certain they are delightful.' It did not matter if they were delightful or not. She needed to be their governess.

'They have it in them to be and many times they are, but they have run off the candidates I interviewed before you.'

'Fortunate for me, then. I assure you, I shall not be run off.'

'My intention is to spend the summer travelling, which I also mentioned in the advertisement. You will not mind caring for my girls while I explore the wilds? I do not feel comfortable leaving them in Cheshire.'

'The wilds of where, may I ask?' Perhaps birds in

the wild would be more amenable to having their images captured than they were here?

'The Isle of Wight.'

'The Isle of Wight? Where artists, poets and even the Queen go on holiday?'

'The very isle. But we will not be staying where they do, I'm afraid. It is into the less civilised areas for us. I am an entomologist and the island has some of the finest insects a man might find.'

She glanced again at the drawings on wall, trying not to flinch.

It was silly to worry that the insects were going to crawl out of the frames, creep up her stockings, and make her lose her composure during the most important interview of her life.

She knew they would not. Still, logic did little to keep her skin from prickling.

'You dislike insects?' Clement Marston touched his chin, thumb on one side of his jaw and finger crossing the other while he gave her a deep look.

The man had an interesting face. Not quite handsome and yet altogether agreeable. Anyone seeing the smile peeking from behind his hand would have a hard time looking away. It was wide and flat, but then took an amusing upward turn at each corner.

Just now he appeared bemused that she did not share his fondness for creepy crawling creatures.

Since she did need to become the governess to his

lively girls, she smiled and lied once more. 'I adore them, of course. Who does not?'

'You do not.'

'Very well, you have caught me out. But I do adore little girls and it is them I am to care for, is it not?'

If his funny crooked smile was anything to go by, her honest answer satisfied him where her lies had not.

'I shall protect you from insects as best I can, but they do have a way of going wherever they wish to.'

'I shall be—'

Oddly enough, in that very instant she felt something...a tickling sensation on her ankle.

Her imagination. It had to be.

Discreetly, she lifted the hem of her skirt to be certain. To her everlasting horror there was a bright green creature creeping up her stocking! She could hardly scream and dash about the study in an effort to dislodge the small monster, not if she wished to appear stout-hearted enough to perform her duties.

She stood and stamped her foot. The insect hung on, digging its prickly legs into her stocking and climbing ever upwards. Surely this was a nightmare from which she would soon awake!

With each movement of the insect, she lifted her skirt higher, modesty forsaken in the moment. The insect reached her knee and seemed to have no intention of stopping. She spread her fingers to swat it, already dreading the disagreeable green stain sure to ruin her stocking and the sticky guts which would smear her hand.

'No!' Clement Marston leapt over the desk, sliding across the surface, scattering pens and papers. He caught her hand, but not his forward momentum.

She lost her balance and they both went down in a tumble.

'Oof,' he grunted, hitting the floor beside her.

She sat up, shaking out her skirt in search of the horrid insect...or a green smear.

Rather than offering an apology, Mr Marston gave her an astonished-looking frown.

'She is quite harmless, I promise.'

'You are acquainted with it, then?' How could he know the insect would not have bitten her?

'Acquainted with her kind.'

He glanced about, probably looking for a squashed bush cricket. Apparently reassured it had made an escape, he seemed to come to himself and noticed they were sitting on the floor.

'I beg your pardon. Please do forgive me. I confess, I get carried away now and again in my enthusiasm for particularly nice insects.'

It was all she could do not to point out that there were no nice insects.

A pair of reading glasses lay on the floor, cracked across the centre of one lens. They must have slid off the desk in the tumble. He picked them up, holding them up to a beam of sunshine coming through the window.

'Ruined,' he commented. 'But I believe the cricket made it safely away.'

Perhaps she ought to do the same. Unless she missed her guess, his daughters were not the only unruly members of this household.

Imagine putting the well-being of a cricket before her own! It might be that the man needed a governess as much as his daughters did.

Oh, feathers! She would not dismiss this position because of his overreaction to a cricket.

'I accept.'

'My apology...or the offer of employment?'

'The apology since you did not actually offer employment.'

'I was about to when our little miss made her untimely appearance.'

Our little miss? Heaven help her.

He stood, offering a hand.

Although she was capable of rising on her own, she took it.

My word, the man might be studious, but his hand did not indicate it. His fingers were strong and steady, helping her up.

'Miss Curtis, my voyage is for next week. I confess, I am desperate for a willing woman.' All at once he seemed to realise his questionable wording for lines suddenly creased his brow. 'For a governess, of course. Please tell me you accept the position.'

'I do accept, but there is a condition to it.' It would be unfair to carry on and not admit her limitation. She must bear in mind her promise to Everett. 'I can only give you the summer. After that I have another engagement I must fulfil.'

'I will gladly take whatever time you can give me.' Hmm, the man had interesting gold flecks in his green eyes. They were probably not glowing in relief, but it seemed so to her. 'Thank you, Miss Curtis. And I promise I will never put a insect's well-being over yours again.'

While his flat, turned-up-at-the-corners grin was not the polished smile of a society gentleman, she found it appealing...genuine rather than practised.

Genuinely confounding, too. Why would looking at his smile make her insides flutter in such a curious way? She had read of such feelings, naturally, but she had never experienced the sensation.

She was not certain she approved of it. The man was her employer, not her... Oh, dear, never mind that.

Three days before the ship was to set sail for the Isle of Wight, Vivienne stood at the head of the lane leading to the Marston home, waving farewell to Grace and George. She felt more than a bit victorious, having only just won a skirmish which, had she lost, would have ruined everything.

It had been a victory of the highest order convincing her sister and her husband to drop her off at the lane while they continued on with their holiday. They had objected, naturally, but Vivienne had been prepared to counter each protestation.

Although Grace had been stunned by what Vivienne was doing, it had not been so difficult to win her over. She and her sister had always been allies. As different as apples and oranges, but they always took one another's side.

'Your parents have entrusted you to my care and in it you shall remain,' her brother-in-law had argued.

To that, she crossed her arms over her bosom and shook her head. 'I take myself out of your care.'

'You are to be married. You cannot become a governess,' again from George.

'I already am a governess,' she parried.

'George, my dear. Surely you understand Vivienne's predicament? Would you not wish for a final summer's adventure if you were in her position?'

'I am a man. It is expected that we will have adventures before we wed.'

'Oh, indeed? And you had such an adventure?'

'Well, I… I did not.'

'Nor were you forced into a loveless marriage, George. Vivienne will have this time to herself before she commits her life to Everett.' George, clearly not convinced, shook his head at his wife. She patted his cheek as if dismissing his concern, then she gave her attention back to Vivienne. 'There is one thing, though. Our parents will worry.'

It wasn't as if she had not already considered that.

'It is why you must keep my secret.' Vivienne handed her sister a stack of letters she had written, to be mailed at different points of the Continental holiday.

'Think of it, George,' she said coaxingly. 'You and my sister will have a far better time without me.'

The glance George briefly shot at his wife, the smile lurking at the corners of his mouth, told her she had scored in her favour with that observation.

Still not convinced he should allow it, she and George had gone around and around while bumping along the country road.

Then Grace brought an end to it.

'We will keep your secret.' Grace gave her husband a look, one which Vivienne had seen her mother use on their father. 'We will, won't we, George?'

'While I do not condone this, yes, I will do as your sister asks.'

At last they had reached the point where the lane leading to the Marston home cut off from the main road.

With a bit more grumbling, George ordered the carriage to stop.

Then there had ensued another discussion because, no, George could not drop her off in front of the house. Nor could he meet her employer to judge his character and intentions.

Mr Marston was unaware of her being the daughter of a marquess and if he knew, she would very likely lose her position. Ladies of her station did not seek employment.

Ten minutes had passed while Vivienne argued in favour of her employer's sterling character, which she actually believed to be true.

Finally bidding them goodbye, she had bestowed on them kisses and her good wishes for their trip...along with her promise to be home at summer's end to announce her engagement. With the experience of a lifetime ready to begin, she sat upon the lid of her trunk to gather her thoughts and calm her nerves.

This quiet moment to savour the coming adventure was lovely. Fresh air, warm and fragrant with jasmine, washed over her. She glanced about, curious to know where it was growing. With the woods being so dense, she could not spot it.

Some people might think it rash to go away with a man she had only met one time. Those people would be correct. It was why she had gone to the village of Whisper Glen to discreetly discover what his neighbours thought of him.

She'd learned that Clement Marston was the son

of one Baron Granville. More than one person had pointed out that the baronetcy was very wealthy. The Honourable Mr Marston had an older brother who was now Baron and had recently married. He also had a younger brother who had not yet settled down. She already knew of the late sister whose daughters she was to care for.

Most importantly, she had learned that everyone thought highly of Clement Marston. He was considered a good neighbour and a man who loved his children.

She'd sensed this about him from their first meeting.

What she also knew of him from that one meeting was that, upon occasion, he valued insects at the cost of good sense…that he was studious, but not soft. Apparently the quest for interesting specimens kept him robust. He probably wore those dark-framed glasses, although she hadn't seen him use them before the lenses cracked.

He had a goal for his life. She envied him the freedom to pursue it. What impressed her most about him was that he not leaving his children behind while he travelled. It indicated a great deal of devotion to them, no matter if he was called uncle or father. She admired him greatly for it.

Although she was no longer under George's protection, she had every confidence that she would come to no harm while she was with Clement Marston.

An out-of-place noise rallied her from her thoughts. Vivienne had spent enough time in the woods of Cheshire over the past weeks, listening to bird calls and other natural sounds, to recognise when something was amiss.

She stood, stretched, giving every impression of being unaware of giggles and whispering from the woods. Unless she missed her guess, she was about to become acquainted with Alice and Jayne. Given that they had done their best to make their prior governesses leave, there was no reason for them to think they would not do the same to her.

Vivienne Curtis, they were about to learn, was one governess who would not fall prey to impish shenanigans. In expectation of battle, Vivienne had packed her weapons...lemon drops and peppermint sticks. She lifted the lid of the trunk, drew out the bag of sweets and slipped it into her skirt pocket.

Armed, she set off down the pretty lane. Strolling in the dappled sunshine of the leafy canopy overhead, she watched for interesting birds and listened to brush being crunched on either side of the path.

The girls did not seem to be terribly accomplished in stealthy tactics. Of course, they were only ten years old. Vivienne, on the other hand was twenty-four and, as a lady negotiating society, had learned to be wily. Somewhere along this path the children would have laid a trap. Very likely it was something which would antagonise, but not cause harm. Only a little something to convince her they were not worth the trouble. How wrong they were. Given what she was getting in return, they were more than worth it.

She glanced above, scanning the branches for something which might spill down upon her. Nothing there, which was a relief. Children should not lay traps in tree branches, no matter what fun it might be. When it came to a contest between gravity and growing bones, gravity often won.

Moments later the footsteps stopped. This might mean the trap was nearby and they were waiting for her to fall into it. Ah, just ahead the ground looked disturbed. Leaves and twigs covered a shallow depression in the centre of the path.

Stepping to the very edge, she noticed a hidden mud puddle. Lifting her foot, she gave every indication that she would step into it. From each side of the path she heard excited gasps. Lovely. She held her foot above the trap for an exaggerated instant, then drew it back and stepped around the puddle.

To the left of the lane was a fallen tree. Using it as a bench, she sat down on the trunk and gave her skirt a fluff while giving thought to which weapon to unsheathe.

Peppermint. It was more easily seen than a lemon drop.

She withdrew the bag, setting it on her lap. Taking her time, she took out a stick, unwrapped it, then licked it with a sigh of delight.

'Please do come out of hiding, girls. Your scheme has failed.'

No response. Not that she had expected them to emerge at once.

'As you wish.' She let the statement stand for a moment and then, 'I offer you one of two outcomes. The first is that I will step in your puddle, jump about quite madly just to make sure my skirt and shoes are ruined. Then you may face whatever punishment your father sees fit to dole out. But you will have achieved your end.'

Silent for a moment, she let the thought settle.

'The other outcome is that you come out of hiding and join me for a treat. I have lemon drops and peppermint sticks. We will become acquainted one way or another. How we go about that is up to you.'

A little girl with a pair of sunshine-blonde braids draping her shoulders stepped out from behind a tree. She frowned at Vivienne with deep brown eyes.

'Are you Jayne or Alice?'

'Jayne.'

The other little girl came out of hiding. She was taller than her sister and also had blonde hair, but on the reddish side. She wore it in one braid down her back. Her eyes were identical to her sister's in colour and shape.

'I am Alice.'

'It is a pleasure to meet you both.' She patted the log in invitation. Hesitantly, they came forward, then sat beside her, one on each side.

What pretty children they were. Time spent outdoors had given their skin a healthy blush. Both of them had a dappling of freckles across their noses and cheeks.

'Which confectionary do you prefer, Jayne?' she asked the child who had called herself Alice. 'And you, Alice. Lemon or peppermint?'

They glanced at one another as if stunned that she had figured them out. Poor babies were not nearly as crafty as they thought they were. It took all Vivienne had not to smile.

Alice chose the peppermint sticks and Jayne chose lemon drops.

'I am Miss Curtis. Given the manner in which you greeted me, I assume you knew it already.'

They sucked on their sweets without answering.

'I will admit, it was a creative trap.'

'Thank you, Miss Curtis,' Jayne said.

'I might have fallen for it if I had not known beforehand that you have undertaken such pranks before.'

The girls exchanged some sort of message with their eyes.

Vivienne smiled, liking them right off even knowing they were not ready to accept her...not yet. They would in time, she meant to see to it.

While it was true that the reason she had sought

the position was to have a summer of adventure before she wed, she took her responsibilities to Alice and Jayne to heart.

'I do not believe that you are finished trying to get rid of me, just as you did my predecessors.' She nodded and smiled at Jayne, then to Alice. 'Please understand, though, I will not be driven away.'

Apparently they were not accustomed to having their mischievous intentions exposed so bluntly. They gave her wide, matching blinks.

'Come now, ladies, shall we let your father know I have arrived unscathed?'

Alice giggled, but probably by accident since she clapped her slender fingers over her mouth.

Clement looked up from the notes that he was jotting down regarding the newly hatched damselfly he had come across early this morning.

He glanced at the clock hanging on the study wall. Oh, curse it! It was nearly three in the afternoon! It was past time for Miss Curtis to arrive. He had meant to meet her at the end of the lane and walk her up to the house…to get to her before Alice and Jayne did.

Miss Curtis had assured him she would not quit her post, that she understood a young girl's mind, but she had yet to meet her charges. He had hoped to guide their first meeting, make sure it was without incident.

Dropping his pencil on top of his notes, he dashed out of the room and through the house. Out on the porch, he came up short. It could not be, but he was witnessing the sight firsthand.

There was Miss Curtis, flanked by his daughters… the three of them contently sucking on…sweets? No one was muddied. Miss Curtis did not appear to have insects in her hair or on her hat, praise the Good Lord for it.

'Good afternoon, Papa.' Alice said, her sunny braids swinging while she walked. 'You were late for meeting Miss Curtis so we did it for you.'

He gave them all a glance over. No one seemed the worse for it.

'Sometimes Papa forgets the time if there is an insect involved,' Jayne explained.

'I apologise, Miss Curtis, I ought to have been there to greet you.'

'What was it, Papa? A butterfly or a beetle? Please say it was a stag beetle!' Of the two girls, Jayne was the one who shared his interest in insects.

'An azure damselfly. I spotted it quite by accident near the stream. Unexpected discoveries are the best, Miss Curtis. It never fails to prove true.'

It was how he felt about the new governess. Just when he had all but given up hope, there she had been, as pretty as said damselfly while she'd hurried up his drive.

For an instant he'd had the sensation of delicate wings batting about in his chest. It was a distinctly odd reaction to seeing a pretty face. Not that prettiness mattered, only that she had been hurrying up the drive and eager to be hired.

Now, seeing her standing in front of the house, a peppermint stick pressed to her lips, he could scarcely believe his good fortune. For the moment his daughters seemed accepting of her, but it might be because of the sticky sugar smearing their mouths.

'Where are your belongings, Miss Curtis?' Why hadn't the hired hack delivered her and her things to the front door?

'I had the driver leave my trunk at the entry to the lane. It is such a lovely day I wanted to walk.'

That made sense. It boded well for their excursion that she enjoyed walking and being outdoors. They would be spending a great deal of time in the open air. He wanted the girls to learn their lessons and sing in French, but not to the exclusion of fresh air and sunshine.

'Alice, dear, please run and ask Mr Chambers to bring the trunk to the house.' He tugged on both of her braids which was a special sign of affection between them.

Alice skipped away, braids swinging across her back.

'Jayne, love, let Mrs Simmons know that your governess has arrived. We shall have refreshments outside.'

Jayne stepped on top of his shoes and gave him a

hug around the middle. This was their special sign of affection.

Clement wondered if he had thanked Miss Curtis heartily enough. For as much as this trip meant to him, he could not possibly leave his daughters behind. He knew parents who had no qualms about leaving children in the care of others while they travelled. His own parents had done so often. As far as Clement was concerned, the whole family had suffered because of their absence.

Perhaps had they not been gone so often, his sister would not have been as in need of affection as she was. She might have been more selective about whom she fell in love with and married. Everything might have been different.

One thing was certain—her children would never feel such a lack of affection. He loved them and would make sure they knew it.

'We shall go to Liverpool tomorrow,' he said while escorting Miss Curtis into the house. 'The day after, our ship will sail on the first tide. Will that be suitable?'

He could not imagine what he would do if it was not.

'Quite suitable. I look forward to it.' And then, to his everlasting relief, she added, 'Alice and Jayne are endearing girls. I look forward to getting to know them better.'

'You do?' She did?

'But of course.'

Since Miss Logan, no governess had said such a thing. Oddly enough, he believed her. There was no indication of insincerity in her eyes, no hint of it in her smile.

'I believe we are off to a brilliant start,' he said.

What he didn't say was that her presence was a gift, as if she'd been magically dropped from the sky. It was not true, of course. He had placed an advertisement and she had answered it. Still, it must be more than co-incidence that a lady who thought his daughters were endearing had shown up in in his moment of need.

Vivienne was still awake long after anyone else in the household had fallen asleep. Even if she had not been too excited to sleep, she was in a new home in a strange bedroom.

The window was cracked an inch which let in all sorts of night sounds that she was not accustomed to. Insects, she imagined, singing their odd songs to one another. Crossing the room, she closed the window. Ah, that was much better.

Now that she was no longer concerned about what the strange clicking sound near the windowsill had been, she could think about what was uppermost in her mind.

Being a governess. She had an employer who counted on her to teach and guide his lively daughters. At the same time, those lively daughters would resist her attempts to teach and guide. She would need a few weapons in her arsenal which did not involve confectionery.

Books...that was what she needed. She wondered if Mr Marston had already packed them or if he meant for her to do it. Better to be prepared, she decided. A visit to Mr Marston's library was called for.

First, though, she sat on a chair, then took off her shoes and stockings. Giving her toes a good stretch, she sighed. This was one of life's delightful pleasures after a long, busy day. She plucked the pins from her hair, not quite certain how she would get it up again without her maid to do it.

A matter to deal with tomorrow, she decided. To-night she must live up to her duty as a governess, even though she was not quite confident of all it would entail. Books, though—any governess she'd ever had carried one under her arm as a part of her attire.

Leaving her chamber, she walked down a long hallway, her bare feet silent on the polished floor. She remembered the way since her employer had given her a tour of his large, yet comfortable, home after dinner.

The only lamp still burning came from under Clement Marston's chamber door. He must be working late on his research. Would he be trying to peer though his broken spectacles or had he another pair? Although it was not his spectacles she was dwelling on as much as his eyes.

They were interesting eyes. Studious, to be sure, but she thought there were brief hints of humour in them, too. Mostly they reflected devotion to the children he quite clearly adored. Not quite green, not quite brown...yes indeed, he had very nice eyes.

Feathers, who was she to be noticing his attractive qualities? His governess, that was all...and a woman who was to become engaged at the end of the summer!

Around a corner, then down a hallway, she came to the door of the room she recalled being the library. The hinges squealed when she pushed it open. It was a lucky thing that the moon was bright since it was the only light in the room. She spotted a lamp on a corner table and struck a match to it.

The book-lined walls came to life with a golden glow. This was far more inviting than the library at home. It was cosy, whereas at Helmond House the library was vast. This place called for a person to sit and live within the pages of a book. Helmond's library was meant to impress guests.

She scanned the shelves, wondering what books she ought to bring to the Isle of Wight. There was great variety in the volumes. She picked a few on arithmetic and history. There were dozens on geography, so she took down a few of those, too. Best of all, she discovered several volumes of fiction she could read with them. Adventure was the very thing which would appeal to her charges, she thought.

There was a book on the shelf near the ceiling which had an interesting binding. In the dim light she could not read the title so she slid the library ladder over, then climbed up to look at what it was.

'*The Fascinating Life of Queen Bees and Drones,*' she read aloud. 'Hmm, what can be so fascinating about a bee?'

'Few insects are more interesting than bees, Miss Curtis.'

The voice coming out of nowhere gave her a start. Her balance wobbled. The book hit the floor with a hard thud. She would have ended up on the floor beside the book except that Clement Marston grabbed her knee, steadying her. With a gasp she clasped the ladder rail, clinging tight.

'I beg your pardon. I did not mean to startle you.'

She started down the ladder.

No man had ever touched her knee and Mr Marston had only done so to keep her from falling. She should read nothing into her reaction to his touch or the pressure of his strong fingers. No doubt the true reason her heart had skipped and stuttered was because she'd nearly fallen.

Or because she'd suddenly realised that from where he stood his gaze would be at the level of her bare feet. What a mortifying way to begin her employment.

'I was looking for books to bring to the Isle.' Hopefully he did not think she was snooping. 'To instruct the children.'

The man did not speak for a moment. He simply stared at her hair as if he had never seen unbound hair before.

If he felt uncomfortable, she was more so. Outside of her family no one had seen her hair unbound. This whole encounter left her disconcerted.

Why had she not remained sensibly in her room?

Then he blinked and gave her his wide, congenial smile which made her feel slightly less flustered.

'Ah, I am ashamed to say I did not think of bringing along any books. But Alice and Jayne will need them, won't they?'

'Books are the tools of a governess,' she announced as if she knew it from vast experience in the profession.

'Let me help you, then.'

With her hair loose and her feet bare? It would not do.

'I shall manage. It is what you hired me to do, after all.'

'Very well, just put the books you choose on the sofa and I will have them packed into a trunk in the morning. I do not know if I made it clear how grateful I am that you accepted this position. I had all but given up on my girls having proper guidance and instruction over the summer. I am relieved to know they will be well tended.' He held her gaze for an instant longer. She held his in return because…well, what was that expression? Recognition of her as a woman?

Certainly not! More likely he was making a valiant effort not to look down at her toes.

'Good night then, Miss Curtis,' he said at last.

'Good night, Mr Marston.'

With a nod, he turned to walk out of the library. She noticed that he had a smudge of ink on his thumb. So she was right about him being up late doing his research.

Once she had picked her books and stacked them on the sofa, she went back to her chamber. Not to sleep though. She would spend the hours until dawn remembering everything that her governess had ever said or done.

Or, she would be awake, recalling how her employer's hand felt bracing her knee. How his touch had been enticing and flustering all at once…

Chapter Three

The only one of them to have survived the ferry crossing in good humour was Clement Feodore Marston.

How the man could be grinning with rain pouring off the brim of his hat, while accompanying three females who had not done well with the rough seas, was a mystery Vivienne would never understand.

'Nearly there,' he announced, doing his best to steady an umbrella over the girls' heads. With the wind wild and contrary, it was a useless effort.

Alice was not likely to notice the rain, being as sick to her stomach as she was. Stepping off the ferry had done nothing to improve her condition. Vivienne and Jayne were queasy, but not as wretched as poor Alice was.

Through the dim light of late afternoon, made gloomier by the storm, Mr Marston pointed towards an inn. Please let it be the one he had reserved rooms in.

'It looks charming,' he announced cheerily. She

wondered if he genuinely felt cheery or was just putting on a brave front for their sakes.

As far as Vivienne was concerned, any place with a warming fire and a solid roof would be paradise.

'Look, Alice,' she said, giving the little girl's hand a squeeze. 'Isn't it pretty?'

Alice gagged so they stopped for a moment, getting ever wetter while the child gathered herself.

Vivienne wished the inn was not so far from the nearest village. She had never been anywhere quite so remote. In the beginning it had felt civilised enough, but then the road had turned slick. The hired carriage had been forced to stop a quarter of a mile from their destination.

The driver had promised to return with their belongings as soon as the weather cleared, but for now they trudged along with only what they were wearing and an umbrella bent at odd angles by the wind. Vivienne reminded herself that she had come for adventure and this would certainly count as one.

Well…it would if Alice was not feeling quite so wretched.

Approaching the inn's drive, she heard surf crashing on a beach, but with clouds pressing close she couldn't see it.

Clement was correct about the place being charming. White paint made it stand aglow against the weather pressing on all sides. Smoke rose from several chimneys and seemed to wave a welcome.

'I am assured the food is excellent,' her employer declared.

Not the most excellent news for the three of them suffering the lingering symptoms of seasickness. He might as well have announced that the beds were damp for all the better it made them feel.

Coming up the front porch steps, Vivienne glanced though a large window draped with lace curtains. She spotted a fireplace with a wonderful snapping fire. A woman sat in a rocking chair beside it, knitting.

Mr Marston rapped twice on the door, then opened it and waited while the three of them filed in past him.

The lady in the chair rose at once and hurried towards them. Her steps were quick given her short, round stature. She patted her grey hair as if to be sure the neat bun was presentable.

'Mr Marston, I assume?' Her welcoming smile did as much to warm the room as the fire did. 'I was afraid the weather would delay your arrival.'

Vivienne had an urge to embrace their hostess because of her resemblance to Great-Aunt Anne.

'It has delayed our luggage, Mrs Prentis, but here we are, no worse for the wear.'

No worse for the wear? Her employer did not see things as they were. Was he always so optimistic in the face of adversity? Or did he simply thrive in the face of it? As admirable an attitude as it was, it was a little hard to take right now. Alice was not thriving in the face of adversity. Judging by her expression, it would be a wonder if she ever ate again.

'Come directly to your rooms, my dears. Mr Prentis has already laid the fires in the event you made it through.'

A room and a fire. Nothing had ever sounded so inviting. The four of them followed her up the staircase to the third storey of the house.

'This room is for you, Mr Marston,' their hostess announced, opening the door to an elegantly appointed chamber with a large bed. It was appropriate for the brother of a baron.

The next door the lady opened had two beds.

'This is for you, my sweet young ladies.'

The room looked perfect for little girls. There were a pair of yellow rugs on the floor. On the wall was a mural of dainty blue flower bouquets with images of frolicking puppies scattered among the blooms.

Vivienne followed the girls inside, noticing that they were beginning to shiver.

'The doors at each end of this room connect all three. The room at this end is yours, Miss Curtis.'

Mrs Prentis opened the connecting door, indicating that she should go inside. 'I thought that you would enjoy a private space of your own so that you can shut the door on your charges when you wish to.'

Bless the woman. Perhaps she should hug her even if she was not Great-Aunt Anne.

A room in Buckingham Palace might not be as welcome as this small, warm space with its plush-looking bed. It did not matter that it was not as finely appointed as the other two rooms. She was the governess, after all, not Lady Vivienne. The truth was she would be blissfully comfortable in this snug chamber.

Leading Vivienne back into the children's chamber, the lady gave a look around, seeming to assure herself that all was as it should be.

'Now, sit and warm yourselves. I shall have Mr Prentis rummage about the attic for dry clothes. Dinner will be served in the dining room in an hour.'

With her guests' immediate needs settled, Mrs Prentis hustled out of the room, her skirts bouncing about her round hips.

Vivienne swung her gaze to her employer, surprised to see him frowning. As soon as he noticed her attention on him, he smiled.

'Well then,' he said, 'I shall collect you for dinner in an hour.'

As soon as his door closed, Vivienne began removing her charges' wet clothing. Pink and bare, she had them sit on the rug in front of the fireplace. She plucked blankets from the beds and draped them over the girls, tent style, until all that showed of them was hair, eyes and noses.

'There now,' she declared with a bright smile meant to rally their spirits. 'Dry clothes will be here in no time at all. We shall feel better once we have eaten.'

Vivienne's appetite was returning and Jayne's colour was looking better. Still, it would probably still be some time before Alice would eat.

'Miss Curtis,' Alice said, giving her an odd look. 'I am sorry I plucked the feather from that woman's hat on the train. I only thought it was unkind that she had it and not the bluebird it came from.'

Alice was quite correct about where the feather belonged, which in no way excused the child's behaviour. As their governess, it was up to Vivienne to enforce proper standards. Whether she agreed with them was neither here nor there.

'It is good that you recognise your mistake. I trust you will not repeat it.'

'Yes, Miss Curtis.'

Not exactly a promise of good behaviour in the future. Still, Alice had apologised for her crime and done it without being coaxed. While she had been contrite about that particular misdeed, there had been others.

The train ride had been stressful with hours upon hours of being tested by the girls. Sadly, as an inexperienced governess, she was not as canny as she might have been in catching them at their mischief.

There had been a moment when Vivienne had envied the titled ladies enjoying their leisure, their every need being anticipated and catered to. It had passed quickly enough when she remembered that she had her freedom for now, which they did not.

By the end of summer she would have photos and memories of adventures she would not have had, otherwise. She would also have the rewarding experience of teaching Alice and Jayne better manners...and balancing the teaching with carefree fun which children needed as much as the other.

'Miss Curtis...' Alice moaned her name. 'I feel like I am going to—'

Luckily the water basin was close at hand.

As it turned out, Clement and Jayne went down to dinner without Miss Curtis or Alice. Poor sweet Alice was not ready to face a dining room. Her governess did not feel she should be left alone. Vivienne Curtis might not have lengthy experience in the career, but she had an instinct for it, he felt. It was evident in the way she spoke to his girls, how she treated them with affection, but not indulgence.

Also, he'd already noticed a change in his daughters. Not that they had become angels overnight, but something was shifting in their attitudes towards Miss Curtis. Although Jayne and Alice might not realise it yet, they were beginning to respect their new governess. That had not happened since Miss Logan.

Clement had offered to bring dinner up, but Miss

Curtis claimed she was not ready to eat. Perhaps not. But it might not be due to residual queasiness. He wondered if she had forgone dinner out of kindness to Alice. No doubt eating in front of his sick child would make her feel even worse.

Sitting down to dinner with their host and hostess, Clement found their company to be pleasant, but he was distracted with wondering what was happening upstairs with Alice and Miss Curtis.

During the conversation, Jayne had mentioned the reason for their visit to Isle of Wight. It was on his tongue to speak at length of the amazing insects he hoped to find along the shoreline.

But no. Surely Miss Curtis was getting hungry and hopefully Alice was, too.

After three-quarters of an hour he began to wonder how to dismiss himself and Jayne from the table without appearing rude. As a guest, he did not wish to misstep.

It had been ages since he'd had dinner in company, but he recalled from his old life in London, before the girls came into his life, that dinnertime could be endless.

He asked to take up dinner to Alice and Miss Curtis. Mrs Prentis assured him that the cook would have it already waiting. If Miss Curtis still had no appetite, she probably would soon. The meal had been worthy of society dining, but with a more homelike flavour.

Entering through his chamber, he and Jayne crossed the room, then he opened the door to the children's bedroom.

Vivienne lifted one finger to her lips, a signal for silence. She tipped her head towards the bed where Alice slept, a blanket tucked up around her chin.

An image formed in his mind. It made him feel warm all over. In it, Miss Curtis was tenderly tucking the blanket about Alice, giving the child a kiss on the forehead as his daughter's eyes dipped closed. It might have happened that way. His sister would have done so, had fate been kinder to her.

'To bed with you now, Jayne,' he whispered, then set the plates of food on a bedside table. 'It is late. Miss Curtis needs time to herself.'

He presented his feet. Jayne stepped on his shoes, gave him a hug, then she slipped under the bedcovers wearing the clean, dry gown Edward Prentis had brought down from the attic. The dress looked as if it belonged to an earlier generation. No doubt it had belonged to one of his children. Not that it mattered how old it was, only that it was clean and warm. Until their luggage arrived, he was grateful for anything dry to put on.

Jayne fell asleep at once.

'It seems I am too late to get Alice to eat.'

'Perhaps if she wakes soon she will have an appetite.'

'Perhaps. But come, Miss Curtis, eat your meal in front of my hearth. The fire is warm and the chairs are comfortable. We will leave the door open in case the children need anything. We can see them easily.'

She hesitated, clearly undecided on whether to do it or not.

Leaping locusts, he ought to have realised how inappropriate an idea it was. Respectable women did not spend time in gentlemen's bedchambers, no matter how sensible it was to do so.

'As tempting as it is, our chaperons are asleep.'

'I suppose I could put my chair in my doorway and you could put your chair in your doorway and we could speak to each other from across the children's beds.'

Miss Curtis cast a glance at the girls, her smile warm upon them. No one had looked at them that way since Miss Logan.

'This is the first bit of relief Alice has had since we boarded the ferry. It would be a shame to wake her, which speaking across the room would do.'

That said, she carried her meal into his chamber, then sat down in one of the chairs in the bay of the window. She lifted the napkin from the plate, breathed in deep, clearly appreciating the aroma.

'It is as good as it smells,' he assured her while settling into the other chair.

It was fascinating, watching her eat. She closed her eyes whenever she took a bite of something she found particularly delicious, giving a quiet sigh. He guessed she was a lady who savoured sensations, making them more intense by closing everything else out.

But what else was she? She spoke like a lady and she moved like one, too. Perhaps she was a vicar's daughter who had fallen on hard times? She might have married, though, and he wondered why she hadn't. She was lovely enough to attract a dozen beaus.

She had not enlightened him on her past situation and he would not ask. It was her business to tell him or not. His business was to attend to his studies, not dwell on the personal life of his children's governess.

Yet Clement found himself dwelling on her none the less. Perhaps he ought to look at the rain beating on the window instead of at the governess. Only the way her hair shone in firelight was too beautiful to glance away from. She had left it loose, probably to let it dry.

Given that he was not a worldly man like his brothers had been and had largely avoided society and its entanglements as much as he could, he'd not had occasion to watch a woman's unbound curls catch and reflect a fire's glow. It was fascinating watching copper glimmers within the dark strands. Made it seem like the fire was coming from the inside.

Lovely. If he did nothing but gaze at her for the rest of the evening, he would be a contented man...warmed at last after the cold trek to the inn.

Early fatherhood had limited his amorous adventures. There had only been two lovers. Odd that he should be remembering them now while sitting across from the governess while she ate her meal. But it was the way she savoured it which made him think of those other intimate moments. The second moment at any rate, not the first.

His first liaison with a woman had been at his brothers' strong urging. They'd insisted he was wasting away his youth with too much study so they pushed him towards an older, obliging lady. The matter of becoming a man had been accomplished in a shockingly short period of time. What he'd learned from it was that he was no less a man before and no more a man after.

He was rather certain that Miss Curtis was savouring her meal more than he had savoured that moment.

The second woman was one he had found on his own. He'd wooed her and believed for a time that they would be a match. In the end, though, he'd found it difficult to fall deeply in love with a lady who did not enjoy children or insects. Vivienne did not like insects either. But somehow her dislike of them seemed endearing, not pretentious. His governess and his former almost-fiancée were quite different women…so what was he doing comparing them?

He and Maisie Smith had bidden each other goodbye within six months. To his knowledge neither of them had shed a tear over the parting. Maisie's lips had never lingered over her food, chewing slowly and with great delight as the governess was doing. Nor had Maisie ever flicked out the tip of her tongue to catch a stray but tantalising crumb. Clement did not know for certain the crumb was tantalising, but the word certainly occupied the forefront of his mind.

He did not think Miss Curtis realised just how sensuous her movements were. But he was quite undone watching her enjoying her meal.

There was a valid reason why gentlemen did not entertain ladies in their chambers. Tantalising went to war with propriety every time.

Vivienne opened her eyes to find her employer giving her an odd look.

Feathers! Mother had warned her not to display overt pleasure while eating. It was not ladylike to sigh and smack one's lips. No doubt Clement Marston now considered her ill-mannered. He might even fear that she would teach his daughters improper behaviour.

She could not reassure him that she had been taught impeccable behaviour from the cradle…that her manners were so polished they shone…well, most of the time they did. If she admitted her station in life she was sure to lose her employment. The second son of a baron did not hire the daughter of a marquess. No one did, as far as that went. It was simply not done.

'The weather continues to be fierce,' she said. Weather was always a subject to engage in when one was unsure of what to say.

'Looking back on it, I ought to have sought us lodgings right off the boat. I am sorry to have dragged you out in it.'

'I hardly think you can take the blame for a storm which came up out of nowhere. Looking back on it now that we are dried out, it was a bit of an adventure.' The pursuit of adventure and photography was the very reason she had become a governess.

'A bit of one, yes. I only hope that, going forward, our adventures are not as wet.'

'I imagine rain makes it difficult to hunt insects.'

'Most of them, but there are some which thrive in moisture...roaches, silverfish and the like. It is easier to find them right after rain.'

How perfectly awful. She meant to keep as far away from those crawly creatures as possible.

'I wonder, Mr Marston—how do you wish for me to focus my time with the girls?'

So far they had not spoken of it in detail. She was to keep them safe, naturally, but what else? 'How advanced are Alice and Jayne in reading and arithmetic?'

'Their previous governesses had no success at teaching them, but I have worked with them on both subjects. They could do with some history and literature. I promise they are bright students when they apply themselves.'

'The academics, I have learned...' from her experience growing up '...are important. However, they must be balanced with free time. There is also much to be learned outside the classroom.'

'They will become proper young ladies one day.' He paused, looking thoughtful as if seeing them grown in a blink. 'For now, though, it is good for them to have a balance of study and free time.'

What a relief to know they were in agreement on it. Vivienne might never have been a governess before, but she did understand what made for a happy childhood.

'I want Alice and Jayne to join me in the field, to be a part of my research. Jayne will be eager, Alice not as much.'

Vivienne not at all. However, as their governess she would be required to be near her charges.

'What will you do with your research?' Surely there must be a point to it all.

There was a point to Vivienne's interest in photography. To capture the beauty of birds and share it.

Mr Marston grinned. He shuffled his chair sideways

to face her. Eyes alight, he leaned forward as if he was about to reveal the grandest secret ever revealed.

His enthusiasm was contagious. She found herself leaning forward in her chair, as eager to know the secret as he was to tell it.

'I am going to write a book with drawings and descriptions of rare insects. My hope is to publish it and establish my name in the field of entomology.'

Vivienne sat up straight, struck by a thunderously grand idea, although she was repelled by it as much as she was drawn to it.

'Are there many in your field wishing for the same?'

'I know of several, yes. I suppose whoever makes the best find, perhaps a new species...or one that has not been seen in years...will win the publishing prize.'

'Clement... Mr Marston, that is.' In her excitement she nearly forgot that she was in his employ. 'If I may be so bold as to suggest something?' She did not wait to hear if she might be bold or not, but pressed on to make her point. 'Perhaps you need something unique to set your work apart, in case you do not find a rare insect.'

He sat back in his chair, cocking his head while he looked at her, brows raised. V-shaped lines etched his forehead. Was this how a rare insect species would feel under his intent speculation?

Probably not, since his specimens were usually dead, while Vivienne was alive...quite alive if the odd little sparks shivering her nerves were anything to go by.

'I wonder?'

'Wonder what, Sir?' She had not yet told him her idea so how could he be wondering about it?

'Out here, life is not strictly formal. The two of us sitting where we are right now is an indication of that. More, we each have Alice and Jayne's best interests at heart. Put those two things together, and it follows that our association would be more easy-going. If you do not mind, I would like to call you Vivienne. It didn't feel inappropriate just now when you called me by my given name.'

'As you say...here we sit quite informally.' How true it was that it had not felt inappropriate. Having permission to call him Clement gave her a ticklish smile inside. 'We shall be Clement and Vivienne.'

'Now, about my book.' He leaned forward again, elbows resting on his knees while he peered at her with his flat crooked smile. 'You mentioned something which you believe might set my work apart from others of its kind?'

'Yes, something unique. But may I ask, if you discover your new species, how would you prove you'd actually done so? It seems that anyone might make that claim.'

'I would describe it in words and then illustrate the creature in exacting detail. Come, I will show you.'

He rose quickly from his chair, then strode past the fireplace to a desk near the window. With a grin and a crooked finger he beckoned her to join him.

He turned up the wick on the desk lamp. A small circle of light shone on a leather blotter and a vase of yellow and blue wildflowers. The desk drawer squealed when Clement opened it. He cast a worried grimace at the doorway. Alice stirred, but did not wake up.

'Ah, here, we are in luck,' he said, keeping his voice low. He withdrew a sheet of paper, setting it on the desktop. Then he picked up a pencil and twirled it between his fingers.

'Let's say this is my journal and I have just discovered a unique wasp...'

'A butterfly, if you do not mind?'

He nodded, casting her a side grin. 'Will a Holly Blue do?'

She supposed so. Holly Blue sounded friendly and could not fail to be more pleasant than a wasp.

'So, just here.' He pointed to a spot on the desk above the paper. 'Imagine a jar containing the butterfly. I open it up and then put the insect on a square of black velvet.'

How interesting that his words, spoken softly so as not to disturb the children, sounded smooth like dark velvet.

He withdrew a pair of spectacles from his jacket

pocket, then placed them on his nose. The lenses made his eyes look larger, his expression more animated.

'I inspect the specimen, consider the colour. Is it all one shade or does it change, light to dark? I look at spot patterns, measure her and then write down what I have observed.'

What Vivienne observed was the excitement in his whispery voice.

'After that…' he waggled the pencil '… I make an illustration of what I have seen.'

He began to sketch the imagined butterfly. His arm flexed with the strokes and shading he put on the paper. Fascinated, she leaned in close while watching him draw. In his enthusiasm he must not have noticed how his arm brushed hers once in a while.

For a bookish gentleman, he was well built. Even through his shirt sleeve she felt how firm his muscles were. Even though she should ignore the pure masculinity of him, she could not. Rather, she let it warm her heart, melt it just a little bit.

'That is beautiful, Clement. It looks as if it might flutter off the paper.' It really did. 'You are very talented.'

'Not really. It took hours of practice,' he answered with his head bent over his drawing, probably making certain every detail was accurate.

Vivienne peered over his shoulder, amazed at how

he could recall the insect from his imagination and bring it to life on paper.

'No matter how you came by it, you do have a gift with that pencil.'

Turning his head suddenly, he looked back at her. His hair was curly on top and it tickled her nose.

My word, she had never smelled a man so close up. What mischief made her take a deep, appreciative breath?

Hopefully he had not noticed. She stood up straight, took a step backwards.

'But what if you discovered a new species and then a competitor accused you of fabricating it? Anyone might draw an insect and call it a new discovery.'

'I would have the insect in my jar. It would be labelled with the date and the location of the discovery... the time of day and even the weather.'

'Yes, but how long would it last in the jar?'

He answered with a one-shouldered shrug. 'Most of them keep well in alcohol or vinegar.'

'What if there was another way to avoid the question of your find's validity?'

He stood up, too, considered her with a thumb on his chin, a long finger crossed over his mouth.

'What is it you are getting at, Vivienne? I have not made such a discovery, nor has anyone attempted to discredit it.'

'I am saying you should have someone photograph

the insects. Publish the photos along with the descriptions and drawings. Even with ordinary insects, it would set your work apart.'

'And where would I find someone to take these photos?'

'Here.' She spun one time in her borrowed, baggy and too-short gown from the attic, pointing at the button on her bodice. 'Me!'

For the longest moment he stood, silently staring while she tapped the button. Chances were he was not seeing the benefits of photography. If she had it to do over again, she would simply have dashed to her chamber and come back with her camera.

'I am a photographer. Or trying to be, but of birds. They are a challenge, of course, since they tend to fly off too quickly for me to capture more than a blur on the glass. Sometimes—most of the time, if you want to know—not even that.'

She was rambling in an attempt to regain her composure. The way he had watched her finger tapping her bosom had made her feel featherheaded. But it was not her finger he had been looking at, was it? She had not meant to draw his attention there, why would she? As bosoms went, hers was not terribly impressive.

'But a dead insect could not scramble away,' she announced before the point she had meant to make could elude her again.

Something was wrong with her. Being around a

man had never made her thoughts ramble. Certainly
she had never lamented the size of her bosom before.
It was a good, practical bosom, easily contained and
never fussed over.

'You wish for me to hire you as a photographer?'

She gave herself a mental shake, bringing herself
back to the conversation she had instigated.

'Yes…well, no.' She went to the doorway to peer
at the sleeping children and regather her position. 'I
do not wish for you to hire me in any capacity except
as your governess. I only wish to be helpful with the
book. Photographing your insects allows me to indulge in my passion at the same time as you indulge
in yours.'

Oh, so subtly, his mouth lifted at one corner. Not so
subtly, her heart flipped in her chest and her cheeks
flamed. Perhaps she should have used a different word
than passion…interest would have been more appropriate.

Somehow, ever since she came into his chamber, it
had been one inappropriate thing after another. And
all on her part. She had never been a flirt and did not
feel like one now. She ought to start calling him Mr
Marston again. It would establish safe boundaries, put
a social distance between them. Not that she was in
any peril except in her own mind. Her employer had
acted like a perfect gentleman.

'You wish to act as an associate on my book? I never considered such a thing. I am not convinced it is wise.'

He would if he understood just what an advantage her photos could give him over his competitors.

'Nothing as important as an associate, Clement.' She liked his name and decided to continue to using it. 'You are the one with the knowledge. Photos will only help to set your work apart from others, that is all.'

'I cannot say I have ever seen a photo of an insect in a book before. Is it even possible?'

Somehow Vivienne must convince him to allow her to photograph his subjects. A dead insect would be ever so much easier than a flitting bird.

'The world of books and photography is changing.' In her eagerness she grabbed his hand and squeezed it. 'Did you know that a couple of decades ago, a book was published with photos of algae?'

The best of it was, the algae had been photographed by a woman. Anna Atkins had probably not been required to wed nobility as Vivienne was, but still, the woman was her inspiration.

Did he realise that her hand was still in his? She would need to take it back, but for an instant she wanted to feel how firm and large his fingers were while they pressed her palm. And hadn't his thumb just skimmed her knuckles? If he was pressing and skimming, he would be aware that they still touched one another.

Aware, both of them, and yet neither of them making the first move to let go.

How confusing. How inappropriate.

How mesmerising. How impossible.

Clement must have come to the same conclusion in the same instant because his fingers uncurled from her hand, one by one.

With a quizzical glance and a hesitant smile, he said, 'I cannot agree, you understand. It is not something I have ever considered. At the same time I cannot disagree. The more thought I give it, the more intriguing the idea is.'

There must be bees buzzing in her mind, scrambling her good sense, because she was suddenly not certain he was speaking of photographs of insects. Sparks of gold flickering his eyes made his expression warm, curious. But he was a scientist and so he would by nature be curious about everything.

'Let's see where it goes, shall we?' he suggested, removing his spectacles, setting them on the desk with a soft clink. While not loud enough to wake the children, it brought Vivienne back to the here and now.

Here, being at this inn because she was governess to this man's children. Now, being for the summer only. Even if she allowed her heart to explore the path it was gazing down, it would be madness to follow. Vivienne Louise Curtis was not mad. She was sensible.

And, sensibly, all they had ever been speaking of was her photographing his insects.

'Once you see how it looks, you will want nothing else. Photo illustrations will be all the rage one day. Mark my words.'

Chapter Four

It had been two days before the rain stopped. Three before the waves subsided enough for safe exploration of the tideline.

This morning a breeze blew in off the sea, drying out the land.

At long last Clement was free to hunt whatever creeping treasures he might find. Today, his focus was on beetles.

He found them to be sturdy insects. More predictable in their movements than those which flitted about looking pretty in sunshine.

Things that looked pretty could be distracting. Vivienne's smile was an example of it. When he ought to be focused on practical matters he found his attention all too frequently drawn to her lips. They were pretty and expressive. Sometimes they were wide, showing humour. Other times they were pressed tight showing a firm attitude. Sometimes they were round, pursed in introspection.

Seeing them round and introspective was particularly troubling for him. It was then that his curiosity was highest, wondering what she was thinking about... but more, wondering what it would be like to kiss those lips.

Last night he had been completely distracted by her. Her lips had pursed for only an instant before she'd smiled widely and tried to convince him to include photographs in his research, but an instant was all it took to make him wobble inside.

Oddly, he'd never been a man to wobble.

She'd been so eager that he'd become caught up in her enthusiasm. Firelight had reflected on her cheeks and lent them a pink glow. Passion for one's calling, he knew, could make a person glow just like that.

In his wobbly state, he'd had a crazy thought. What if, in part, the glow had to do with him...with her reaction to him as a man?

It was incredibly forward of him to imagine such a thing. They had only just met. When she'd grabbed his hand it had been out of excitement for her idea. It was unlikely that she had meant anything else by the gesture.

What he must keep in mind was that simply because her lips were round and pouty, it did not mean it had anything to do with him. It was simply how they looked...in the moment.

Birds circling and calling overhead brought him

back to the here and now, to the wonderful hours spread before him.

Life was good.

Walking over a grassy dune, he scanned the sand watching for whatever might scuttle across.

'Papa!'

He looked up, saw Alice waving her arm. What a relief to see her fully recovered.

Turning away from the path he'd meant to follow, he approached his daughters and Vivienne. They sat on a blanket several yards from the surf rolling tamely onshore. A pair of grey plovers dashed in and out with the tide, pecking holes in the sand.

Evidently Vivienne had taken the morning lesson outside. He approved of that.

The three of them made a pretty scene. Vivienne had a book open in her lap, her blue skirt spread out like a fan. Alice sat on one side of her and Jayne on the other. Their skirts spread across the sand in the same way but smaller, one green and one yellow. If he were not so eager to go exploring, he would sit with them and go along with them on whatever adventure was in the book.

Not that he would be paying much attention to it, he realised. Watching the sunshine glimmering in Vivienne's dark curls was far more interesting. Not properly contained, her hair blew about her shoulders, fingered by the breeze.

'What did you find, Papa?' Jayne asked.

'Nothing yet.'

He noted that the girls' braids were not as neatly plaited as when he did it.

Plaiting hair was clearly not one of Vivienne's skills. Who was this woman he'd hired? Accomplished in some ways and yet not in others. He wondered now if she might be a gently born lady who'd been forced to seek her own way in the world... If so, such a woman was only to be admired.

In the end, he felt it was better to have a governess who the girls seemed to nearly like than one they loathed who could fashion proper braids.

What did a neat hairstyle matter out here in the beautiful wilds, anyway? Who was nearby to judge them for it? Their host and hostess were the only other people nearby and they took life quite casually.

Vivienne tipped her head, presenting one cheek to the sunshine while she looked up at him, shielding her eyes from the brightness with her hand. It was her left hand. The same one he had held. The same hand a wedding band would go on.

Now there was an odd thought which had come out of nowhere. He reckoned she would be stunned if she could hear his thought. He was stunned. Not horrified, though. Random thoughts came at men all the time. He would count this as one of them.

'Have a good lesson, my dears.' He bent to kiss Jayne's cheek, then Alice's.

In what might be one of those random thoughts, he saw himself kissing the governess. On the cheek, he amended in his mind. He was finished envisioning improper actions.

Which, he reminded himself, even a kiss on the cheek would be.

'I shall see you at tea,' he announced, his voice suddenly tight. Striding away with a brisk step, he did not allow himself to dwell on what it would have been like to kiss Vivienne. If he did, it would no longer be a random thought, but an invited one...which would not do at all.

It was too early to rise, Vivienne thought, snuggling deeper under her blankets while looking the window. Sadly, life as a governess began earlier than life as a lady did.

There were still lingering stars on the horizon when she heard Clement begin to move about in his chamber. Apparently, life for an entomologist began earlier, too. Hopefully he would not wake Alice and Jayne. With a bit of luck they would sleep for another two hours.

After what happened yesterday, Vivienne needed some time to herself in order to practise a skill which she was clearly lacking. She had seen the look on Clement's face when he had stopped by to greet his children while they read on the beach. He had been looking at their hair, his brow slightly furrowed. Obviously, he had been thinking their grooming was not up to standard.

Feathers, but he was not wrong. The only experience she had with styling hair was having it done to her. Her lady's maid had a gift when it came to containing her perverse strands.

Alice and Jane had far better-behaved hair than she did and yet she could do nothing with it. Suppressing a groan, she rose from the bed, crossed the room, then sat at the dressing table. She picked up her hairbrush and stared at the mirror.

'Practice makes perfect,' she mumbled, not really believing that in this case it was true.

She simply must conquer the skill if she wished to fulfil her tasks properly. And she did wish to. Accomplishing her goal of photography was all well and good. However, she was being paid a wage to care for Alice and Jayne.

Keeping their hair in order was all a part of it. Keeping her hair neat was, too, if she wished to play her part believably. A governess who was orderly in every way. By the time the girls woke up, she would be properly groomed.

First, she brushed her hair thoroughly. To show its gratitude, it made a curly puff all around her head. Dividing the mess into three equal sections was challenging. When they were somewhat even, she began the process of crossing the hanks, one, then two...and didn't neglect to do the third in proper order or the process must be begun again.

The problem, she decided, was with the mirror which made all her movements look backward. No wonder her fingers got tangled. Resigned to failure for the moment, she tied her hair in a blue ribbon instead and fashioned a bow at the back of her neck.

She frowned at her image but then noticed that the mirror reflected the sky growing lighter beyond the window. She turned on the bench to see clouds pulsing with pink and gold...in some places they were red, making it appear as if there was fire glowing within.

This sunrise gift would only last for a few moments. She hurried to the window and looked out. A figure strode across the beach towards the dunes, cast in the same pink hue which reflected off the sand and the water.

Clement. Who else would be setting off at this time of morning with a pack slung across his back? His posture was straight, but he leaned forward slightly, as if the angle would lengthen his long strides and somehow carry him more quickly to his goal.

Efficient, orderly...this was a man who would expect his children to have neat hair. Perhaps she would make a better job of it today than yesterday.

She watched him reach the crest of the dune. He

paused. Long grass teased the knees of his trousers. He lifted his face as if he were sniffing the morning breeze, appreciating the scents of sand, sea, and dawn.

While she watched, the clouds faded from bright pink to golden.

Not as brilliant, but just as beautiful in its way. Rather like Clement, it occurred to her.

So many society gentleman were like peacocks, flashing their bright feathers, so handsome and re-fined. To Vivienne's way of thinking, not one of them was more interesting than Clement Marston was. Watching him disappear around a stony embankment, she wondered why some perceptive lady of London had not grabbed him up.

While he was not titled or as blatantly handsome as some men, she thought that he was, somehow, more than they were.

It came back to hair, she decided. When she had met Alice and Jane for the first time their braids had been neat and tight, no wild ends poking out at odd angles. There was only one person who could have done it. She could not imagine another father in London who would braid a little girl's hair and make certain she began her day properly.

How many fathers even looked at their daughters, let alone were responsible for their immediate care? She had known many fine gentlemen over the years. Now she was discovering what went into making a genuine man. Clement Marston was proving to be genuine in every way a man could be.

By now the sky was bright blue, the clouds fluffy white.

She squared her shoulders, firmed her resolve. It was time to begin her day. This morning she would not be beaten by unruly braids. Today she would be a better governess than she was yesterday.

She might never convince Clement to include photographs in his books. She might never be a professional photographer. But no matter what came of her life after this, she would succeed for this summer as an employed woman.

Other than herself, Grace and George would be the only ones to know she had done it, but she would feel pride in her accomplishment for ever.

That afternoon Jayne and Alice came to tea with blue checked ribbons holding their hair in place. For all her effort, Vivienne still failed at weaving braids. However, she did have a talent for fashioning a nice bow.

While their father might not be pleased with the freer look the girls wore, Vivienne had gained some favour in her charges' eyes.

Earlier this morning while she had brushed their hair Jayne had wiggled, Alice had squirmed. Both had glared at her. All in an attempt to sabotage her efforts, she was quite certain.

While the girls tolerated her better than they had the governesses who preceded her...indeed, even seemed to like her at times...they had not finished testing her.

Matters changed a bit when she tied their hair in bows and openly admired how grown up they looked. They had preened before the mirror, run fingers through their hair and giggled.

It was in that moment she felt the tide turn in her favour. She could not be certain, but for the first time she had hope of being accepted by them.

But now, while waiting for their father to enter the cosy parlour for tea, she wondered if he would be accepting of the change in his girls.

She had not asked permission to make this alteration in their appearance so perhaps she had overstepped.

Alice and Jayne were happy with how they looked so Clement might have a struggle of it if he made them go back to neat plaits.

The fact that Mrs Prentis had gushed over how pretty the girls looked would not help his cause if he sided with braids. Especially after their landlady had run upstairs to the attic and brought down a dozen more bows which her own daughters had worn.

If there was a confrontation over their hair, Vivienne would be to blame. And so here she sat, watching steam curl from the spout of the teapot, waiting for Clement to arrive and give his verdict. There was more than a hairstyle at stake here. How much authority did she have as their governess?

For a normally self-assured lady, she was jittery. It might be wise not to pick up a teacup and risk dribbling on her fingers. That would show a great lack of confidence. Governesses, as she recalled them to be, were ever self-possessed.

When she heard heavy footsteps in the hallway, she pasted on a smile.

Passing though the doorway, Clement was smiling. He nearly always entered a room smiling, she was learning.

His hair looked damp. The lingering scent of shaving soap hovered about him.

As he saw his daughters sitting beside Vivienne on the sofa, his eyes widened. Of course she had expected him to be surprised. What else was he, though? Other than that immediate widening of his eyes, he revealed nothing.

'Papa!' the girls exclaimed in chorus.

Jayne reached him first. Stepping on his shoes, she hugged him as she always did.

Alice stepped forward for her braids to be tugged but, of course, there were no braids.

Vivienne held her breath. She had forgotten about this special show of affection between Clement and Alice.

'Hello, my dears.' With a smile he tugged on each

side of Alice's bow. 'I hope you have had a good day. Come, sit with me and tell me all about it.'

There was another sofa facing the one Vivienne sat on. Clement sat down, one little girl pressed to each side of him. Jayne twirled a lock of strawberry-blonde hair around her finger, grinning.

'Do we look grown up now?' Alice asked.

'And pretty?' followed Jayne.

'Well, let me see...' He turned Jayne's chin this way and that, slowly looking her over, but smiling when he did. 'Very pretty.'

He did the same with Alice and said, 'You do look grown up. But you must not do it too quickly, for when you grow up and move away from me, I shall be sad.'

'We won't go away, Papa, we love you too much.'

'Good girls... Now, did you remember to thank Miss Curtis for arranging your hair so prettily?'

Alice slipped out from under her father's arm, dashed from one sofa to the other, then gave her a hug. Jayne followed close behind. Wrapped up in small arms, Vivienne felt her heart swell. She hadn't known how having their affection, which apparently she now had, would touch her to her soul.

She glanced across the rug at Clement. His smile seemed genuine, but it might be for the sake of not hurting his children's feelings.

Later, when the girls were sleeping, she would discover the truth.

* * *

Later that evening after his daughters were asleep, Clement left the door adjoining theirs open. He hoped that Vivienne would notice and take it as an invitation to join him.

Most of his nights were lonely ones after the girls went to bed. It had always been that way, but never really troubled him. He had not minded that his days went on, one after another in a familiar rhythm. With his mind attentive to his work, he had rarely noticed.

Being set apart was what he was accustomed to. He had never been kindred spirits with his brothers, him being a studious young father and them being society bachelors. Lately, he had noticed. The difference between then and now was Vivienne. The first evening they were here, when Alice had her stomach trouble, the governess had spent time in his chamber. He had enjoyed that.

He had his girls and it was wonderful…and yet, perhaps no longer enough? He was a lonely man and could no longer deny it. What he needed right now was a way of getting her attention without rapping on her door and blatantly announcing he wanted company.

It would not do to appear needy. He decided to hum. It might draw her attention.

Sitting at his desk, he withdrew the scribbled notes he had made while exploring the tideline this morning. He began to copy them neatly in his journal. If the off-key tune did not attract her notice, nothing would.

His voice must be even worse than he thought for it took only a moment before he heard her door open. There was an unobstructed view from his desk, across the children's beds and to her doorway. He glanced up with a smile.

'Oh, good evening, Vivienne.'

'May I have a word?' she asked.

'Of course.' He stood, sweeping his hand towards the pair of chairs he had placed in front of the fireplace. 'Nice fire tonight.'

From the corner of his eye, he watched how her skirt swished around her hips when she walked around the children's beds. Paying attention to the way a woman walked was not what he was used to doing. So many things lately were not. But he did not mind in the least.

It occurred to him, not quite out of the blue given the way he had been thinking about her lately, that he was glad he was not the titled brother. An untitled man and a governess might make a match of it if—

But there was nothing like putting the cart ahead of the horse. They were employer and employee, nothing more than that. He did not know why the thought had even come to him.

'The girls were pleased with the way you did their hair.' He sat down, then she took the chair beside him. 'What is it you wished to speak with me about?'

Relaxing, he stretched his feet towards the fire. Ah, the evening felt better already.

'Just that, their hair. I hope you do not mind the change. Braids and I have always been at odds. I do not have the patience for them the way you must.'

'Necessity, more than patience, I assure you. When Miss Logan, their nanny, resigned, there was no one to do it except me.'

'I have been wondering, Clement—why do Alice and Jayne dislike the women who care for them? They seem like sweet girls except when it comes to that.'

This was not a subject he liked to discuss. It cut him to the quick every time. She ought to know, though, since she was the one being bedevilled by those sweet girls.

'I told you they are not my children, but my nieces.' He paused while she nodded. 'An hour after my sister died I took them home with me. I also took the neighbour who had been caring for them during the week Alice Jayne lingered. She had just lost a child and so it was a good fit. Miss Logan loved them and they her. You might imagine how they felt when she left us to begin her own family.'

'As if they had lost their mother, I would think, not having known another.'

'They were only seven years old then. I could not explain that Miss Logan did not belong to us. They cried for her every night. I admit that I cried once or twice, too, once they were asleep. Seeing them suffer was not easy for me.'

'So, then…is it your belief that they rejected their governesses because they were not Miss Logan?'

'That is part of it, naturally. But more, I think they did not wish to have another woman leave them. Better to reject them from the beginning.'

Vivienne bit her lip, looked away. Even though she hid her face, he knew she was frowning.

'What is it, Vivienne?'

She did not answer, but shook her head. He reached across, covered her hand on the arm of the chair.

When she turned her face to look at him, her brown eyes shimmered.

'Your daughters and I are growing close. They no longer see me as an intruder.'

'But that is wonderful!'

She jerked her hand out from under his. 'No, Clement, it is horrible. Have you forgotten that my employment is only until summer ends?'

Hardly. He would have reached for her hand again, but she folded her arms across her middle, making herself unapproachable.

'What if I offer to double your wage? Would that be enough to make you cancel your next service?'

Summer was such a fleeting season. It was true that his girls were bound to be heartbroken again.

'Please, Vivienne, stay on with us.'

All of sudden she stood, shaking her head. 'I cannot.'

And with that, she rushed from his chamber. Passing through the centre room, she paused to gaze down at Alice, then at Jayne. She pressed the back of her hand to her mouth, then fled to her own chamber and closed the door. Not walked, not strode, or even hurried...but fled.

Why had a simple question upset her so deeply? It was curious. She had not given any indication of anything being wrong, yet the mention of her service ending seemed to distress her.

There might be more to her turning him down than he was aware of. There was so much that he did not know about her...or her past, really. But it was not for him to pry or coax it out of her. When she was ready, she would confide in him...he hoped.

Chapter Five

It was Vivienne's day to herself. Her time was her own to do with it what she wished.

Standing on the inn's porch, she watched Clement and his girls walk along the path towards the sand.

What did she wish to do with her day? Read, walk, attempt to photograph a grey plover?

No, not the last. She would only have taken the cap from the lens before the bird flew away. Surprisingly, photography wasn't what she wanted to do today. There was still a great deal of summer left in which she could take her photos.

What she wanted to do was go with the Marston family on their exploration of a group of rocks and boulders Clement had discovered a distance down the beach.

'Don't be foolish,' she reminded herself.

It was important to keep her relationship with Alice and Jayne friendly, but not intimate. After speaking with Clement the other night, the last thing she wanted to do was break hearts, her own heart notwithstanding. Joining them when she was not being paid to do so would cross that line.

At the crest of the dune, Jayne spun about, waving her hand in invitation.

Cupping her hand to her mouth, Alice called, 'Come with us!'

Vivienne shook her head, a clear 'no'.

It was far too tempting to give in. She must remember what was at stake. Only sorrow would come of her becoming too involved with this family. She would not take their hearts with her when she left, nor would she leave her own here.

Alice tugged on her father's arm. Drawing him down, she whispered something in his ear. He straightened and nodded, then walked back across the sand towards the porch.

He stood at the bottom of the steps, wearing a big floppy hat which hid his eyes but not his smile. Wide and flat with brackets on each side of his lips, she saw the invitation in it.

'Will you come?' he asked.

'It would not be wise.'

'You are worried about becoming too close to them and then leaving them heartbroken. It might happen. I cannot stop that. But consider this—are they to live their lives not ever having a close connection with a motherly figure? You are the only one they have allowed in since they were seven years old. I fear that if you reject their affection it will be worse for them than losing it.'

What he said made sense. At some point there would be an emotional price to pay in one form or another. However, it would not be called due today.

He reached up. 'Come, Vivienne.'

She placed her fingers in his broad, long-fingered hand. A calloused palm and a bookish mind? What a fascinating contradiction he was. It was a lucky thing she could not fully see his eyes under the hat brim. If they were looking at her with glimmering gold flecks, well, she could not be blamed for becoming infatuated with him on the spot.

What woman with a smidgen of sense would not?

The walk towards the rocks was not long or difficult. It was why Clement had saved the excursion for a time when the girls were with him.

The place he had in mind was ideal because the rocky area he wished to inspect was near the shoreline. This meant he could explore with Jayne and at the same time keep an eye on Alice, who did not like peeking in dark places for creatures which scurried from the light.

Butterflies were more to her liking. And to Vivienne's. While she was not trying to get them to land on her finger as Alice was doing, she did smile and point out how pretty they were.

Having Vivienne come along hadn't been part of his plan for the day. His intention had been for her to have time away from the children to do whatever she wished.

He was glad she'd agreed to come. More and more he found he enjoyed being in her company more than being away from it.

'What will we find under here, do you think?' Jayne asked, kneeling beside a stone and reaching to lift it.

'Remember what I taught you? Turn the stone and have your specimen jar ready in case you find something. If it is a spider, put the rock back down and call me over.'

He repeated those instructions each time they went on a hunt. Not all insects were harmless.

He watched while Jayne carefully turned the stone. His attention was not completely on it, though. He could hear Vivienne laughing, Alice giggling.

While he watched for what might be under the stone, he imagined hands reaching for butterflies, sunshine on upturned faces…bare feet in the sand.

He did not know that Vivienne had taken off her shoes, but it was the practical thing to do so it was what he pictured. Stockings might have been removed, too, so his mind's eye saw bare ankles. If she was leaping for, say a damselfly, her skirt might fly up. It was why he pictured her smooth, bare calf.

What was amiss with him lately? His thoughts tended to roam too freely when it came to his children's governess. And why wouldn't they? Vivienne was becoming more than an employee. Friend was not the precise word. Was there a word for a person a man liked with equal parts admiration and longing? Longing for her company, naturally.

Although there was the other, too. Being a man he could not deny the physical attraction to her, the itchy longing to be closer to her than was acceptable in their situation. Her casual company, friendly companionship as it were, all he was free to indulge in.

When he glanced over his shoulder he did not see Vivienne leaping barefoot after a damselfly. What he saw rocked him more than his ridiculous imagination had: Vivienne sat in the sand with Alice on her lap, the pair of them studying a seashell.

He saw his child in the arms of a woman who cared for her. Vivienne might not wish to form a bond with his girls, but there was no denying the affection he saw when she bent her dark head to Alice's fair one. No mistaking the tenderness in her touch when she drew his child close while they studied the shell.

All at once, Jayne gasped. He had not noticed her wander to a fallen log several feet away.

She lifted one finger to her lips and pointed down at the rotting wood.

His quick but silent dash to the log must have caught Vivienne's attention. She and Alice crept forward.

What interesting find had his daughter made?

'Will he attack her?' Jayne whispered.

It looked rather as if he would, but, no, the impressively large stag beetle had something different in mind while he circled his lady with antlers raised.

'It might look as if he will, Jayne,' he whispered, 'but he will not injure her. Now had this been a case of two males they would battle one another fiercely.'

He waved for Vivienne and Alice to come and have a look at this rare sighting. How often did one see a mating ritual between two magnificent insects?

Alice came slowly forward. To all appearances, Vivienne meant to remain where she was, but then she hurried after Alice. The expression in her eyes, the set of her lips, indicated that she meant to conquer her dislike.

She peered over his shoulder, much as she had done when he drew the illustration of the butterfly. Her hair tickled his ear. Being so close, he sensed it when she shivered.

For all that she tried to put on a brave front, he knew that, for her, this was not a fascinating moment.

'Well, then,' he announced. 'Shall we give them a bit of privacy?'

'Why do insects need privacy, Papa?' Alice asked while clinging to Vivienne's hand.

'Because they… The natural way of things is… Well, you see—' There was no explaining the mating act to a ten-year-old girl.

'It is because they have a secret which is between the two of them only,' Vivienne explained. 'It is a dance which no one else may be privy to.'

'Oh, it is very good then that we do not watch,' Alice declared.

He'd heard of shoulders sagging in relief. It turned out to be a true thing. This was one discussion he did not wish to have with his daughters. But with no woman to guide them, he feared he must one day.

In only a few years there would be certain things his girls would need to be made aware of. Physical changes that he could not bear to consider, let alone disclose.

Perhaps he ought to wed.

He had not considered marriage in the past but maybe he ought to have. The girls needed a woman's guidance. They needed it from a woman who cared for them. Since Miss Logan, no woman had. Not until Vivienne came into their lives. She would be perfect for the girls.

But he could hardly marry his children's governess…could he? No matter that he was attracted to her, it would not do.

'Shall we have lunch?'

Food was what was needed. A bit of sustenance for his body and a few moments to get his mind straight.

Vivienne had made it clear that she had another engagement at the end of summer. It would do him no good to indulge in thoughts of anything more intimate between them. Not for him. Nor for his daughters either.

When lunch was finished, the girls dashed down to the water to splash their feet in the waves.

'Thank you for coming up with that story about the secret dance,' he said. 'I was floundering trying to explain it. And you were right about it being a dance; it's all a part of the courtship, you see.'

'Insects courting?' Her quiet, disbelieving laughter snared him. 'I shall never view a ball in the same way again.'

'Have you seen one, then? It is what I think of whenever I must attend one, which is hardly ever.'

She nodded. The sweet biscuit she was holding crumbled, fell from her fingers and on to her lap. 'Whoops, that was clumsy of me.'

'The insect world is intriguing. Most people have no idea how fascinating it is. Would you like to know something truly astonishing?'

She tossed biscuit crumbs in the air. A seagull swooped down, snatching two before they hit the sand.

'More astonishing than that?' she asked, arching a brow at the bird and giving him a grin.

He gave her back the same look. 'Termites are monogamous.'

'Clement Marston, you are making that up!' She flicked a finger of sand at him.

'Oh, it's true. I promise.'

'You shall write that in your book, I hope.'

'I must. It would be irresponsible to leave it out.'

'Well…' She turned to more fully face him, her eyes bright, eager and pretty. 'How much better would it be if you had photos to go along with it?'

'I would never ask that of you, Vivienne. You would be miserable having to handle insects.'

'I would get over it.'

'The creatures will not become any more endearing. They are what they are.'

'I already look more kindly on termites.'

'A test, then. Are you willing to prove you can change your feelings on the matter?'

'Indeed. Test me.'

'Go back to the log and bring me back one of the stag beetles.'

'That is not a test. It is torture. Nor is it an indication of how well my photographs would improve your book.'

'Since I do not wish to torture you, I will get by with my drawn images.'

'Feathers,' she declared, then joined the children at the waterline.

* * *

Later in the afternoon, Vivienne decided there was only one way to prove her point and that was to show Mr Clement Marston she was correct.

Vivienne slung the case holding her camera and three glass plates across her shoulder, then took the children towards the kitchen to spend time with Mrs Prentis.

'But where are you going?' Jayne asked. 'We want to come along.'

'Not this time. I am only going to the cove to take a photo or two. I will not be gone long.'

After seeing them settled in the kitchen, she hurried outside.

With a bit of daylight remaining and the walk to the log containing the amorous beetles only taking fifteen minutes, there was plenty of time. With any luck the insects would still be smitten with one another and she could get a photo of them.

Surely that would convince Clement of the benefit of her photos. It would also prove that she was up to the task even if she did not care for her subject matter.

Walking along the shoreline, she went around the rocks which created the alcove where the log was. To her relief the insects were there. If they were still courting or done with it she did not know. The main thing was, they were quite still. If she hurried she might get her shot.

The surf sounded louder than it had a few moments ago, but she did not take the time to look at it. Her attention was on putting the camera in the exact spot she needed it to be before she lost the daylight.

She had not noticed before, but there was a third beetle there and it was dead.

Lifting the cap from the lens, she allowed what she estimated to be the right amount of light. Just…right… there. She replaced the cap.

Something about the sound of surf rolling onshore seemed different than it had before…closer .Glancing over her shoulder, she gasped. Those waves really were closer. Larger, too. Only a narrow strip of sand remained when moments ago there had been a wide swathe.

She would need to work quickly. It was important to take two more photos. One could never count on only one. Especially when what she was going to present to Clement had to be outstanding.

Being caught up in capturing their image, she forgot how repulsive beetles were. She bit her lip, closed her eyes and then nudged the dead one with her fingernail in order to scoot it closer to the others.

With her attention focused, everything else faded. The world narrowed to two satisfied beetles and one expired suitor.

And then her feet got wet. Startled, she glanced down. Water rushed around her shoes, dragged at the hem of her skirt. Another wave splashed on the log, sending up a tall spray of saltwater.

She screeched, then snatched up her camera and the bag containing her glass plates an instant before a wave would have carried it off. Lifting her treasure high above her head, she turned to wade back to safer ground.

Too late! She had left it for too long and now there was no safer ground. The sand had completely disappeared. While she watched, the water grew ever deeper. What to do? If she tried to walk back through the water, she might get jostled and drop her equipment.

Scrambling on top of the log, she gazed about. There really was no place to go except up and she was as high up as she could get. Behind her there was only a rocky cliff.

How long did high tide last, anyway? How high did it get? She had been out here longer than she'd expected to be and the sun was beginning to set.

Naturally she was frightened. Who would not be, facing the prospect of being swept away in the dark and not knowing how to swim?

Oh, dear, the log was beginning to rock with the force of the water rushing over and beneath it. She lifted her equipment over her head. No matter what, she was not going to let go of it until the waves ripped it from her hands.

* * *

Where was Vivienne?

Clement checked one room after the other without finding her. He needed to apologise for taunting her with that challenge of bringing him a beetle.

The moment had been light-hearted and so he had teased her. He'd hoped to see that charming expression she had...the one where her brown eyes grew warm while she gave him a reprimanding glance. The opposing expressions given at once were charming.

It had not turned out that way. She'd gone to splash in the surf with the children. Between then and now he had not found a private moment in which to beg her pardon.

Going into the kitchen, he found Mrs Prentis stirring something in a pot, his daughters looking on.

'Do you know where Miss Curtis is?' Whatever was in that pot made him anxious for dinner.

'She went to the cove to take a picture, Papa,' Jayne said.

He glanced out the window. Wind stirred leafy branches of shrubbery in the garden, casting long shadows in the dusky light.

It would be approaching high tide in the cove.

'Are you certain she has not returned?'

'She hasn't,' Alice said. 'I've been waiting for her.'

Hurrying outside, he scanned the path to the beach. Vivienne was not on it.

The surf was loud, crashing hard as it rushed on-shore. In the cove there would be no shore at all.

He ran, hating the drag of sand slowing his steps. While the water in the cove would be no more than hip high, it would be swirling fiercely. A woman with water weighing down her skirts would have little chance of wading out of the cove.

By the time he came within sight of the cove wall, water soaked the soles of his shoes. The closer he got, the deeper it became. Waves swirled around the rock wall, cutting the cove off from the rest of the beach. Up and over was the only way to reach it. He started climbing, but it was slow going with the rocks being slick with sea spray.

Once on top, he had a view of the cove. Peering hard through the dim light, he spotted her. She was standing on something. It must be the log where they'd discovered the stag beetles. It did not appear steady. Vivienne rocked and swayed, trying to keep her balance.

'Vivienne!' he shouted.

She looked up sharply.

'Hold on! I'm coming!'

With that, he scrambled down the rocks, then jumped into the water. The tide swirled around his hips. It tugged him backwards when it went out, then gave him a push forward when it came in. Rough going, but he made it across without slipping.

When he reached Vivienne, he lifted his arms. 'I will carry you,' he called over the noise of the water.

She looked at the swirling tide, then shook her head. He could not blame her for hesitating.

'Wet skirts will drag you down.'

She had been gripping her camera to her heart. With a nod, she opened the case she had slung around her shoulder, put it inside, then snapped the lid closed. Placing one hand on his shoulder, she bent her knees. She hesitated, clearly uncertain about which was safer, the log or his arms.

'I won't let go of you. Come down now.'

All at once the log shifted.

She tumbled. Her legs flailed awkwardly and yet she managed to lift her case away from the water. Only good fortune landed her smack in his arms.

In spite of his best efforts to keep them dry, Vivienne's skirts got soaked. The extra weight made it tough going. His thighs pressed hard with each step. His arms ached with the effort not to let her go.

Getting back to the cove wall seemed to take a very long time, but he made it without losing Vivienne or her camera. He set her on her feet, but kept her pinned between his body and the rocks.

'We need to climb over.' He had to speak loudly because the water was noisy, crashing all around.

She nodded as if she understood, but she still kept

the case lifted over her head. How did she think she would manage to climb without using her hands?

There was no time to argue the point. The water was cold and they would soon be growing weak with exertion. They needed strength for the climb.

He lifted the case off her and slung it around his neck.

'Go up, Vivie. It's steep and wet, but I'm behind you. I won't let you fall.'

She started up, slipped, but he caught her with a hand under her thigh. He boosted her higher, one hand pressing her ever upwards and the other finding purchase in rock crevices.

Making the top, he took a moment to catch his breath. The hardest part was over. Only the descent remained and gravity was with them this time.

By the time they reached the safety of dry sand, night had settled. It would be dark if not for the huge moon on the horizon casting its bright, bluish glow.

He sat down, bringing Vivienne with him. They sat silently for a few moments while their ragged breathing eased.

'I am sorry,' he managed to say at last. 'This is my fault. I should not have teased you about bringing me the beetle. I should have made certain you knew about high tide. I should have—'

'You are hardly to blame. Going to the cove was my choice.'

'Because I said—'

'No, Clement. I take full responsibility for what I did and now, because of you, I am not drowned. And my equipment is safe.' She touched his cheek with cold fingers. 'You are my hero.'

Then she leaned towards him as if she meant to kiss him. Yes, she did mean to. Why else would he feel her breath on his face? Her eyes would not look like melted brown sugar if she meant to do something else. Then all at once she dropped her fingers, sighed and then leaned away.

'Vivie...' He cupped her cheek in his hand, drawing her back towards him. He would have that kiss.

And so he did.

Nothing felt more perfect in this moment. She must have felt the same for she leaned into him once again and wrapped both arms around his neck. It was not proper. Logically he knew that. But his longing didn't know it and that was what was speaking in the moment.

When the kiss ended, logic slowly regained control, pointing out that he had not behaved like a gentleman. He could blame it on moonlight, or a reaction to the danger they had faced. It would be a lie, though. It was his overwhelming attraction to her and his inability to control his desire at fault.

'And now I must apologise for this, too.'

'Apologise? I think not, Clement. You saved my life and I kissed you in thanks.'

In thanks? He'd been on the other end of that kiss and knew better. There was much more to it than she was willing to say. It was, however, a graceful way out of what they had so impulsively done.

'I'll admit, I've never been thanked in a nicer manner.' He stood, reaching a hand down to help her up. And then, because he would likely never have the chance to do so again, he dipped his head and gave her one more kiss. 'Now I thank you, too…for forgiving me when I challenged you to fetch the beetle.'

'Did I say that I did?' She gave him that soft-eyed look, her lips still glistening from the kiss while they walked towards the lamps glowing in the inn's front windows.

'You did. It was when you nearly kissed me first.'

'Oh, then,' she said and then did not speak again until they reached the porch steps.

She looked up at him with moonlight on her face, with her hair dampened by sea water.

'I liked it when you called me Vivie. But, Clement, you must not do so again.'

He liked it, too, but she was correct. The endearment was far too intimate.

The end of the summer would come. She'd go away.

The less she took of his heart with her, the better. Unless he was very careful indeed, she would take more than a little.

Chapter Six

Vivienne was a liar. This was the third, or maybe fourth time she had accused herself of being one while she worked in the dark room which Mrs Prentis had allowed her to set up in the corner of the cellar.

That moment she'd shared with Clement had nothing to do with gratitude. Except that she had been grateful she was kissing him. Grateful indeed. Once she wed Everett she would never have a kiss like it again.

How was it that Clement's lips could bring her blood to a simmer, yet at the same time make her nerves shiver? Deliciously hot and cold all at once. What a confusing state to be in…wondrous in the oddest way, too.

It was unthinkable to even imagine giving Everett Parker the kind of kiss which made her go blurry and fuzzy. Just because he was a good man and a match society would approve of, he had never made her heart go wild. He was her father's friend, not her heart's desire.

Mr and Mrs Stag Beetle probably had more passion in their union than she would ever have with the Marquess of Winterfeld. She was about to begin worrying about how there could ever be an heir to Winterfeld, but just then the image on the glass plate came into focus.

It was amazing! Far better than she could have dreamed it would be. The live insects were as sharply focused as the dead one was. She found it a stunning revelation, but insects were clearly co-operative creatures when it came to holding a pose.

All of a sudden she did not dislike them quite so much.

It was late when she rushed up to her bedroom with all three images in hand. Too bad. She was itching to show them to Clement, but after this evening's misadventure he was probably exhausted. It would be better to show him the photos and then press her cause once he was refreshed.

Oh, feathers! How was she to sleep? She was far too excited to close her eyes. Once Clement saw the images of the stag beetles preserved for ever, once he imagined them in his book, he would surely relent and allow her to help with his project.

Vivienne opened the door between the rooms to

check on Alice and Jayne. Since they would never know she did it, she gave each girl a goodnight kiss on their forehead.

She had always expected she would have children one day, truly wanted them. Now that she had kissed Clement, now that she understood more about the nature of what led to conceiving them, she could not imagine how it would happen.

Not with the man she was promised to.

Going to the window, she stared out at the full moon, thinking about her sister and her husband. For the first time, she envied Grace having her love match.

Having spent so much effort avoiding marriage in favour of independence, Vivienne had not given proper thought to the benefits of it. Marriage meant you had a friend for ever. A lover for a lifetime. Everett was pleasant and considerate. She supposed she would at least have a friend once she married him.

Now, though, she was not convinced friendship on its own was enough. Now that Clement had kissed her and shown her what it could be like between a man and a woman, how intimate moments were a bond which set a couple apart from anyone else, the independence she'd believed so essential seemed less than fulfilling.

Kisses were fulfilling; indeed, one could get quite addicted to them!

Feathers, but she was confused. She was not sure

of anything anymore except that her future was not with an entomologist.

'I am certain there is no one like him, but you must know that,' she murmured to the moon even though she understood that it had no answer for her.

Was there a way out of her promise to Everett? In society, once one gave one's word on such a thing as marriage it was often binding. Alliances were made, family lineages ensured and social status fortified.

She tapped her lips with one finger, deep in thought. The engagement had not yet been announced. Not that it mattered greatly. If she did not go through with it, she would let down the people she loved most. And even if she did refuse to go through with the engagement, what then? She must still marry some noble fellow of the right rank.

All at once she noticed her reflection on the glass, her finger touching the very lips Clement had kissed.

She sighed, turned away from the silent, unhelpful moon and stared at his closed bedroom door.

In that very instant, it clicked open.

'Can't sleep, Vivienne?'

If only she had not been forced to tell him not to call her Vivie. It had sounded so nice when he did.

'I did not mean to wake you, Clement.' The only noise she had made was to whisper and sigh. He could not have heard her unless he was awake and listening.

Was it their kiss leaving him restless? Unlike her,

he probably had many to compare it with. What to her was unforgettable might be ordinary to him.

That moment, while constantly on her mind, was not the reason she was awake. She had only just run upstairs from the darkroom, all aglow and frustrated that she must wait on showing him the photos until morning. What a bit of luck that she might not need to wait after all. Once he saw the three images, he would understand how extraordinary...how unforgettable they were.

'You did not. I wasn't sleeping,' he said.

'Good, then.' She turned to rush for her chamber, but then spun back. It was late and... 'Do you mind having company? There is something I wish to show you.'

Did he mind? Not at all, because more than ever he craved her company. And, yes, he did mind, because more than ever he craved her company...her kisses. This had certainly not been his first kiss, but it had shaken him as if it was. Somehow, after Vivienne, he could not even recall the others.

What he must do was learn to enjoy her companionship while he could and yet understand that his time with her was not for ever. Summer would end and she would take up her new position.

For all that he wished to, the one thing he must not do was kiss her again. He must guard his heart or it would be far too easy to fall in love with her. He must have a care for his daughters' feelings as well. No one was better off with a saddened heart.

Vivienne returned from her chamber, smiling when she passed through his doorway. She smelled odd. Like chemicals of some sort. 'Wait until you see, Clement!'

She set a folder on his desk, then whirled to look at him with a smile glowing in her eyes…sparkling on her lips. 'Come and look. Here is proof that I will not be tortured by helping you in your work. And you, my friend, will be greatly helped.'

He opened the folder and saw three photos of the stag beetles. The images were sharp, clear in every detail. He could not speak for a moment. While the living creatures had sadly been washed away in the tide, wonder of wonders, here they were preserved for ever.

'You see? I brought you not one, but three beetles. As I recall you asked me to bring one, not touch them. I did touch the dead one with my fingernail, though, so it would be in the frame of the picture.'

'Clever and brave,' he said. How was he to resist her? 'It means a great deal to you to be a part of my work, doesn't it?'

'You cannot imagine how much. And not only for my own sake. As you can see, my photos will give your book a great advantage over your competition.'

'Hmmm.' He snatched his reading glasses from the

corner of the desk, then leaned down to peer more closely at the photographs. 'Excellent work, Vivienne.' He straightened, took off the glasses and set them back in their corner. 'I think you are correct. And what you said before about being able to validate any find I made, a photograph would do that. No one could dispute it then.'

'You never know what sorts of unscrupulous people are out there.'

'Indeed, even in the scientific world.'

'Will you let me be a part of this project, then?'

It would be a risk. They would be working shoulder to shoulder on it. Which would mean their lips would not be so far apart.

Maybe he was already safe and she never wished to kiss him again? How was he to know what she truly felt about what had happened earlier tonight?

The photos fanned out on his desk had to do with research, not romance...so perhaps they might manage to work together...

'Tell me, why is this so important to you?'

'As you can see...' she waved her hand before her face, before making a sweeping gesture from hair to hem '... I am a woman.'

Indeed, he knew that all too well. It was the only thing keeping him from giving her an enthusiastic yes.

'As a woman I am not free to pursue a career the same as a man is. I have an obligation to wed, to produce an…to have children. I am speaking in general, of course. I do have a career as you well know, but I will never be free to open a little shop and sell my work.'

'Some women do…hat shops and the like.'

'I do not wish to sell hats. Trust me, Clement, working with you is the only way I will ever see my photographs for sale.'

No doubt she was correct about that. The odds of her having the career she wished for were rather slim. Easier for a woman of her station than a lady of high society, but difficult none the less.

'Join me, then. Let's see what we can do about getting ourselves a successful, published work.' He extended his hand, a gesture of agreement.

Rather than take it, she threw herself against him, giving him a quick, tight hug. Then, as if remembering herself, she backed away. 'I apologise; that was not professional.' Then she shook his hand. 'I will be far more circumspect in the future.'

No doubt she would.

No doubt he would be sorry for it.

Clement stood at the shoreline watching his helper, her photo equipment slung across her back, while she rattled the branches of a bush. When she bent over, her skirt swayed and shimmied with her search. No entomologist had a more appealing helper, he would wager.

Or a more dedicated one. To his surprise, she became bolder by the day in their quest for specimens. She no longer backed away in revulsion when she spotted a creepy crawler. Only an hour ago she had called him over with a grin, pointing to a dung fly. Just this moment she was in pursuit of a cricket.

Now that Vivienne was involved, excursions were far more entertaining. Everything was more entertaining. No longer were his late-night studies lonely.

Each evening after the children were asleep, Vivienne came up from her darkroom to show him the photos she had taken during the day. No more yawning over tedious illustrations for him. There was nothing routine about her leaning over his shoulder and admiring his drawings. They were still necessary to illustrate the finer points of the insects' bodies…and make notations on size and colour.

More and more Vivienne began to ask questions regarding the insects he wrote about. He did not think her interest was feigned. Especially when it came to butterflies. She often admired the Creator's artistry in the beauty of their wings.

Last night when Clement had explained how the creatures looked delicate but were, in fact, not, her eyes had grown wide, sparkling with incredulity. Her lips had parted in amazement.

Which had meant he'd had to fight the urge to kiss

her again. He'd managed by explaining how a butter-fly could carry forty times its own weight.

'If only a photograph could capture colour,' she had said with a sigh. 'Wouldn't it be a wonder?'

And so the nights went. All this time—his whole life, in fact—he had not noticed how lonely he had been. Study had filled his hours and seemed satisfactory. Now that he knew the difference, how would he get by when he was alone again?

Although he was not really alone, he knew, while he watched Jayne and Alice building a sandcastle at the water's edge. His heart was fulfilled for the most part.

Not all, though.

'Found it!' Vivienne called.

He hurried over, but the cricket jumped away before he could capture it in a jar.

'Ah, well. We have other crickets to put in our book and tomorrow we will search inland, see what is to be discovered there.'

Interesting that after only a week's time he no longer considered it his book, but their book.

'The girls will miss their afternoons at the beach.' Vivienne inclined her head towards Alice and Jayne. 'That is an impressive castle.'

'How are their studies advancing this week? Are they giving proper attention to them? And behaving?'

'You would be proud of your daughters, such quick

learners. Both of them are studious when they put their minds to it.'

'I hope they have stopped testing you. From what I can see, they have.'

He recalled the seashell, how Alice had snuggled close to Vivienne while they studied it.

'We have found our peace. Not that they do not enjoy a good prank now and again. It is all in good fun, though, not like before.'

'They are like their mother. I've always thought so.'

'I imagine it is a special moment whenever you see their resemblance to her.'

'Quite. She would have liked you, Vivienne. I think she would be pleased if she could see you with them.'

She nodded, but looked away. It might have been better if he had not said that. He knew she feared growing too close to them.

'Mrs Prentis is going to town tomorrow,' she said after a moment. 'I thought the girls might like a morning off from their studies. It will be good for them to explore the shops and have a bit of girlish fun.'

'Girlish fun…that is something I have not been able to give them.' Honestly, he knew far more about insect anatomy than he did about girlish fun. 'Thank you, Vivienne.'

'No need for thanks. I will enjoy the outing as much as they will. In my opinion there is a great deal that goes into making a well-rounded young woman. A balance of studies and outdoor playtime...and shopping, naturally.' She gazed at the girls, smiling with her hand over her heart.

It was impossible to look away from the soft, affectionate light in Vivienne's eyes.

He was ever grateful to have found a governess who truly cared for them. Loved them a little even, he believed.

'You have given them a brilliant start, Clement. They will become modern independent ladies. You should be proud.'

Modern? Independent? For all that these were enlightened times, he was not certain an independent attitude would be in their best interest.

As Baron Granville's nieces they would need to take their place in society. Perhaps Vivienne did not understand that. Not existing within the stricter requirements of the upper class, she had a bit more freedom.

Not that he knew for certain her station since she kept that part of her past to herself. A vicar's daughter or perhaps a genteel lady from the fringes of society fallen on hard times was his best guess.

Still though, Alice and Jayne were only ten years old. There were several years before they would need to settle down and behave by society's rules.

Let them have their fun, he decided. For as long as Vivienne remained their governess, let them have it.

* * *

Vivienne walked across the children's bedroom, watching them sleep and thinking about what a splendid sandcastle they had made. It had been the four of them at the end, building towers and a grand moat.

They had screeched when the tide rushed in and filled the moat, then moaned when a wave knocked the castle over. With shrieks of feigned outrage, they'd dashed about, stamping and splashing in the water which had carried off their creation.

It had all been great fun but now, hours later, the best part of Vivienne's day was just beginning. This was the fulfilment of her dream. The reason she had become a travelling governess. What did it matter that she was taking photos of insects instead of birds?

What she had never imagined when she'd set out on this adventure was how much she would enjoy working with Clement. His enthusiasm for his subject matter was contagious. Tonight, she might try to impress him by picking up an ugly insect. Ugly to her, at least. Her partner considered them all to be wondrous creations, each with a purpose for being in the world.

As was her custom, Vivienne stopped beside Alice's bed, bending to kiss her forehead. Perhaps she should not. It would only make it more difficult to leave them. But that was still weeks away. This was now and she would indulge in the moment.

Turning to Jayne's bed, she stroked the hair from

her brow, then gave the child a goodnight kiss as well. But wait…something was wrong. Her skin was too hot.

Vivienne turned back to Alice's bed, touching her skin in order to compare. Humm…cool, moist. She swiped her fingers over Jayne's cheek. Hot, dry. Rushing for Clement's door, she knocked.

Clement smiled when he opened to her. His grin fell at once. Her expression must look quite worried.

'Jayne is ill.'

Clement walked towards the girls' doorway, not looking terribly alarmed. 'Children get sick. It is not unusual.'

'It is for me.'

He touched Jayne's forehead with the backs of his fingers, then bent to kiss her cheek. 'You have never had one of your charges fall ill?'

Never, not one single time. How could she? She was an imposter.

Now Jayne would pay the price because Vivienne had absolutely no idea how to deal with this situation. How irresponsible of her to have taken this job. What she had believed was that she would simply keep the girls entertained for the summer. She ought to have anticipated that one of them might become ill.

Please do not let it be something horrible, she silently prayed.

'I wonder if Mrs Prentis is still up,' she said. 'She

did raise six children and will have dealt with fevers many times.'

'Of course she has. Try not to worry. If Mrs Prentis is alarmed, we will send for a doctor in the morning.'

And between now and then, she would sit by Jayne's bed and watch her breathe. It was what her mother used to do, she recalled now, watch at her bedside until the physician arrived.

Chapter Seven

Before dawn Jayne developed spots on her back.

Mrs Prentis diagnosed them as chickenpox. Each and every one of her children had had them, so she knew the signs.

'I shall go for the doctor at once.' Clement rose from his daughter's bedside.

'Surely not.' Mrs Prentis bent lower to look at the red welts on Jayne's back. 'The poor man will not be pleased to be called away because of a common childhood ailment.'

'It isn't dangerous?' Clement asked.

'It can be, but usually it is merely uncomfortable for a week or so. I suggest we wait and see. If it seems more serious, we will call for the doctor then.' Mrs Prentis tugged the blanket over Jayne. 'There now, my dearie, how are you feeling?'

'Bad in my head.'

'No need to fret. It will soon pass and then your father and Miss Curtis will do all they can to keep you entertained.'

Jayne smiled, closed her eyes and went back to sleep.

'Alice, lift your gown, will you?' Vivienne asked. 'Spots tend to jump from one child to the next in a blink.'

This did not sound at all good, but Clement kept the thought to himself. No need to add to the anxiety.

It was somewhat reassuring that Vivienne did not seem worried when moments before, she had.

'Ah, there one is. It is to bed with you, too, then.' Vivienne eased Alice down, covered her up, then kissed her cheek.

'Not to worry, Mr Marston.' Mrs Prentis patted his arm. 'Having them get it at the same time is for the best. Why, when one of mine came down with it, I put them all together to make sure they all got it at once. Better to get it over and done, I say. And it is far safer to have it when they are young. Once they recover they will never get it again.'

'I never had chickenpox,' he said. 'Will I catch it from them?' He might since he would not avoid them, especially when they were ill.

'Why, of course you did. That little scar near your eye is from it. You are quite safe to be around your children,' their landlady reassured him.

He must have been very young when it happened. He did not even recall the event.

'Vivienne, have you had chickenpox?' he asked. If she had not, she must leave the room at once. He would not allow her to risk her health to care for Alice and Jayne. She had already taken a risk by kissing Alice's cheek.

'I have—both my sister and I caught it when I was nine years old.'

'All is well, then,' Mrs Prentis declared. 'I shall go to the kitchen and make a good nutritious broth.' With a smile and a nod, she bustled from the bedroom.

'And I suppose that leaves us to find a way of entertaining them until they recover.'

'I will do it. If you will stay with them for a few hours, I will go with Mrs Prentis when she goes into town. I'll purchase a few things Jayne and Alice will enjoy.'

'Thank you, Vivienne. I cannot imagine how I would get along without you.'

She bit her lip, glanced away.

Dash it, he'd done it again. Reminded her that the time would come when she must leave them. Growing closer to the girls was not something she could prevent. No wonder it grieved her to think about it.

He would be careful not to say such a thing again. Not that he could keep from thinking about it, though... and wishing circumstances were not what they were.

* * *

It was the oddest thing, but looking back, Vivienne recalled those two weeks of her childhood when she was sick with chickenpox to have been a good time.

Once she and Grace had got over the fever, they'd had a great deal of fun playing games with their mother. Great-Aunt Anne had been visiting at the time and had spent hours each day telling them stories.

The trip to town today had been a great success. She had brought back paper dolls, coloured chalk and chalk boards, as well as too many books to be carried upstairs at one time.

Coming into the girls' bedroom, she found Clement sitting on a chair placed between his daughters' beds. The girls were asleep and so was he. A large book with paintings of butterflies lay open across his lap. His head lolled back on the chair and his lips were parted ever so slightly in sleep.

She set the armload of books she had carried upstairs on the desk. Crossing to Clement, she meant to wake him before his neck grew stiff.

Instead, she stood over him, looking at the scar Miss Prentis had pointed out. She had not noticed it before, but there was no reason she would have, never having had the opportunity to watch his face in repose before.

What a good face it was. Bold, humorous, studious and, most of all, loving. What sort of man, and barely a man at the time, put his dreams on hold to raise his infant nieces?

Indeed, this was a very good face. Not refined, not swoon worthy, but by far the most handsome she had ever seen. Here was a man who gave love without hesitation no matter the sacrifice to himself.

And he had wonderful lips, so warm and expressive. She did not mean only when they were smiling, either. No, just now she was thinking of how they had felt when he'd kissed her. How those lips had spoken in emotion rather than words.

Slowly, his eyes opened, he blinked once and then smiled. 'You're back from town,' he murmured.

Yes, clearly she was. What he probably meant was why was she standing over him?

'I just arrived. I was about to wake you. You fell asleep with your neck at an angle. I thought it might be getting stiff.'

He turned his head this way and then that, up and down as if testing for soreness. 'You rescued me in time, but thank you for your concern.'

It was a fortunate thing he could not be inside her mind right then. If he could, he would find that concern was only a small part of what she had been feeling.

At that point Alice woke up. 'I'm itchy,' she complained.

'Let me see, then.' Vivienne went to the bed and

lifted the back of her gown. 'You are coming along nicely.'

'It doesn't feel nice.'

'It will once you begin to recover and are able to play with the toys I brought from town.'

'Toys!' Her eyes brightened a bit at the news.

'They are the very type my mother gave me when I had chickenpox. Now, the most important thing you must remember is not to scratch. If you do, it will leave a scar.'

'But it feels so itchy. I might.'

'I will dab some calamine lotion on your spots. It should help.'

'You are lucky girls to have such a splendid governess.' Clement smiled at her, his eyes soft and his grin wide.

And all at once, for the first time, she did not feel like an imposter. She was a governess.

Clement sat at his desk, Vivienne shoulder to shoulder beside him. He stared at the insect he was drawing without really seeing it. His mind wandered, he needed sleep. Photographs might have kept him focused but there were not any tonight. His assistant had been caring for sick children all day, insects forgotten.

Even though she sat here beside him, she must be far wearier than he was. She was the one who cooled their fevers with damp cloths, who dabbed their blisters with soothing lotion and fed them broth.

He had tried to help, but she'd shooed him off with a wave of her fingers. This was her job, she'd insisted. The reason he had hired her was to care for the girls and she meant to do it. Even so, he was exhausted. There was nothing like worry to drain a soul.

Just because Vivienne and his landlady's children had come through chickenpox unscathed, and just because he apparently had as well, did not mean that all children did. In spite of the ladies' sunny attitudes in the face of this illness, he well knew that some children did not survive it.

Until the fevers passed his nerves would be on edge.

'Clement…' Vivienne wriggled the pencil out of his grip '…you just drew a line across the paper.'

Had he nodded off for an instant? For the first time that he could recall, his research was unfocused.

Seeing Vivienne's bemused expression, he frowned. 'I will need to start the drawing again.' He reached for a blank sheet, but she put her hand on the stack, preventing him.

'The damselfly will not mind waiting for her portrait until you have rested. We are finished here for the night.'

'I cannot do her justice in this state, anyway.'

'Go to bed, Clement. I will watch the children sleep.'

Would she? Her lids drooped with weariness. There

were dark circles under her eyes and her shoulders sagged.

'No, Vivie, you sleep while I watch.'

It took a moment for him to realise his mistake in calling her by the endearment. The fact that she did not mention it only went to prove how exhausted she was.

'I will earn my wage.'

It's what she always said, but he knew that her motivation in caring for the girls was not financial. In fact, she seemed remarkably unconcerned with money. Everything she had purchased in town had been with her own funds. Naturally, he had tried to reimburse her but, oddly, she had refused. How puzzling that a young lady fallen on hard times would have any funds to spare. Since he did not wish to pry, he kept the thought to himself.

'We will sit together,' he decided. 'Take turns watching them breathe.'

'Listening so they do not unknowingly scratch.'

Vivienne got up from the desk and then went into the girls' bedroom. She sat on a chair, a hard wooden chair with no cushion. He'd spent enough hours in it to know it was not an ideal place to pass the night.

There was a small sofa in his chamber. He looked it over to see if it would slide through the doorway. Good, it would clear with half an inch on each side.

He made a space for it along the wall under a window where they had a clear view of his fitfully sleeping daughters. Funny how he had long since stopped thinking of them as his nieces. That was the relationship they had with his brothers. As far as uncles went, though, they were not terribly doting.

The distance between London and Whisper Glen was further than the miles accounted for. If they wished to, his brothers could easily take the train and visit. But they had only done so a handful of times.

Clement could have taken the girls to London, but Miss Logan had not liked travelling and the thought of taking them by himself was daunting. Better to keep them at home where life seemed safer and healthier.

'Where have you wandered, Clement?'

What? Having become lost in his thoughts he discovered he had been standing beside the sofa, gazing out the window. Below in the garden, he saw bushes being lashed in a stiff wind. One pane of glass vibrated, apparently loose in the frame.

'Ah, I'm just thinking about my brothers.' He indicated the sofa with a sweep of his hand. 'I imagine you are as done with that chair as I am. Sit here with me instead.'

'Quite done,' she said, then eased down and snuggled into the cushions. 'This is heavenly.'

It was, but in a way she would probably not guess. The sofa was not as wide as most and so it put them close enough that he caught a whiff of rose water in her hair.

'Tell me about your brothers.'

'Duncan is the older one, Eldon the younger. Both of them live in London.'

'Alice and Jayne must enjoy having uncles.'

'The truth is, they barely know their uncles. Duncan used to spend all his time entertaining himself in various ways. He wed six months ago and now his bride keeps him fully occupied. Eldon is now sniffing about the marriage mart. Busy fellows.' He yawned, stretched. Since there was little room on the sofa, he rested his arm along the back behind Vivienne. 'You mentioned a sister. Any brothers?'

'A brother-in-law only. He is a wonderful man and I am happy for my sister...did you hear scratching?'

He shook his head. 'Are you and your sister are close, then?'

She nodded, 'Oh, yes. Grace and George are on holiday on the Continent. They must be in Paris now.'

All of a sudden she blinked, frowning. 'Not on holiday so much as business. George has ties in industry.'

'Did you hear Jayne miss a breath?'

She shook her head, then rested it on his shoulder. 'No.'

Under normal circumstances she would not do something so familiar. Surely even now she meant nothing by it except that she was hours beyond weary.

Because he was in the same condition, he let his

arm slip off the back of the sofa and settle around her shoulders.

'I'm sad for your brothers,' she murmured. 'They have no idea what they are missing by not being good uncles.'

'Distant uncles. There is a difference.'

'I have a great-aunt. I see her several times a year even though my family lives in…oh, in a distant city from her. But families are all different. Mine are not like yours…yours are not like mine…'

Her conversation seemed unfocused, but it hardly mattered since his own attention was wavering.

'Clement, did Alice just miss a breath?'

'No, I would have noticed if she had.'

She closed her eyes. He closed his, resting his head on top of hers. Rose-scented curls tickled his nose and made him smile.

'Vivie, did you just hear scratching?'

Vivienne felt warm…and so comfortable snuggled against her pillow. She nuzzled her cheek into it. Sighed.

'Jayne, are Papa and Miss Curtis allowed to curl up all over each other?'

'I think not. You must be married to do that.'

'Perhaps they wed in the night.'

What?

What!!

Vivienne exploded off the sofa. So did Clement. They banged their heads together...then stared at one another in horror. She smoothed her skirts while he rubbed the sore spot on his chin.

'Papa, did you get married in the night?' Jayne asked. 'Is Miss Curtis our new mother?'

Clement cleared his throat, 'No, we did not wed.'

'Then why were you sleeping all over each other?'

'We were not sleeping, exactly, we were merely resting our eyes while we watched over you.'

A change of subject was called for and in a hurry.

'But look at you! You both seem much improved,' Vivienne declared.

She pressed her cheek to Jayne's and then to Alice's. Glancing up at Clement, she said, 'Nice and cool, no more fever.'

She saw it when a prayer of thanks crossed their father's eyes. And for good reason. It was wonderful to see the sparkle return to the children's expressions.

'We wish you did wed in the night, Papa,' Alice declared.

'We need a mother, after all.' Jayne smiled at Vivienne when she said so.

'Perhaps one day I will,' Clement stated. 'But for now you have very fine and dedicated governess. Wait until you see the gifts she's brought you.'

At the same time the girls leapt out of bed.

'Ouch!' Alice pressed the top of her head.

'That hurt!' Jayne sat back down on her mattress.

'And no wonder. You cannot leap about so suddenly. You need to rest so that you can fully recover. After breakfast, if you are still feeling better, I will show you what I have for you.'

'Maybe we won't mind being sick, Jayne,' Alice suggested.

'Not if there are new toys and we have Miss Curtis to play with us. We will have a merry time.'

The sooner Alice and Jayne recovered, the better, in Vivienne's opinion. An opinion which was not all to do with their health. Quite clearly she and Clement could not spend another night keeping watch together.

Their intentions had been well founded. Sick children needed attention. Two people guarding them was safer. One could not be too careful. They had not meant to doze off. Certainly had not intended to wake up entwined and have the children believe they had got married.

Caution was called for when it came to her employer. The last thing she should do was put herself in a position where she would be forced to marry Clement Marston.

Why, the very thought was— Not intriguing...no, never that. Unacceptable was what it was. Her father had made an agreement with the Marquess of Winterfeld. Everett and her parents had been generous in allowing her this time to go on holiday...with her sister. How thankless was she to have let the thought of wedding Clement cross the corner of her mind.

Well, she would not allow it to happen again. If Clement decided to give his children a mother, it would not be their governess. Even though he was not a baron, at this point in time he was next in line to be. Therefore he would feel he owed it to his family and children to marry to the best advantage.

Clement kissed each of his girls, then said, 'I will go to the kitchen, bring us all some breakfast. Mrs Prentis will be happy to know you two are on the mend.'

Once the door closed behind him, Alice and Jayne bent their heads together, whispering and smiling... casting Vivienne sidelong glances.

Perhaps it should not be, but it was reassuring to see them plotting a prank, for clearly it was what they were doing.

Vivienne would overlook a dozen mischievous plans if it meant seeing the fevers gone and the worst over. There would still be the blisters to deal with, but there would be games and books to get them through.

Soon they would be back to their studies and looking for specimens for their father's book...her book, too, now. While her name would not appear on the cover, her photos were on every page. Her heart was on every page. Afternoon excursions with Clement and the girls, evenings spent assisting him...oh, yes, her heart was in all of it.

* * *

Clement leaned against his doorway, looking into the children's bedroom. Vivienne and the girls sat on the rug. They looked like a flower bouquet, the way their skirts swirled about them in a blend of red, yellow and green.

The three of them were caught up in cutting out paper dolls so he did not think they noticed him. Good. Watching them in unguarded moments was one of his favourite things to do. Now that Vivienne was added to the mix, it was all the better.

They were laughing while they snipped paper dresses. It seemed a dull way to spend time to him, but Alice and Jayne were enjoying it and Vivienne, too, by the looks of it.

They attached elegant gown after elegant gown to their dolls. Apparently they were preparing for the most important ball of the year and deciding whose dress would best win the attention of the gentlemen.

Their fevers had been gone for a week and a day. The blisters were healing so well that the girls wanted to go outside. Vivienne would not allow it, telling them that they must not risk their trip to town by venturing out too soon.

Alice and Jayne did not give her more than a second's argument since they were quite anxious for the trip that chicken pox had thwarted.

Jayne glanced up.

'Look, Alice, Papa is here.' A smile passed between them...but not an ordinary one. Intuition and experience warned him something was brewing.

But then they hopped up from the floor and ran to him. Jayne stood on his shoes and gave him a hug. Nothing out of line in that.

Alice came up to him, chin pointed up while she smiled and waited for him to tug the bow in her hair.

Perhaps he'd imagined the look he had seen a moment ago, mistaken it for something else.

'Would you like to join us?' Vivienne smiled up from her spot on the floor. 'Each and every gown you see here is the height of fashion. All straight from Paris. Every woman will be wearing them this Season.'

'Our governess knows all about elegant gowns and shoes and hats and...everything,' Alice declared.

'Every single thing about jewels,' Jayne added.

'You must have attended many balls, Vivienne.' He gave her a teasing wink. He had been asked to join, after all. 'How else does one know how to dress a debutante in her finest?'

She gave him back a wink, a laugh. 'It says how to do it, right here on the illustration pages.'

Jayne whispered in Alice's ear. There went that secret look, putting all his senses on alert again.

'Papa, we would like for you to read us a story,' Jayne said.

That seemed innocent enough, on the surface.

'Of course, it would be my pleasure. Which book would you like?'

'One of our new ones. It is up high in the cupboard,' Alice told him. 'We cannot reach it.'

'What is it called?'

'"The Tail of Lost Dog".'

He went into the built-in cupboard. It was dim inside. Without his reading glasses he could not tell one book from the next. 'Which side is it on?'

Alice sat down on the wooden chair that had no cushion. 'On the left, up high.'

He reached up, felt a stack of books. Any one of them could be the one they wanted.

'What if I read the top one?'

'We have our hearts set on hearing that one. Maybe Miss Curtis can help you find it.'

There was little room for two people, but Vivienne squeezed in, going up on her toes to better see the book titles.

Fine hairs on his neck came to attention. Too late he realised this was a trap.

In the instant the door shut, he heard Jayne giggle.

He reached for the knob, but too late. A chair scraped on the floor, the knob jerked under his hand when one of the girls jammed the chair under it, making it impossible to open.

They were trapped. In the dark. With barely enough room to turn around without touching.

'Open this door immediately or there will be consequences!'

Skipping feet sounded across the floor.

'Alice! Jayne! You must let us out. I am terrified of the dark,' Vivienne called.

'Papa will keep you safe, just like he does us.' Alice's voice came from the hallway now.

'Come back here this minute, girls.' He gave the order in his deepest, most commanding voice.

'After we get cake from Mrs Prentis, Papa.'

'And after you fall in love.'

He heard the bedroom door close. After that, silence.

Nearly silence. Inside the cupboard he heard Vivienne's breath coming quick.

'You are afraid of the dark?'

'No, I was merely appealing to their tender mercies.'

'Apparently they do not have any. I apologise for their behaviour. This is unacceptable.'

She turned, something soft brushing his arm. He did not allow himself to dwell on what it was, but it wasn't an elbow, nor a shoulder.

'Please do not be too hard on them. Every little girl longs for a mother.'

'Longing is one thing. I know they do. But causing trouble in order to get their way will not do.'

'I wonder how long they think it will take for us to fall in love,' she mused.

The small space filled with the delicate fragrance of

a rose. It would be coming from her hair he thought, but it might also come from the tender spot behind her ear where ladies liked to dab their scents.

'They must think we will emerge from here magically engaged. I have brought up monsters, I fear.'

She laughed, which he felt as much as he heard.

He pressed his back against the door, hoping to put some distance between them. Or, rather between him and temptation. It did no good. She was still so close that he felt it when the fabric of her skirt wrapped around his trousers. Even with no part of him touching her, he felt things he should not be feeling. He could so easily kiss her again, tenderly call her Vivie.

The one and only thing keeping him from doing both those things was that she was helpless to step away from him if she wished to. And yet, in the dark, both of them breathing hard, feeling one another's heat, the sensation was already as intimate as a kiss.

'How long does it take them to eat cake?' he grumbled.

'Not long enough, I fear.' Her whisper was soft and he thought he must have misheard.

'I beg your pardon?'

'Long enough, I fear,' she said.

He frowned. 'You have nothing to fear from me, I promise. I will protect you in the dark, just as my daughters said I would.'

She nodded, then said nothing else for what seemed a long time.

'I know.' Her whisper was once again under her breath. If he thought he heard regret in her tone, he would be as mistaken as he had been a moment ago.

And so they stood, nearly touching, breathing and wondering...at least he was—what would happen if he gave in to temptation and did what he wanted to do? What if he kissed her long and hard? What if this time it was not disguised as a thank you? Only confirmed that he wanted her. Would she reconsider her next engagement?

Beset by questions, he continued to breathe, in and out, long and slow...fighting the realisation creeping into his brain. He did not want to acknowledge it...it could not be and yet it was.

He curled his hands into fists and accidently caught a bit of lace in his fingers. Lace was utterly feminine. He ought to let go of it. To let go of the fog obscuring his good sense. In the moment all he knew was that his children needed a mother. They loved Vivienne, they wanted her.

And he...dash it...he was not going to lean closer to her lips, hinting at a kiss. He had promised she was safe with him. Safe was what she would be.

Pressing harder against the door, he suddenly fell backwards into the bedroom.

'Oh, my gracious!' He looked up from the floor to

see Mrs Prentis leaning over him, fingers pressed to her round, rosy cheeks. 'They did lock you in!'

'And they shall pay for it.' This prank had gone too far. He had nearly gone too far.

'Oh, yes, Sir, you must discipline them.' Mrs Prentis's shoulders heaved ever so slightly. The woman wasn't taking this as seriously as she ought to. 'Just as soon as they finish their cake.'

As soon as they finished their cake! What nonsense was this?

'Do you realise what they intended to do?' She must not or she would not be taking this so lightly.

'The poor dearies were hoping to get a mother, I would expect.'

'In the most inappropriate way possible.'

'No harm was really done,' Vivienne said calmly.

No harm? He'd come within seconds of losing control, of doing something which would compromise his children's governess…his assistant.

Looking at her now, seeing her expression cool and unconcerned, he wondered if the temptation had been only on his part. It had to have been. Vivienne's cheeks were not flushed. Clement was pretty dashed certain all of him was flushed.

While he reflected on it, Alice and Jayne came into the room. Alice held her cake, grinning though a smattering of crumbs on her mouth.

'Did you fall in love?' Alice asked.

'That is not quite how it is done, my dearies.' Mrs Prentis tried to frown, but it did not come across as severe as it ought to have.

A pair of bright spots bloomed in Vivienne's cheeks. She walked to the window and looked out, apparently trying to hide her reaction. How was it that being alone with him had not made her blush, but Alice's question had?

'I will have a moment alone with my children.'

'Come, Vivienne,' Mrs Prentis said. 'There is more cake in the kitchen.'

Vivienne cast him a sidelong frown while she walked out of the chamber, side by side with their hostess.

Did she, like Mrs Prentis, not believe discipline was called for here?

He understood his daughters' feelings. Naturally they wanted a woman to love them and be their mother.

It was not their need for such a woman he was chastising, it the way in which they'd attempted to get one...to capture one, more to the point.

'Sit down. Give me the rest of your cake.' He held out his hand.

Jayne swallowed hard. Alice dumped a few dozen crumbs in his palm.

He paced before them, his mind churning.

'Please tell me you understand what you did wrong.'

They glanced at one another...holding their silence.

'What you did was unacceptable.'

'We are sorry we locked you in the cupboard,' were the words which came from Jayne's mouth, but he doubted they were sincere.

'I hope you are sorry. And I expect you to think over what you did during your punishment. For the next week you will not play with paper dolls, nor will you read any book which is not a textbook. And no cake.'

'But we only meant for us all to be happy.'

'I do not believe your governess appreciated being locked up in such a small space.'

With him, where the only thing to do was breathe, sweat under the collar and resist fiery temptation.

'Do you understand why you must face consequences?'

For all that he understood them wanting a mother and that they wanted their governess to be that special lady, what they had done must be addressed.

'I understand this is hard for you, not having a mother. But you cannot lock people up together in order to get one.'

'But don't you love Miss Curtis?' Jayne gave him a wide-eyed glance of disbelief.

'You cannot simply force people into a small space and expect them to fall in love. It is not done.'

Having said all he could on the matter, he walked towards his chamber to give them time to think over their misbehaviour.

'Only you needed to,' Alice mumbled.

That brought him up him short. He turned slowly about.

'What was that?'

'Miss Curtis is already in love with you,' Jayne said with Alice nodding agreement. 'So only you need to fall in love now.'

'You are ten years old. You cannot know such a thing. No one is in love with anybody.'

'Yes, Father,' the two of them said at the same time.

They were little girls and did not know what they were speaking of. Vivienne would get a good laugh out of if he told her.

Perhaps, though, he would keep this to himself. He was not sure why, only that it felt the wisest thing to do.

Chapter Eight

Vivienne sat on the front seat beside Mrs Prentis while their hostess drove the carriage towards Sea Mist, the village nearest the inn.

She glanced around at Alice and Jayne sitting on the back seat. The children looked as healthy as if they had never been ill.

During the week of their punishment the children had behaved so well that at the end of it, their father consented to let them go to the village for the long-awaited outing.

They would visit shops, make some purchases and then admire them over tea and sandwiches at the bakery.

Vivienne was in high spirits over the excursion, as much as the girls were. In a sense, their punishment had been hers, too. Only textbooks for entertainment had been a great bore.

The nights had been better when, after the girls were asleep, she had her time with Clement.

Seeing the book come together was exciting. Clement's drawings and detailed descriptions, enhanced by her photographs, were going to make it a great success.

No doubt their work would stand above the others. Publishers would gather at their door... Clement's door, she meant.

While she watched birds sweeping over rolling stretches of grass, her mind wandered to the time she and Clement had spent in the cupboard...because that was where her mind tended to wander when left free to ramble. Even when it was not rambling it cut into her thoughts.

It was not easy to ignore the delightful afterglow of being confined in the small space with him.

He had been so...so very...responsible. He'd wanted to kiss her. She could nearly smell the desire calling them to act on it. How noble he had been fighting the battle to remain respectful of her.

She admired him for it, of course. Admired him for a great many things. He was brave when the occasion called for it, unrestrained in vulnerable moments and restrained when it was prudent to be.

But feathers. Far better to keep her affection for him a special secret within her heart. Let it glimmer in private since that was the only place it could exist.

Arriving at the village, Mrs Prentis secured the carriage at the livery and then left them to go about her own business. They agreed to meet at the bakery in two hours.

One only had to look at their faces to see how excited Jayne and Alice were. Living with only their father, they had not experienced a shopping trip like this one.

Vivienne was as excited as they were. To be able to share this first-time experience with her girls—

Very well, not really her girls, but she was as happy to share this day with them as if they were.

They were of an age to learn the pleasures of browsing the shops, looking for pretty hats, and the nicest gloves in which to clutch sweet little reticules.

They would not need any of those things yet, not having been exposed to society. Which Vivienne considered to be a good thing. A child's early years were meant to be carefree...days packed with sunshine and outdoor adventure. Balanced with study, naturally, but, in all, childhood was a time of happy exploration.

The day would come when they would need to put society's pretty trappings to use as tools, but not today.

Today was for having fun. Seeing it all through their young eyes was a treat. Vivienne recalled the days when she and her sister had shopped for adventure, not necessity.

In her real life as a high-born lady, making purchases was expected. A lady must be seen spending her father's wealth to a certain degree. Also there was the obligation to keep the shop owners in business.

What a lady purchased was often noticed and copied. Not Vivienne since her tastes were on the plain side and no one copied her, but her sister—people did tend to notice what Grace bought and wore.

Sadly, when shopping became something of an occupation, it took away from the pleasure. Today, with Alice and Jayne, it would be pure enjoyment.

'What shop would you like to visit first?' she asked, hoping it would be the hat shop…or the book store would be lovely, too.

'Mrs Fortune's Feathers and Frocks,' Jayne declared, her gaze seeming spellbound by a hat having red plumage, which arched majestically from a satin brim.

'Very well. We shall visit Mrs Fortune's. Now tell me again… What are the rules of polite behaviour?'

'One may speak and chatter, but not too loudly. It is rude to cause a distraction for other ladies who are shopping.'

'Excellent. What else?'

'Ask permission before you pick something up. Treat the merchandise with respect.'

'Excellent again. But what was that last bit we talked about?'

Matching grins lit their faces, ear to ear.

'If we see something we would like to purchase, tell you what it is and you will consider it.'

'Come then, we will have a grand time.'

With a happy screech, they hopped up and down, racing for the front door, eager to explore the feathers and frocks. It might not be all their fault that they forgot rule number one so quickly. There were flashy, pretty things wherever one looked.

Alice and Jayne made an effort to control their enthusiasm, but each item they asked to inspect shone brighter than the next. The volume of their admiration remained acceptable until they spotted a bird's nest, complete with eggs, nestled into the brim of a hat. It was a gaudy thing with a purple satin band and red streamers.

A woman standing in front of an oval mirror picked it up, placing it on her head. She gazed at her reflection, chin up, chin down, then side to side. She must have liked the look because she gave herself a pouty-lipped smile.

Undone, the girls' gasps of dismay were loud enough to be heard from the front door to the fitting rooms in the back.

The woman paused in her preening to give them a disapproving stare, or rather her reflection in the mirror did. She lifted one finger to her lips in a shushing gesture.

Jayne gave Alice a look. Oh, dear. Alice gave it back. They giggled which gained a harsher frown from the woman at the mirror.

Vivienne sided with the girls about the absurdity of wearing a bird's nest. No sensible woman should be seen in such a thing.

Not only did she not reprimand Alice and Jayne for their reaction, she was within a breath of pointing out that this was a business establishment and not a library.

'Pity the poor bird who lost her home and family in the name of fashion,' she told the girls, not as quietly as she might have.

'We should put it back where it came from so mama bird can hatch her eggs,' Jayne said, her gaze narrowed on the hat.

'It is too late for that,' she answered. 'Those will not be real eggs. Only paste.'

'The nest is real,' Alice declared, 'We should put it in a tree so mother bird can lay more eggs to hatch.'

'I am afraid we cannot, my dears. We do not even know where it came—'

'Miss!' The woman at the mirror spun about, pinning Vivienne with a glare, complete with narrowed eyes and a turned-up nose. 'You must control your charges.'

Vivienne began to simmer. Who was this person treating complete strangers, children no less, with such a haughty attitude?

'Do you intend to purchase that outrageous hat?' she asked, her voice crisp with indignation for Alice and

Jayne's sake. It was all she could do to behave like a lady and not reveal her real identity.

The woman turned to the young lady standing behind the counter who had been watching the exchange in wide-eyed interest.

'I will not patronise your shop unless you remove this disruptive person and those children.'

The girl glanced back and forth between Vivienne and the woman, clearly not sure of what to do.

'I will pay you three times what you are asking for the hat,' Vivienne said.

'Of all the impertinent nonsense,' the woman declared, tying the purple ribbon under her chin.

The assistant grinned. 'The hat has been sold, Miss. I must ask you to remove it.'

And so in the end, Vivienne and the girls walked out of the shop only moments behind the offended patron, being the proud owners of an overpriced, ridiculous-looking hat.

Alice and Jayne carried it between them, gazing sorrowfully at the nest.

'No need to fret, my dears. When we get back to the inn we will find a tree to place it in. Perhaps a mother bird who's lost her nest will discover this one and then use it to hatch her eggs.'

'How brilliant!' Jayne grabbed her in a hug from one side. Alice hugged her around the middle on the other side.

'We love you, Miss Curtis,' they said, their sweet voices coming one on top of the other.

It was terribly difficult not to say the same back to them. But proprieties must be observed. A governess might express passing affection for her charges, but nothing more.

Vivienne bit her lip, blinked back a tear.

'May we take turns wearing the hat?' Jayne asked.

'Oh, please let us!' Alice hopped about on her toes. 'We may never get to wear something so horrid again.'

It was the truth and so Vivienne laughed when she wanted to sniffle.

'You may, but only if you share it with me.'

'And Papa, Miss Curtis paid three times the price of the hat so that we could put the nest in a tree for another bird to have,' Jayne told him while they stood a distance from said tree, watching Alice scramble out on a limb.

Vivienne stood underneath, her arms spread, apparently thinking to catch her if she fell. The branch was low so he resisted the urge to run to the tree and add his support.

'Three times?' Clement asked in case he had not heard correctly.

'Yes, Papa.'

Humph…how had she managed that? It must have cost her a month's salary.

'We still think you should fall in love with her.'

He was saved from having to argue the point by a carriage turning on to the drive. Perhaps Mrs Prentis had let out another room. But, no, as soon as the carriage stopped in front of the inn, he recognised it. How surprising to get a visit from Baron Granville here on the island. He hoped it was not to deliver some sort of bad news.

'Run along and help your sister and Miss Curtis place the nest, my dear.' Jayne stood on his toes, gave him a hug and then dashed away.

He walked to the carriage to greet his older brother. There were no trunks on the roof so they must not intend to stay.

The driver climbed down, opened the door. Duncan stepped down.

'It is good to see you, Brother,' Clement said, thinking that surprising would have been a better word.

They pounded one another on the back while the driver helped his sister-in-law down.

As always, Mildred dressed above the occasion. As far as Clement knew, there was no ball being hosted in the vicinity tonight.

'Clement! It is so wonderful to see you.' Mildred came forward as if to embrace him, but then stopped short. She twirled about in her gown then waited, he thought, for it to be admired.

'You look quite fetching this afternoon, Mildred. What a surprise to see you and my brother here.'

'It happens that we are here on holiday. When Duncan mentioned you were here as well, I insisted that we must pay you a visit. You know, I have never met my nieces. I have been anxious to, ever since I married your brother.'

'It is true,' Duncan said with an indulgent smile at his bride.

'They will take their place in society one day and I must guide them, see them settled into advantageous marriages,' Mildred declared. 'After all, the higher they wed the better it will be for my own children when they come along.'

'While I appreciate your interest, that day is a long way off. They are only ten years old.' Naturally, his new sister-in-law would put position over childhood.

'I know that, of course. But as their only female relative, it is my duty to launch them into society. Such an undertaking cannot be begun too early.' Mildred touched her hat, fluffing a mound of silk flowers. 'I know all about them and how they came to live with you. It was kind of you to take them in.'

Kind?

Something about this conversation was beginning to set him on edge. Mildred set him on edge. She had ever since he'd met her.

In his estimation, she was a social climber. Being

the youngest of four daughters, her prospects had been limited. When Duncan had shown a small interest in her, she'd reeled him straight in. A fish on a hook was the image he'd always had.

However, she was family now and so he did his best to treat her with courtesy.

'Please do not make us wait a moment longer, Clement. Where are our little darlings?' his brother asked.

Our little darlings? This from the uncle who had made so little effort to see them over the years.

There was more going on here than a family gathering.

'Over there, by the tree,' he said.

His gut rolled, uneasy. He had a feeling he was going to regret this visit in some way.

Vivienne noticed the coach as soon as it turned on to the drive, but did not pay a great deal of attention to it. Alice was wriggling about on a tree limb. A responsible governess would not let her attention wander.

'Why is Papa hugging that man?' Jayne asked.

'We will know soon enough, I expect. Give me the nest, will you, so I can hand it up to your sister.'

After a few moments, Vivienne was aware of Clement coming towards them across the grass, a man on one side of him and a woman on the other.

'Jayne, Alice!' Clement called. 'Come and greet your uncle and aunt.'

Uncle? The newlywed baron who had not visited his nieces in far too long? Interesting.

She helped Alice down from the tree, took the bird nest from Jayne and then set it in the grass to be attended to later. Alice and Jayne held hands, walking towards the visitors. They seemed uncommonly shy. She followed behind them, doing her best to appear a retiring, blending-into-the-background governess. With her eyes to the ground, she did not really look at them.

Not until Jayne blurted, 'It's her!'

Her, who?

'She's come to take our hat.'

Vivienne looked up sharply, stunned to see her adversary from yesterday.

'You!' Oh, there went that pert, superior nose, lifting in the air as if she were a queen instead of the wife of a baron. 'I cannot believe it!'

'She has come to take our hat, Papa.' Jayne crossed her arms over her chest.

'Tell her she may not have it,' Alice pleaded, then clamped her lips in a pout.

Clement looked at Vivienne, eyes narrowed in question, but the corners of his mouth twitching up ever so slightly.

'Three times the amount?' he asked. 'That hat?'

'Your governess stole it from me. I had it on my head yesterday and she robbed me of it. I cannot believe this woman is in charge of Jayne and Alice. It will not do.'

'No, she didn't steal it, Papa,' Jayne said.

'Our aunt is telling a fib.' Alice's mouth fell open in apparent shock at hearing such a blatant lie.

'Miss Curtis, would you mind taking the girls inside?' Clement asked. 'And if you will, please let Mrs Prentis know she has unexpected guests for tea.'

'Come along, girls,' Vivienne called on an inner well of composure, reminding herself that she was a lady. Well-bred ladies never flouted their social position. A lesson the new baroness had clearly yet to learn. 'Perhaps Mrs Prentis will have a treat for you.'

Vivienne would need one, too, along with a few moments to gather herself. She would never have dreamed that abandoning her position in society for the summer would be so difficult. Until this moment she had not fully appreciated having it.

'Well,' Mildred stated, rising from the couch in the parlour. 'Since there is no one to serve tea, I suppose I shall do it myself. But where is that Mrs Prentis? One would expect her to do it.'

'I rent rooms at her inn. I do not pay for her social services.'

'I am only glad that Duncan and I are staying in Ventnor and not this uncultivated…' She waved her hand towards the window which had a beautiful view of the beach and dunes.

'Seaside?' he suggested. 'I find it as close to paradise as an entomologist can get.'

Mildred answered with a dismissive sniff.

'How have you been, Brother?' Duncan asked. 'You look well.'

'I am well. You would not believe what a boon this place is for my research.'

'It is all so silly, if you ask me. No one really cares about insects.'

'Mildred.' Duncan smiled at his wife in the doting way he had developed since his marriage. Seeing him like this made Clement miss the brother who had been a carefree bachelor. 'Clement is happy in his pursuit. We are happy for him.'

'But of course. Please do forgive me. We have not come to criticise. What we wish to do is discuss our nieces' futures.'

His gut clenched harder. Surely Mildred was not suggesting she and Duncan were equally accountable for his children. Until this moment neither of his brothers had been involved in any decision regarding them.

'I have their futures well in hand. You need not be concerned.'

'I am, of course. How are they to become proper young women without a woman's guidance? That woman you hired to be their governess will not do at all. I assure you, she is not a proper influence on them. Really, Clement, she was allowing Jayne to climb a tree!'

'It was Alice in the tree,' he pointed out.

'I do not doubt the governess is qualified or you would not have hired her,' his brother put in, taking a long sip of tea and smiling as if he enjoyed it. He'd always disliked tea. 'But I wonder if—'

'She must be terminated, naturally. Especially after the way she behaved towards me.' Mildred had an unattractive way of lifting her nose and sniffing to emphasise a point.

Clement set his teacup down too hard. Hopefully he had not cracked Mrs Prentis's china.

'I appreciate that you wish to help, Mildred.' He did not appreciate it. Her meddling was beyond annoying. 'But I will handle my daughters' affairs.'

'Your daughters?' There went Mildred's nose again, but this time her eyebrows shot up, too. 'They are our nieces. Ours as much as yours.'

Clement stood, agitation making it impossible to sit. When he found his voice, he addressed his brother in firm tones.

'What part did you play in raising them, Duncan? What gives you the right to claim any part of them?'

'My husband is the Baron and you are not. Really, it is not as if we wish them any harm.'

'Mildred!' For the first time Duncan looked perturbed by his wife's attitude. 'You must not use my position in the family against my brother. He has done an admirable thing in raising Alice and Jayne when Eldon and I were…when we were finding our way. Clement always was the responsible one.'

'And I respect that, of course,' Mildred said. 'However, now that we see how things are with the children, we shall proceed with what we discussed.'

What they'd discussed?

'If you have had a private discussion regarding my family,' Clement said more coolly than he felt, 'I insist on being informed of it.'

'Tell him, Duncan.'

'Indeed, please do that, Brother.' Before his temper got the better of him and he said something he could never unsay.

'We all know the girls will need to take their place in society eventually,' his brother explained awkwardly. 'Make matches to enhance the family name and position. What we propose is, when the summer is over and we have finished our travels, that you bring the children to London. We will engage a highly qualified governess and they will be strictly trained by her to fulfil their roles.'

Nothing in his life had made him angrier than hearing someone else make plans for his children. To direct their lives as if they had a right to!

'My daughters will not do well in that environment.'

'They need to have their manners refined,' Mildred said, looking at Duncan. 'Many of the finest ladies have flourished under a strict governess, as I myself did.'

If there was ever an argument against such a course of action, Mildred had just presented it.

'My wife is correct, Clement. Rest assured we shall find the very best governess for them.'

Clement yanked the door open, needing to go out before he punched his brother. They were no longer children and fighting was not acceptable to settle a disagreement.

To his surprise, there was Vivienne. Had she been eavesdropping? No matter. He had never been so happy to see anyone in his life. Calmed somewhat, he uncurled his fists.

'I am sorry to interrupt, Mr Marston. Mrs Prentis is asking for you.'

'Tell her we are not finished with tea.' Mildred insisted, looking lofty in spite of the fact that she was seated.

Vivienne looked at him, brow lifted. She would stay if he wished her to was what the gesture indicated.

'You are dismissed.' Mildred nodded at Vivienne, who ignored her.

'Stay if you do not mind, Miss Curtis. The matter we are discussing involves the children, which in turn involves you.'

'Of, course.' It was good to have an ally who was willing to spy behind a door on his behalf. He was certain that she had been doing so. 'What about the children?'

'They are not thriving under your care, Miss, and so Baron Granville and I will find them a proper governess.' Mildred did not address herself to Vivienne, but to him. 'I fear that your governess will need to find another position.'

'Miss Curtis's position is secure. Now, we would like to get on with our day. Alice and Jayne have a bird's nest to place in a tree.'

'I will take the nest and my hat with me.'

'But it is not for sale, Mrs Marston,' Vivienne announced pointedly.

'Duncan, tell her to address me as Baroness Granville.'

'Finish your tea, Mildred.' At last Duncan sounded put out with his wife. Possibly regretting he'd married her. 'We must be on our way.'

'Very well, as long as we have an agreement on our nieces' education.' Mildred set her tea cup on the tray and stood.

'We do not have an agreement. You are mistaken if you think you have any authority when it comes to my family,' Clement declared.

'Alice and Jayne are misbehaved hellions who need a much stricter hand.' Mildred reached for her reticule.

'Since they do not have a mother to do it, an older, more authoritarian governess it must be. They will be set straight within the first few months, I am sure.'

While he scoured his mind for a scathing defence of his children, a perfect rebuttal, Vivienne spoke.

'You are greatly mistaken, Baroness.' There was a quality to her voice when she pronounced the title that made it sound dismissive instead of respectful. 'They are sweet children who naturally took offence to a bird's nest being used for a decoration instead of a home for hatchlings as the Good Lord intended it to be.'

'I insist on having that hat. It ought to have been mine all along.'

'You may have it, and with my blessing. However, the nest will remain with Alice and Jayne.' Vivienne delivered the verdict with a genteel smile.

'This matter has gone awry,' Duncan said with a resigned sigh. 'Please do keep the bird's nest and the hat if it makes the girls happy. Now, to the matter of their futures. We all wish for what is best for them. Since they do not have a mother, I believe they need a lady of standing to guide them in society. My wife is willing to take on this responsibility. I am sure we are all grateful, my love.'

His sister-in-law responded with a preening smile.

'I would suggest that we wait on the decision about hiring a new governess until the autumn. We shall see then what you have done to make sure the children have had proper guidance as young ladies.' Duncan glanced between him and Mildred. 'Will you agree to that, Clement?'

'I agree that they should learn what they need to. I do not agree that they have to learn it from some stifling, old-fashioned tartar of a governess.'

'Put your foot down, Duncan. You are the Baron and the decision will be yours. Apparently your brother believes they can learn what they must under the guidance of a common governess with hardly any experience.'

'Baroness...' Again Vivienne's voice dripped with dismissiveness, as if, somehow, the position of governess was higher than that of a baroness. 'We have met only once before and so I do not expect you to understand what I am capable of teaching my charges. I assure you, Mr Marston does not need to have you engage a martinet to teach his children in order for them to learn how to act in society.'

Once Mildred found her voice she said, 'You, Miss Curtis, have a very superior attitude.'

'Indeed? It is something I was born with.'

Mildred opened her mouth, but closed it again without speaking.

Who was this woman? Holding her own, no...surpassing his sister-in-law, in 'superior attitude'. It left him dizzy.

Clement and his brother said their goodbyes, but

rather awkwardly. Still, awkward was better than angry. If he let his true emotions rule, words would have been spoken which could not be recanted. Contrary words would only divide the family. Nothing would be accomplished by creating such a rift.

Alice and Jayne were his children and he did not mean to lose them to anyone.

Once the front door closed, Clement turned to Vivienne.

'Who are you?'

She looked down and then back up. She blinked. 'I am myself, of course. Your friend and partner.'

'It is good having a friend and partner. I admit that I have rarely faced a more challenging moment.'

Late in the afternoon, Vivienne took the girls back to the tree so that they might set the nest in place.

She wore the gaudy bonnet. Long purple ribbons fluttered behind her in the breeze. Flags of victory was what they were.

It had taken her last thread of self-restraint not to admit who she was and put Mildred Marston in her place. If she had, there would be no question of her ability to teach the girls what they needed to know about becoming society ladies. Her hands were rather tied about it, though, unless she wished to admit her grand deception to the Marston family. Unless she wished to face the scandal that would be sure to follow.

And it would not be only her it followed. There was Clement's reputation to be thought of. This would surely be the very excuse his brother and his wife needed to snatch the girls away to London. She must teach Alice and Jayne what they needed to know and do it as their governess. The thought of them being taken from their father and sentenced to a strict, unloving governess was too outrageous to even consider.

Also, she had a book to finish, a dream to fulfil.

More, she was not ready to give up her friendship with Clement. The last thing she wished was for him to know she was a deceiver. He would never look at her the same way again.

She very much liked the way he'd looked at her lately. The interest in his gold-flecked gaze was not like anything she had ever seen before. Many gentlemen of her acquaintance considered her to be awkward, not interested in feminine matters. She was interested of course, only not in the things which usually appealed to society ladies, such as balls and fashionable gowns.

There was no reason whatsoever a lady could not be a proper woman while at the same time following her own pursuits.

Herein lay her dilemma when it came to the girls. She must teach them what society required of them and yet show them that they had worth of their own.

That what they wanted for themselves mattered as much as what others wanted of them.

And she must do it in a very short amount of time. When summer ended, who knew what the attitude of the woman caring for them after her would be?

'Is that a good place?' Alice asked from up in the tree. 'Will it fall down?'

'It looks splendid,' she answered. 'Come down, now. We are going to play a game.'

'Will there be a prize?'

'Every proper game must have one. But it will not be easy to earn. Let's visit the shoreline where we can play the game before the sun goes down.'

'What sort of game?'

'I will teach you how to curtsy. Whichever of you performs it best will win.'

'But who will judge?'

'Your father, of course.'

Clement felt too unsettled go to his study and make notes regarding an interesting moth he had seen towards sunset last night.

It was unusual for him to be so worried about a matter that studying did not offer relief.

From the hallway window he saw the sun getting ready to set. It was pretty tonight, with clouds drifting slowly across. In a few moments the sky would turn pink and orange.

178 *The Truth Behind the Governess*

With the girls being entertained by Mrs Prentis, he decided to go outside, walk the sandy path over the dunes towards the beach. Blowing grass made whispering sounds in the breeze which tended to come up each evening. Nature's lullaby, it seemed to him.

Ah, good, he would not be alone on the beach. Vivienne sat in the sand, very likely seeking solace the same as he was. After the way Mildred had treated her, she was probably feeling belittled, although, she had not seemed belittled or even particularly offended.

'It's uncommonly pretty tonight,' he said. 'May I sit with you?'

She smiled and nodded, patting the sand beside her. A cool, moist breeze lifted a strand of her dark hair, blowing it across her face. She swiped it away with the back of her hand.

Maybe he should not sit here with her. The temptation to kiss her was pressing. If he indulged, she might very well feel she had to resign her position.

What would he do then? He needed her to care for his children for as long as she was willing to do so.

This afternoon she had taught them to make pretty curtsies. As nice as it was, they would need to learn far more than that in order to avoid Mildred's plan for them.

Settling in the spot beside Vivienne, he let go of his troubles in favour of the glory of the sunset.

He breathed...beauty in...worries out.

'That was a difficult position you put me in, earlier,' he remarked, but smiled so she would understand he was only teasing.

'Appointing you as judge of the curtsies, do you mean?' Brilliant clouds over the sea turned her cheeks pinker than they normally were. 'You made a wise decision, though. Jayne being the champion for grace, then Alice for precise execution. Everyone was happy.'

'I hope you have a few more skills to teach them. Not that I expect you to know as much as...'

He hesitated, then thought better of hinting that her skills might not be refined enough to please his sister-in-law. It would be unfair to expect her to know all that a lady born and bred would know...all the ins and outs of what it took to be presented to society.

Then again, his governess was rather a mystery... Who had she been before she came to him? A shop girl? A merchant's daughter or a seamstress? No, definitely not. He'd wondered before if she might possibly be a gently bred lady, maybe from the lower echelons of society, who'd fallen from grace. But that didn't seem likely now as Mildred would probably have recognised her.

A well-educated vicar's daughter, then. It was the most likely explanation...or at least as good a guess as any.

'Do you think I should wed?' he asked after a moment, remembering that his lack of a wife had been mentioned in the recent argument with his brother and Mildred.

She caught a strand of hair whipping about her face, twirling it around her finger while she watched nature's show. It was as if the sky had caught fire.

'Well, it depends upon why you would be doing it, Clement. If it is because your children need a mother, perhaps…but be very careful who you choose. Do not sacrifice your own happiness. It will only make for an unhappy family in the end. If it is only to appease your family… I urge you not to wed for that reason only.' She was quiet for a moment, sifting sand through her fingers. 'But if you are in love…then by all means you should marry.'

'It all sounds so wise presented that way. Why then am I so confused?'

'Probably because there is so much at stake. Alice and Jayne's futures depend upon you making the right choices. I imagine there is no more difficult job than being a parent.'

'There is not.' But at the same time, none more rewarding.

'I admire you…choosing to become a father when you were barely grown yourself.'

'Ah, well. I will admit I did not fully know what I was getting into. In some ways I was as much a babe as they were. I don't know what would have become of us except for Miss Logan.'

'I have learned a great deal about her from the girls. I understand why they acted up when she left. In their eyes, she was their mother and so naturally they did not want anyone taking her place.'

'They don't want anyone taking your place, either.'

He ought to have left that unsaid. She had made it clear she was leaving at the end of summer. The problem was, he could not imagine his girls blossoming under another woman's care the way there were doing with Vivienne.

For a moment he got lost in thought. When, one day, he did get married, would there be any more of a sense of family than they already shared with this woman?

'I will confess, I have allowed myself to get more attached to them than is strictly professional. It is difficult not to when it comes to children.'

'Has it happened to you before? It must be hard on you, always leaving them behind to take another position.'

She did not answer with words, but gazed across the water, slowly shaking her head. He was far from a mind reader, but clearly she was dispirited over the prospect.

He caught her hand, gave it a squeeze. It seemed natural, not awkward. But then he brought her hand to his lips, kissed her fingers…and got sand in his mouth for his pains.

'Vivie…'

He should not push. She had her plans and was not willing to change them. And yet for his daughters' sake, he must ask again. But, no, that was not honest. It was for his sake, too.

Now that she had told him how fond she was of them, perhaps she would reconsider.

How to find the perfect words…

While he rummaged his mind for them, liked one and rejected another, she drew her fingers out of his, then she used one finger to brush the sand off his lips.

Her gaze was soft…could she be wondering, like he was, what a sand-dusted kiss would feel like? They were not stranded in a cupboard this time. Unlike before, she could resist his advances if she wished to.

For a moment life would be titillating, sublimely delicious. Then the kiss would be over. And if he saw regret in her eyes afterwards, it would be miserable.

Not only that, but what he needed to ask her was of more importance than a moment's elation…of knowing what a kiss with sand-chafed lips would feel like.

'Vivienne,' he said again. 'About your next engagement…would you not reconsider leaving? It would mean a great deal to us.'

Once again she sifted sand through her fingers. 'It is impossible, Clement.' Her expression transformed from soft to stricken. 'I cannot change my plans.'

'Surely you know how badly we need you, especially now.'

She closed her eyes, nodded. When she opened them, they were glistening.

'Ah, I'm sorry Vivie, I should not have pressed you. Please forgive me.'

'Yes, of course. If I could stay and help you, I would. But I simply cannot.'

It was nearly dark now so he almost missed seeing the single tear slipping down her cheek. He swiped it from her chin, stroked the shape of her jaw. It would be all too easy to swoop in for a kiss. Easy to do and hard to get over.

He dropped his hand. 'I will be grateful for whatever help you can give us before we must say goodbye.'

Dash it, why had he used those words. 'Goodbye' caught his gut and squeezed. Life was better since Vivienne had come rushing up his path seeking employment.

Imagining going back to life before her hit him hard. He feared he might not be the same man. What if his studies and explorations were no longer enough to satisfy him? Having shared them with her, they might not be.

'I suppose we should go inside. Mrs Prentis will have dinner waiting,' he said heavily.

He stood, reaching a hand down to her. She took it. Fine sand grated between their palms. Not a kiss, but nearly one in his mind.

Chapter Nine

Two days had passed since Vivienne had watched the sunset with Clement. Those stunning clouds had brought rain which went on and on.

Earlier in the day he had gone out in his raincoat and rubber boots, hoping to spot water-loving insects, he said.

Vivienne thought this was an excuse to get out of the house. Being used to the outdoors, he probably felt confined after two days of being inside.

Vivienne and the girls had kept themselves busy in the kitchen, helping Mrs Prentis prepare meals.

They had studied arithmetic and read books. Their lesson in etiquette had covered how to properly and elegantly hold eating utensils. But at ten years old, how vital was that?

In real life not terribly useful, but to keep from being consigned to a dragon of a governess, it was vital. Vivienne preferred real life where little girls were meant to have fun, not become small replicas of debutantes.

This was especially true for Alice and Jayne, being accustomed to living freely out of doors.

By the end of two days they were as restive as their father had seemed.

For all that they begged and pleaded to go out with him, he would not allow them out in the elements. Chickenpox had been one illness too many for the summer. No matter how Alice pouted and Jayne scowled, he insisted they remain safely inside.

Which had made for an endless day for Vivienne.

But now here her charges were, tucked under their blankets looking as content as slumbering kittens.

She kissed Jayne, then turned and kissed Alice. She should not allow herself to indulge in this nighttime habit. She had also begun the ritual of stroking the hair back from their brows before she kissed them. There was something about stroking hair...it was such a tender gesture of affection. Indulging in it was only going to make it that much harder to say goodbye to them when the time came.

But that time was not now and so she would stroke those soft strands, kiss those smooth brows.

Rain pelted the window. She tucked the blankets around their shoulders and then looked through Clement's open doorway.

At last she was free to join him at his desk. She wondered if his outing had resulted in anything other than release from the indoors. Perhaps it had. He was bent over something on the blotter. He had a magnifying glass lifted to his eye even though he wore his glasses.

To her surprise, she was interested to see what the creature was. Incredible as it seemed, over the course of the summer, she'd lost some of her distaste for crawling creatures. Some of them were even pretty.

This one, for instance. It was such a pure white, it did not seem real.

'What have you found? Something for me to photograph?' she asked, peering over his shoulder. She liked looking at his treasures this way. It gave her an excuse to breathe in his scent, for one thing. He smelled like fresh sea air. It clung to him at all hours of the day, but only in this position could she fully appreciate it.

Also, this vantage point gave her a better look at the insect so that she could see how to best position it for a photo. It was acceptable to be this close to him in the name of research, of absorbing knowledge. And yet it was more than knowledge she was absorbing. It was memories. Each night brought her closer to the time she would be forced to leave him.

So she memorised the scent of his skin, the raspy feel of his wool coat…his breath which tended to come quicker when he was fascinated by a particular aspect of a many-legged creature.

Summer's end was creeping closer and she meant to hoard the things she loved about him for a day when she missed him.

'It looks delicate. What is it?' she asked.

'A White Plume moth.' He turned to smile at her. One more reason she liked standing over his shoulder. It always brought his smile so close that she could feel his delight. 'It must not have taken shelter in time. I found it in a puddle of water.'

'What a shame. It's beautiful. Those wings are so bright and reaching. Makes me think of a small dragon who has moonlight shining out of it.'

'Or an angel with her wings spread.' He glanced quickly away.

Not quickly enough that she did not feel a jolt of awareness zip through her. He meant the comment about her and not the insect.

He would look at her far differently if he knew the truth about her. That she was a deceiver, who had used his family to achieve her own goal. It would crush her heart to see him look at her with reproach. She must be very careful to make certain he did not discover who she really was.

The time was coming when all he would have of her was a memory. She needed it to be a good one. He must remember her with the same affection that she would remember him.

She sat beside him, watched him sketch.

'I think our book will be a great success,' she said. 'Your drawings and descriptions make it seem as if the moth will flutter off the page.'

'Your flattery will give me an inflated head. I have colleagues who are as talented. All of us wish to have our work published.' He set down his pencil, gave her a conspiratorial glance. 'But they will not have photographs.'

'Photographs will make the book unique, but your talent and your knowledge are what will sell it in the end.'

'I do hope so.' His gaze was soft, it nearly felt as though he touched her...as if his eyes were fingers stroking her hair, her cheeks and her lips.

'Teach me to draw the moth,' she said to cover the fact that she had reacted so intensely to a simple glance.

It would not do for either of them to look too closely at this friendship of a special nature thrumming between them. While they could not look directly at it, neither could they deny seeing it. The only thing to do was ignore it...to find ways of becoming distracted in moments of temptation.

Which was why she had asked to be taught to draw the moth, quite grateful it was something pretty and not a spider.

He handed her the pencil. 'Give it a try.'

She did. While his lines were precise and created an

image which was accurate in each fine detail, her line meandered, looking more like a worm than a moth.

'Here, hold the pencil just so...' He arranged it in her fingers, then drew her hand along under his. 'It isn't so hard. It only takes practice...and patience.'

He pressed her fingers so that they made strokes on the paper which gradually took the shape of a wing.

'At times you may not recognise what's coming into shape.' The line she drew under his guidance looked like a heart. One, two, three of them. To her eyes it was romantic. 'Then, all at once, what it's meant to be is revealed.'

The hearts became the slender body of the moth.

Slowly, he let go of her hand. 'You see?'

She did, more than he probably realised. Any tracing could have been used to form the moth's body.

'And now you must show me how to take a photo,' he stated. 'It is only fair to exchange lessons.'

Fair, yes, and fun. But now, with the household asleep and the cellar dark, it was also too risky. Temptation would far outweigh distraction.

At least for her it would.

'Yes, then. Tomorrow. It will be a thrill for Alice and Jayne to watch the magic happen.'

He nodded, holding her gaze for a second too long. What she read in his smile was only two of the words she had spoken.

Thrill and magic.

She was not overly experienced with flirtation nor, did she think, was he. Which could only mean, what they were seeing in the moment was truth. To be romantic with Clement would be a thrill, more magic than she had ever experienced.

She glanced away. So did he.

If she allowed him to look too deeply within her, he might see deep regret and sorrow. He might see the lies.

Feathers, there was no way he could do that. Still, even if she kept her secrets as tight as a miser kept his funds, one day the truth might be revealed.

Not today or tomorrow, though. She would probably make it through the summer keeping her secret.

Oh, but one day when the girls were older, Clement might return to society.

What if she and Clement saw one another at a social event…would he recognise her? The Marchioness of Winterfeld would look very different from his governess. She'd act differently, too.

But if they happened to meet and their gazes collided, he would surely know her. Know her to be a liar who'd taken advantage of him and his children and all for her own gain…for a summer free to follow her own dream.

Her dream, his nightmare.

'What is wrong, Vivienne?'

'Wrong? What could be?' Except that she was a

wretch, deceiving everyone she cared for. 'I am only missing the sunshine. Perhaps tomorrow will be a brighter day.'

'Perhaps it will.'

Sunshine did return the next morning. So did his governess's normally cheerful attitude.

Her troubles of the night before must have run their course. While he was curious to know what had been bothering her, he would not press. Everyone had private matters which they wished to keep to themselves.

He certainly did, as much as anyone. Especially when it came to Vivienne.

While he had asked her to stay on more than one occasion, he had claimed it was for the sake of the children...mostly that was true. Far from the complete truth, though. What would happen if he told her the rest of it? If he admitted that his affection for her was growing quite deep.

Would it make a difference if he confessed it? If he told her that he believed they would work well as a family...mother, father...

Husband, wife. Especially that.

Would she trade her next assignment for his heart?

He no longer questioned that she affected it in a way no woman ever had. If things went very well, perhaps they might one day find themselves in a love match.

Ah, but it was better not to look at that possibility

too closely. For now, surely it was enough to feel exceptionally fond of her?

Working together had shown him how well they got on. If only she would open her mind to the idea, he was certain they'd be content. However, it was not her mind which needed to be opened. It was her heart. How was he to know which key to use to unlock it?

This afternoon, the four of them were to go to the meadow and discover whatever interesting specimens the rain might have unearthed.

Alice and Jayne would be happy for the outing since this morning they would be spending their time in an etiquette lesson. His suggestion to Vivienne had been that it should be how to properly greet a gentleman.

She had laughed, reminding him that the way a ten-year-old would greet a gentleman, if she even did, was far different than how a debutante would. In her opinion it was inappropriate for them to be learning manners beyond their age. Indeed, he agreed with her in that. He greatly feared that other young girls in London were learning such things from their strict governesses.

If Mildred had her way, his girls would, too. Proper little society marionettes was what they would be. He only hoped that Vivienne had the skills to teach them enough to appease his sister-in-law.

If it came to it, he would fight his brother, but he'd

probably lose. After all, a baron would always have his way over a younger son.

It did not bear thinking of how miserable his girls would be. They would rebel. Jayne might add moths to the governess's soup. Alice might put something crawly in her bed.

His brother might feel shamed if there was any gossip about how badly behaved his nieces were.

His sister's memory would not be honoured. Everything he had done in raising the girls had been out of love for Alice Jayne. He wanted to her look down from eternity and be reassured that her children were being well cared for.

Quite clearly, the girls must be raised at home with him, under the watchful eye of someone who loved and understood them.

Vivienne loved them, he was certain she did. He only hoped that she could teach them manners in the short time they had left with her.

Just now, he could see the three of them a short distance from the house where a swing was hanging from the branch of a tree. Alice was getting off the swing. Jayne took her place and laughed while she reached her toes for the sky, then swung back towards the ground and then up again.

The swing had not been there before the rain. It looked a great deal of fun which did not keep him from wishing it had not been installed. The time spent playing might be used in practising social greetings. Not only that, but children had been known to become injured on swings. Just like he had.

One day while trying to prove to his brothers that he was better at it than they were, he'd gone too high, then launched from the swing as if he were not subject to the law of gravity. It took a long time and a great deal of discomfort until his sprained ankle had healed. That was not the worst of it. His mother had the swing removed and ever after his brothers had blamed the lack of it on him.

Marching towards the laughter, he decided to follow his mother's example and take the swing down. Better to prevent an injury before it happened.

'Papa, look!' Jayne cried, flapping one arm. 'I can fly! I'm a butterfly!'

'Hold on to the ropes!'

'But she cannot flutter if she does,' Alice pointed out.

He tried not to be influenced by the joy both his children were experiencing. Joy they would not have in London if they were forced to live there.

'Vivienne, may I have a private word?'

She grinned, clearly enjoying the morning's play as much as the children were.

They stepped several feet away, but his eyes remained fixed on the swing. Perhaps he was too worried because of what had happened to him. Then again, danger was danger no matter how much fun it was.

'Where did that come from?'

'That? The swing, you mean? Mr Prentis brought it down from the attic. He remembered how his children used to enjoy it, so he set it up for Jayne and Alice.'

He might have grunted because Vivienne frowned at him. 'It was thoughtful of him, you must agree.'

Since he could not condemn their host's motives, he did not. 'Of course. I only worry about accidents.'

'We take a risk rising from our beds every day, Clement. We cannot control everything when it comes to our children.'

He blinked. Our children? She did not mean it quite that way, he was certain. Our children did not mean their children. More likely she used 'our' in the general sense.

'I suppose I feel more protective of them since Duncan and Mildred made their threat. If anything happens to Alice or Jayne, they might use it to say they would be better off living in London where they can keep a closer eye on them. Funny, but I never worried about them playing in the woods at home. Didn't have a swing, though.'

'You had a bridge with water running underneath instead.' She touched his arm, smiled. 'Do not worry. Alice and Jayne will not go to London. We shall make sure they do not.'

Then they ought to spend their time practising something, he nearly pointed out. Swinging would gain them nothing. Except fun...a childhood they could look back upon with smiles.

'I see what you are thinking.'

He shook his head. 'I don't know how you can. My thoughts are in my head...private.'

'Perhaps I cannot know them, then. But it doesn't change the fact that children need playtime as much as learning, otherwise they will not know how to play as adults.'

'Very well, that was something of my thoughts. You made a lucky guess. What am I thinking now?'

She studied his face, looking at him this way and that. He hadn't really had a thought in his mind when he'd offered the challenge. He did now. When her gazed settled on his mouth...he had something in particular on his mind.

'You are right. I cannot read your thoughts.'

Since she was blushing, he figured she might have read them perfectly well after all.

'Jayne, get off the swing. It is time to study manners,' he said.

'But I have not had my turn,' Alice complained.

'I saw you having a turn before I came over.'

'I have not had my third turn. It isn't fair if Jayne gets three and I only get two.'

It wasn't fair that they might have to act like small

replicas of polished ladies, either. Not fair that the uncle who was baron would have more say in their upbringing than the one who was actually raising them.

Duncan and Mildred ought to be thinking of a family of their own and leave his family in peace.

'Come now, girls. Listen to your father,' Vivienne called. Then quietly to him, she said, 'You need to let Alice have another short turn.'

This wasn't something a hired governess would say to her employer. It was what a wife would say. Someone who was as equally invested in the children's well-being.

'I suppose you are right. Fair is fair. Alice, you may take your third turn.'

Vivienne's smile spoke of satisfaction in victory, but not without good humour. She gave him a playful elbow in the side. 'You are a wonderful father.'

And one day she would be a wonderful mother, only not, it seemed, for his children.

His chest felt heavy, knowing it was not ever to be.

'It just came up out of nowhere,' Mrs Prentis commented about the wind whipping around the corners of the house and huffing at the windows.

Black clouds, heavy with threat rolled in across the sea. A wicked-looking storm was aiming for the coast.

'It happens this way, every good while,' Mr Prentis announced. 'I wish our young ladies had picked a different day to go to the village.'

Clement, done with staring at the road and seeing no one on it, announced, 'I'm going to get them. Do you have a tarpaulin?'

'Oh, no, Mr Marston, you must not do that.' Mrs Prentis shook her head firmly. 'It is not safe to be out. And more likely than not, they have taken shelter at an inn in the village.'

More likely than not? That was no reassurance.

'I understand it is not safe. It is all the more reason to go out and fetch them.'

'I will get a tarpaulin from the attic right away. But my wife is right. While we stare out of the window wringing our hands, they are probably sitting beside a nice fire sipping cocoa.'

'And I shall make us a nice spot of tea.' His hostess bustled from the room.

Clement raced up the stairs to get his raincoat and rubber boots.

For all of their reassurance, Mr and Mrs Prentis had not successfully raised six children by drinking tea while their offspring were in peril.

Clement shrugged into his heaviest coat, dragged his boots out from under the bed and stepped into them. Snatching the blankets from his bed, he wrapped them up in his raincoat.

He glanced out of the window while rushing for the

door. Dash it, but there was not much chance of getting to them before the downpour did.

In whatever condition he found his family, the blankets ought to be welcome.

The best outcome would be that he did find them waiting out the storm at an inn. In that case, they would have dry blankets to offer him.

Considering how the weather had been bright and pleasant one moment and then a freakish wind sweeping a storm onshore the next, reason would indicate that Vivienne and the girls had been caught unawares.

He knew what time they'd meant to leave the village for home. According to his calculations, they would be halfway between there and here.

Running down the stairs, then across the hallway, he caught the scent of tea.

'You really mustn't go,' Mr Prentis advised, but he handed him the tarpaulin anyway.

'Keep the tea warm for our return, my friend.' That said, Clement closed the door.

Gusts of wind fought his progress down the steps. It whipped left, then right. Once on the drive he had to lean into it in order to fight his way forward to the road.

Luckily, he was still ahead of the rain. Not by much, he figured. Glancing back towards the shore, he saw a wall of rain dumping from clouds which looked an odd shade of green. The downpour could not be more than a quarter of a mile away.

Acres of grass pressed flat to the ground. Wind hissed around his ears. Even this far from the shore he heard waves pounding on the beach. They had to be huge.

He pushed harder. No normal storm, this, it was working up to be a beast—a beast which would not consume his family.

He was about halfway to the village when the first splatter of rain slapped the back of his neck.

A moment later he spotted the Prentis wagon. The horse stood with his head bent to the wind, his mane whipping madly about. The good beast was making a valiant effort to hold his stance against the wind.

But where were Vivienne and the girls? Not in the wagon.

He glanced about, but did not see them. His stomach churned at how dim the afternoon light was becoming.

It was only when he was close enough to pat the horse's flank and praise his courage that he spotted them.

They had taken cover underneath the buggy. Vivienne must have decided it was a safer place to be than on top. There was some shelter there, but not much.

The worst of the rain was nearly upon them. He could see a line of water advancing across the land.

The air had an unnerving tint to it. It was the same murky green shade as the clouds.

The horse was beginning to look nervous. Poor beast. There was nothing to be done for him until the storm blew over.

Clement checked the wagon brake, relieved to see that Vivienne had thought to set it. If the horse panicked and ran, the result might be disastrous. With the wind rocking the wagon and a sense of violence in the air, it was not out of the question.

Peering under the wagon, he only saw Vivienne. In the instant that fear crushed his belly, he spotted the tops of his daughters' heads. Vivienne had them wrapped up in her skirt. A hen protecting her chicks. Vivienne's face was hidden by a shawl she had drawn over her head so she was not aware of his approach.

Ducking under the wagon, he touched her shoulder. She jerked, startled. And then she wrapped her arms around him, squeezing tight. Next, his daughters were hugging him, too.

Rain dumped from the sky all at once. It seemed as though they sat within a waterfall. So far it was dry underneath the wagon, but it would not be for long. He hadn't much time to fashion the shelter he had been planning while he looked for them.

On his knees, he scrambled to unwrap the blankets.

He spread the raincoat on the ground, indicating the girls and Vivienne should sit on it. His hope was that it would keep them dry from beneath while the tarpaulin would do the job from above.

He draped blankets over Vivienne and the girls.

Next, he snapped the tarp open. It seemed a good thick one so his plan might work.

Vivienne moved under the blanket, settling the children on each side of her. He draped the tarp over their heads, tucking the ends under the raincoat.

As makeshift tents went, he thought this one might just hold.

Then he crawled under, tucking the loose ends beneath himself.

The wagon creaked, the horse snorted. For now they were dry and safe. He had done what he could. All that was left to do was pray that the wind did not upset the wagon and the horse did not panic.

'We knew you would come to get us, Papa,' Alice said.

'I am your father. I will always come.'

'That is what Miss Curtis told us. Those very words.'

Had she? It touched him, knowing that.

'It's not scary any more,' Jayne said, snuggling closer against Vivienne.

He was sitting next to Alice and he reached out and gave her shoulders a squeeze. It was warm under the tarp, too, with all four of them to ease the chill.

'What shall we do to pass the time?' Vivienne asked, her voice whispery under the canvas.

'Practise sums,' he suggested, smiling at the moan he knew would follow.

'It is Miss Curtis's day off from teaching us things. It is our day for fun.'

'Ah, then we shall tell stories,' he suggested brightly, even though bright was the last thing he felt.

The truth was, he was worried. The wagon rocked harder. The tarp snapped around their heads…wind blew more fiercely.

'I'm a little bit scared.' Jayne pressed closer to her governess.

'I'm not scared.' Alice announced. It might be because she was wedged between him and Vivienne and therefore had an illusion of safety.

'Tell us a story about someone brave, Jayne,' he suggested.

Jayne told a tale of the bravery of the horse standing stout-heartedly against the storm.

'Your turn, Alice,' he said.

Alice told of how brave Mr Prentis was when he'd climbed the tree to put up the swing.

While they talked, he began to think the tent would hold. He relaxed somewhat and the others seemed to also.

Alice's story went on for a while and Jayne fell asleep during it.

'How long will this last, Papa? It's dull with nothing to do. Then having said so, Alice fell asleep, too.

How content they looked with their heads resting on Vivienne's bosom. Oddly enough, there was nowhere he would rather be than here, in this moment. Again, he had a sense of them being a family. It was nearly impossible not to wonder what could be if Vivienne was not set on leaving them.

'We've lost them, it seems,' he said quietly to Vivienne. 'Tell me your story of someone brave.'

Perhaps he would discover something about her father, perhaps? A former love? He really knew very little about her other than that she had a married sister. There was nothing he would like more than to know about her life away from here. But, no…he would be patient and in time she might confide in him.

'I have a daring tale of bravery to tell, Clement.' She snuggled closer to him, whether by choice or necessity, it was hard to know. 'I met a man once, the bravest I have ever met. He carried me through swirling water to take me and my camera to safety when I was stuck on a rock.'

'That was brave…your heart must have been aflutter over his courage,' he added in the light-hearted spirit of her story.

'Oh, it was. But he did something even braver than that.'

Now wasn't this a pleasant way to pass the time, hearing his praises being sung by a desirable woman.

Even though he still heard fierce rain pelting the tarp, he did not mind so much.

'Braver than rescuing you from an incoming tide?'

'Oh, much braver. You see, this hero took orphaned children to his heart. He loves them as if they were born to him. He has as kind and loving a heart as any man I ever met.'

The story was getting better by the moment. He waggled his brows. 'And I suppose he is a handsome fellow, to go with all that gallantry.'

She could not properly turn, being pressed on all sides by his children. Nor could she reach her hand from under the blanket without disturbing their fragile shelter.

What she did do was slide her fingers over, press them on his chest where his heart was going through some odd manoeuvres.

'His eyes are an interesting colour, green and brown mixed with nice gold flecks in them. And his mouth...' She looked at his lips for a moment as if she were waiting for them to move, to say something. Not that he would know what to say even if he could speak in the moment.

'His lips are funny...at times they do not know whether to smile or frown.'

'It's because this brave fellow does not know what to do with them in certain circumstances. Laugh... or kiss.'

'Kiss, Clement. I would say this moment calls for one...but only one.'

'Two would not be prudent, I agree.'

She nodded and touched the button on his shirt. She rubbed it with her thumb.

So, before the moment passed, before real life invaded the intimacy of their canvas shelter, he kissed her once. And then again, despite everything, because it seemed that once was never enough when it came to Vivie.

A thousand or a million might not be either. Not for a woman—this woman—that he was in love with... Denying that he loved her, as he had been doing, was useless. The truth was the truth...and it broke him a bit.

What was he to do, fight for her? Let her go away as she intended to do? Watching her eyes, her lids still closed in pleasure, he nearly wept because the conclusion he came to was no conclusion at all. The reality was, there was very little he could do.

When she opened her eyes and gazed up through the dim light cast by the canvas, he gulped down a welling pressure in his throat. He was as certain that he loved her as if he had researched the matter all his life.

There was no going back from it.

Chapter Ten

What? My word… Vivienne could not believe she had fallen asleep. But here she was waking up, so apparently she had.

Well, then…show her a lady who would not lay her head on her hero's shoulder and drift away to sweet dreams?

He had a strong shoulder, a manly one. She'd shifted position so that her head now lay in the pillow-like area between his collarbone and his throat.

It was dark now and she could not see who was awake and who was asleep. But judging by the sound of their even breathing, everyone was asleep.

It was no longer raining, nor was wind flapping the canvas as it had done for the past few hours.

The storm had passed.

At least the storm outside the tarpaulin had. There was another one still doing considerable mischief and it was inside her. This storm was not so easily waited out. It tossed her emotions every which way, leaving her confused…and at the same time content.

What a mess she had found herself in after allowing him to kiss her again. Feathers…not allowing, but encouraging. She had all but demanded a kiss…and then received two. If she was to make it to the end of the summer without breaking hearts, she would need to do better than this.

She wriggled, sat up straighter. While it would be ever so nice to continue sleeping entwined like a litter of puppies, it was quite wrong to let the horse shiver in the dark.

'Clement.' She poked him in the chest. He stirred, sat up straighter. 'The rain has passed. We should go.'

She jostled Alice, then Jayne.

'Mama?' Alice blinked her eyes.

For a second, Clement's expression looked stricken. He must have thought of his sister, perhaps reminded of all she had missed by dying.

'No, dear. It is me, Miss Curtis.'

'She had a dream again,' Jayne explained. 'She always dreams you are our mama.'

'Come now.' Clement lifted the tarp off them. The air was suddenly cooler. 'We should get home. Mr and Mrs Prentis will be worried.'

Emerging from under the wagon, they found the ground to be a mass of puddles.

Clement unhitched the horse. Pulling the wagon

through deep mud would burden the beast who had already stood out in the storm for too long.

They walked towards the inn, Clement leading the horse and Vivienne holding the children's hands.

The sky was black but spangled with stars. They walked for a very long time with no one speaking.

'I wonder what time it is?' Vivienne said, at last. There was no way of knowing for certain how long they had been sheltering under the wagon.

'The stars indicate it is about….' He was silent for a moment, glancing up, pointing his finger at this group of stars and then moving his finger left and up. 'Eight-seventeen.'

'About that? Eight-seventeen seems fairly precise.' Walking in the dark with a scientific man had its advantages.

'Give or take a few minutes. No, I'm just jesting with you. I've got a watch. I wonder if Mrs Prentis has held dinner for us. I hope so.'

Such an interesting man…completely heroic…she had meant every word of her story. At the same time he was practical…thinking first thing of his appetite once the danger passed.

If only she had not agreed to marry Everett. The more she got to know Clement, the more of her heart he took. Day by day she regretted giving her word to become engaged.

Not that she, a prime conquest in the marriage mart, would be allowed to wed an untitled man. Feathers…

she was of an age to wed whomever she wished to in the eyes of the law. But she knew well that marrying a man who had no title of his own would severely disappoint her father, who'd always had his sights set very high for his daughters.

More than that, her marriage was supposed to unite the families, fulfilling Great-Aunt's dearest wish.

Oh, but Alice had called her Mama. No title could be grander than that one. In a choice between Mama and Marchioness, she would pick Mama every time. She wasn't going to be allowed to pick, though. No more than she was allowed to pick a career.

What she ought to do was rebel. It was in her nature to do so.

Feathers. What a muddle since she'd been raised to be obedient to her father. Her father who, in turn, had been raised to be mindful of the dictates of society.

If only she had been born to a different family. But even then that might not have done her a bit of good when it came to wedding Clement…who, she reminded herself, had not even hinted at a proposal, only requesting that she remain in his employ.

She directed her mind back to her first thought. Even if she was from a well-established but untitled family, Clement might not wed her. Being the brother of a wealthy baron, he'd be unlikely to wed his children's governess. Not that such a thing had never been done. It happened rather frequently in romantic novels.

Feathers…feathers…a mattress full of feathers! What a mess she had got herself into. It was only by a thread in a tattered, old coat that she was not falling in love with Clement Marston. At any point the thread might break and then what would she do? Wed one man while in love with another?

It might work for some ladies of society, but not for her.

If only she could be more like Clement. How fine it would be to go through a storm and then have her first thought be of a warm dinner.

So much easier than—

'Papa, my feet hurt. Carry me,' Jayne complained.

'No!' Alice whined. 'Mine hurt more. Carry me.'

'You are too old for being carried. But here, give me your hands.'

They dashed to their father. He handed the reins off to Vivienne. She walked a few paces behind, thinking what a sweet sight they were.

'I don't like being too big to carry,' Alice muttered.

Clement picked up her hand, kissed it. Then he kissed Jayne's hand.

'But I do carry you. Right here in my heart. Always.'

And then he turned about, gazing through the dark at Vivienne.

She thought she saw sadness in his eyes…and longing.

She might be mistaken, though. It was dark after

all. But she was not mistaken about the sadness and longing in the smile she gave him back. Right then, the thread in that old coat broke. She was irrevocably in love with Clement Marston.

What a fortunate thing Clement and his children walked ahead of her. The only one who knew she was silently weeping was the horse.

He whickered, nudged her in the arm.

'I do not suppose you have any advice for me?' she whispered.

He blinked his great brown eyes, but naturally had nothing to confide.

The situation she had got herself into, she must now get herself out of. And she had no idea how to do it. Grace, the one person she could confide in, was in Europe, mailing letters meant to deceive their parents.

By the time the inn came into sight with its welcoming lamps aglow in the windows, she had managed to stuff her heart back into its proper place. Her eyes were dry and she had gathered the fortitude to continue with what she must do for the remainder of the summer.

More, for what she must do when it ended.

The problem for her now was how to go away without breaking hearts. As far as her own went, it was too late...it would simply have to stay broken.

But the children's hearts? She nearly wept anew.

Alice had called her Mama. Mamas were not supposed to go away and yet the girls had lost two already. The one who'd given birth to them and their first nurse. Imagining how they would feel when they lost her, too, was nearly too much to bear.

And Clement? She believed she had seen something in that last glance of his, too.

What a mess she had made of everything. When summer ended, she would have caused such damage. And if she did not leave, what about her parents and Great-Aunt Anne? They were rejoicing at the prospect of her marriage to Everett. The only one who would not be affected was Everett. He was only fond of her. No one languished over losing fondness.

When they were several yards from the front door, Mr and Mrs Prentis rushed out, looking relieved to see them safely returned.

'I am so grateful to see you, my dearies.' The couple hurried down the steps. 'We were so worried. Come in to dinner now. I've kept it warm.'

Mrs Prentis bustled them inside, resembling a hen flapping after her chicks.

'We are relieved to have you home safe.' Mr Prentis clapped Clement on the back and then took the horse's reins from Vivienne.

Home. She could not say she had ever felt more at home anywhere than she did here. It had been said that home was where the heart was. But soon she and

Clement would part ways. If the saying was true, her heart would remain here. This place, these people, would be a moment out of time for ever. Nothing was ever going to be the same again.

She gave herself a good shake. So much drama within one's heart could drive her to despair if she wasn't careful.

If this was all the time she had left with Clement, she did not intend to spend it morosely. Indeed, it had never been in her nature to be a gloomy puss.

She had a job to do. Teach the girls to be little ladies so that Clement would not be separated from them. That would simply not happen, not while she was in charge.

And as for the book, she had a job to do there, too.

Wasn't it wiser to live in the moment and take what joy one could from it? Of course it was. Why take misery from a future which had not even happened yet?

With her mind settled, she gathered her resolve and declared, 'I am so glad you were right about dinner waiting for us, Clement. I am quite hungry all of a sudden.'

'As am I,' he said with a look in his eyes which did not seem to relate to the prospect of a warm meal.

Joy in the moment, she reminded herself.

The look could go nowhere as far as a future went.

This, though, was not the future, it was now, so she allowed herself to fall into his gaze.

* * *

Clement was grateful for his family's safe delivery from the storm. Last night he had lain in bed counting his blessings, but fallen asleep before he came to the end of them.

Now that it was day, worries crept back. He stood on the porch, watching the grass on the dunes gently swaying.

Yesterday, while under the tarpaulin, two things had happened. One, Alice had dreamed of Vivienne being her mother. It seemed that, once again, his poor child was headed for heartbreak when it came to losing the women in her life. He hoped that when Vivienne left them, it would not be like when Miss Logan had.

He was not certain he could manage their tears again. And he pitied the woman who tried to fill their governess's shoes.

It did not make him feel good, realising that as his daughters grew, he might no longer be enough for them. Perhaps had they been boys, he would have been. But girls needed a mother.

He tapped his fingers on the porch railing, absorbed in thought. He was in love and he didn't yet know if it was an affliction or a blessing.

Poets had written thousands of words on the wonder and the misery of falling in love. Until now he had thought them a bit dim-witted. Now here he stood, feeling as dim as a fellow could get. How was it possible to feel elated and deflated in the same breath?

What he really needed to do was speak with Vivienne. Find out what was so pressing about her next engagement. If he knew what it was, he might convince her to change her mind.

He wondered—would telling her he loved her make a difference?

It might not go in his favour if he did. It was a fact that she responded well to his kisses...indeed, she seemed as overcome by them as he was. And yet in every instance it had not served to draw them closer, but more distant.

Last night had been no exception. He had waited for her to come to his chamber so they could work on the book, but her bedroom door had remained shut.

It might be that the events of the day had worn her out. That was what he'd like to think, but had he not kissed her, he thought she would have come.

What had come over him? He had been determined not to kiss her again, yet he had done it without hesitation. He would like to put the blame on water and on being in danger, as both times he had kissed her, those elements had been present.

What, though, was more pointless than lying to oneself? For a researcher, factuality was everything. He must speak to Vivienne...now.

It might be difficult to get her alone since she was

no doubt instructing the children in how to act in any given social situation. Each day that passed made him more concerned that Vivienne would not have time to teach them enough to satisfy Mildred.

He would like to believe that having acted as their father all their lives he would prevail in an argument with Duncan. Regrettably, his brother had two things which he did not. A title and a wife.

There was nothing he could do about the lack of a title.

But a wife? He could wed.

Vivienne had advised him not to do so unless he was in love. And here he found himself…in love with her. Her social position might not be acceptable to some, but for the most part, he doubted society would give whom he wed a thought.

More, he did not care if they did.

Clement looked for Vivienne and the girls in the study, but they were not there. Good, then, it was for the best if they spent their time learning to use a fork or make a curtsy. Reading and arithmetic could wait.

Walking back through the parlour, he paused to look out of the window. Maybe Vivienne had taken them outdoors for a lesson.

'Are you looking for Alice and Jayne?' he heard Mrs Prentis ask from behind him.

He turned, smiling. 'Indeed I am.'

'Miss Curtis has taken them down to her darkroom.'

'Ah, thank you.'

Darkroom? Was there really time to be time to be indulging in their governess's passion when it was etiquette they needed to learn?

As interesting as the process was, Mildred would not be impressed that the girls knew how to coax a photograph from a plate of glass.

Coming down the cellar steps, he heard Jayne's voice.

'I don't want to learn manners. They are dull.'

'You must learn them, though. One day you will take your places in society.'

'I want to be an entomologist like Papa.' Jayne's statement warmed his heart, but saddened it, too. His daughter might wish to follow in his footsteps, but her 'occupation' had been determined at her birth.

'I think that is wonderful. You must have something that is your own.' Vivienne stated. 'Something apart from what will be asked of you when you are grown ladies. You must never give up who you are.'

What? It sounded as if she was encouraging them to reject their future roles. Just because a governess was allowed such freedom, did not mean the nieces of a baron would be.

As much as he wished it was the case, it was not. The world they must live in was what it was.

'I don't want to be a lady,' Alice said.

'But you will be. And there are many rules to learn.

It is important to pay careful attention to everything I have to teach you.'

Oh, good. He had misunderstood. The fist gripping his middle eased.

'I would rather learn to take photos like you do.' Alice said. 'It seems like magic.'

'Only chemicals. But it is fulfilling. Which is what I meant when I said you should find something of your own. Something that fulfils you while you are going about the rest.'

'Curtsies are not fulfilling.'

'But they can be. Performed just the right way…if you challenge yourself to make each one more perfect than the next.'

'Mine will be better than yours, Jayne. That will be fulfilling.' Although he could not see his daughter's expression from his shadowed hidey-hole on the stairs, he knew she would be making a face.

'No, it won't! Mine will be.'

'Here is what you must keep in mind. Your father has asked you to learn manners. He deserves for you to try your best. He loves you both very much.'

Alice and Jayne did not know what was at stake for them. How was one to tell a child such a thing?

'We shall both make perfect curtsies then.'

'For Papa. We love our papa…' Alice said.

'Do you love him, too?' Jayne asked.

Clement nearly choked on his breath even though it

was not possible to do so. Clearly his little matchmakers were making another attempt to have Vivienne as their mother, bless their yearning little hearts.

'I admire your father. He is a good man.'

'But you should love him,' Alice said. 'He loves you.'

He should not stand here, breath lodged in his throat, eavesdropping. And yet...how was Vivienne going to answer that?

She did not, but instead swished a glass plate in chemicals.

'You could be our mother if you married our papa,' Alice said, her voice gone soft.

'One day you will have a mother and you will love her very much.'

'Not as much as you,' stated Jayne.

'Come now, girls, let's go up to the kitchen and see if Mrs Prentis has made anything we can have as a treat.'

Not wishing to be caught on the stairs, he quietly went back the way he had come.

Then, standing several feet from the cellar stairs, he made it appear that he was only just walking towards them.

'There you are!' he exclaimed. 'I have been searching for you.'

'We watched Miss Curtis make picture magic.'

'That sounds as if it was fun. Now, you may take an hour away from your lessons while I have a word with Miss Curtis.'

* * *

Whatever conversation Clement wished to have with her, he asked to have it while they walked along the shore.

With the storm having moved on, the weather was ideal. One of those days when the breeze brushed softly against one's face and waves sweetly lapped the beach. Not like yesterday when they'd pounded like a furious beast.

Not like yesterday when emotions had pounded her heart. She felt better about everything today. Or she had until Alice and Jayne said their father loved her.

Of course, they were children who wanted a mother. No doubt they were seeing what they wished to see.

The last thing she wanted was for him to love her. It was the first thing she wanted as well…but it simply could not be.

They walked for quite a distance without Clement coming to the point of this stroll.

'What is it you wished to speak with me about, Clement?' Someone must begin.

Her guess was that he wondered why she had not come to his room to help with the book last night. She had been simply too raw inside, not that she could admit it.

'Do you mind if we sit?' He gestured to a sandy mound several feet from where waves lapped at the shore.

'I do not mind.' Sitting in the sand was one of the things she had come to enjoy this summer.

He was quiet for so long that it became uncomfortable. Extended silence was rare between them. Most of the time, conversation came as easily as breathing.

'Look at that, Clement. There is an unusual butterfly. What is it?' Perhaps casual chit-chat was what he needed to warm up to what he wanted to speak with her about.

He did not look at the pretty creature fluttering about her skirt, but rather into her eyes.

Intently into her eyes, as if he were trying to see secrets which she meant to keep to herself. No one would be better off if he knew she loved him.

'I have asked before and now I am asking again. Vivienne, please stay beyond the summer. The girls... they need you. I—'

'But you know I cannot,' she said quickly to keep this from going any further. 'I am committed to...to my next assignment.'

Which was exactly what it felt like...an assignment. One which she would be fulfilling for the rest of her life.

'Whatever your next employer is willing to pay, I will triple it.'

'It is not the money. I have an obligation.'

'What can I say to change your mind?'

Or do, was the clear intention in his eyes. Gold flecks in the green glimmered with purpose.

But, feathers! Kissing would only lead to worse trouble.

'You know how deeply I care for Alice and Jayne. Surely you do. But I cannot stay. It is impossible. Nothing has changed.'

'Hasn't it?' He touched her hair, drew it back over her ear. He stroked the curve of her cheek. 'How deeply do you care for me?'

'Deeply enough, Clement. You know I do.'

She looked away so that he could not read how deeply. Those few words confessed too much as it was. She must make an attempt to amend them.

'I have not had a better friend. I admire you as a father and as a colleague. I am grateful you have allowed me to help you with your book.'

'Our book now.' He turned her chin back towards him. Unable to look away, she glanced down.

Under no circumstances must he see her heart in her eyes.

'Yes, our book. I will always think fondly of our time working on it.'

'On our time…or on me?'

'Both, of course.' She made her voice sound crisp. If she used the tone coming from her soul, it would be too soft with affection, he would surely recognise love.

'My children need—'

'A mother? Yes, I heard Alice say so.'

'Vivie, what she said is that she wanted you.'

It would be so much easier to utter the words she must if he had not called her Vivie. The endearment never failed to make her want to hand over her heart… as if she had not already done so.

'I am certain they will have a devoted mother when the time is right.'

'Look at me, Vivie, and tell me the time is not now.'

He leaned forward as if he would kiss her…prove to her that it was, that they were—

No! She could not! Standing quickly, she shook the sand from her skirt.

The children had not been wrong when they claimed he loved her. She could not stand here, looking at him and not believe it. Even if she had not been looking, there was no denying the longing each felt, one towards the other.

'Now is not the time,' she said, tears swelling her throat.

'Now' would never be the time for her. Love was not in her future. Everett was. He would never care for her this way, no more than she would him.

If she walked away without letting Clement declare his love, she would never hear it from anyone else.

Then she fled, kicking up sand behind her. She could not hear one more word from him or everything would be ruined. Once he offered her his heart there would be no postponing what must be done. As it stood now she could pretend she did not know, carry on as before…work on the book, teach the children.

Stopping at the foot of the inn steps, she pressed one hand to her middle, caught her breath. What she must remember was that staying, especially in the way he hinted at, would only result in Clement knowing she had deceived him all this time.

There was no way possible for her to join this family without them knowing who she really was.

When they did, they would not want her…a woman who was deceiving not only them, but her own family as well. What, really, was the importance of pleasing herself for the summer in comparison to Alice's and Jayne's deep need for a mother?

She did not deserve their affection.

Chapter Eleven

Clement stood on the path to the shore, insect jar in hand.

His attention was not on insects. It was on watching through the large parlour window while Alice and Jane competed with one another to perform a perfect curtsy.

At least competing was what he assumed they were doing. The window was open to the warm afternoon air and he heard the three of them laughing.

Laughing…while he had been going through his days, a man in misery disguised as a cheerful one.

Three days had passed since Clement had nearly revealed his heart to Vivienne. In part it had been an attempt to convince her, once again, to stay with them. But also because he simply needed for her to know it. Needed to know if she returned his love.

For a moment he'd thought, yes, she must. But in the next she'd called them friends…colleagues…and had run for the house when he was on the verge of pressing his suit.

There was nothing for it but to smile through his confusion. He would not let on how perplexed the encounter had left him.

Insects. He reminded himself they were the reason he was standing on the beach with a jar in his hand. What he needed to do was delve into the quest for one more perfect specimen. Exploring ought to set him to rights.

One exquisite insect was all they needed in order to finish the book. Quite soon it ought to be ready to send to a publisher.

Before he decided which direction to go in search of the perfect insect, the front door opened, then closed. Jayne tiptoed down the porch steps and across the yard. She gave the parlour window furtive glances while she dashed for the tree where the swing swayed in the breeze.

He had his mouth open to call her to account when Vivienne lifted the window and peered out.

'Alice Marston!' she called. 'That is not the way to the water closet!'

Head down, his daughter walked back inside the house. The sight of her pout gave him the first chuckle he'd had in hours.

Turning towards the west side of the inn, he decided to see what he could find in the meadow.

Last week he'd thought it would be a fine thing to join Vivienne in her darkroom. He'd been curious to see how a small plate of glass could reveal the image of an insect.

No longer, though. Now, being alone in the dark with Vivie? His mind would not be on glass plates and that was a fact.

He forced his attention away from what it would be on. Focused it on what it should be on.

What he needed was an insect so fascinating, so absorbing, that he would not be aware of Vivie working closely beside him at the desk, would not feel the tickle of her hair or the scent of her skin while she peered over his shoulder.

'If you exist, make yourself known,' he announced to whatever creatures called the meadow home.

Not so much as a rustle of leaves.

He found himself watching a bird circling, dark against a bright blue sky.

Which meant he was not absorbed in the hunt.

How could he have guessed a time would come when his daughters and his research were not all he needed in order to be fulfilled?

Now he needed his daughters' governess.

To his everlasting regret she, quite clearly, did not need him.

Vivienne sat at her dressing table, drawing a brush quickly through the tangles she had acquired during the day. Over the summer she had not learned to style her hair properly, so she'd continued to wear it loose or fastened at the back of her neck with a bow. She found she liked it better this way than swept up in stiff curls.

When she went back to her old life, her maid would style a stiff pile of curls on her head. If she attempted to wear it free and swinging, there would be no end to the talk.

If only she did not have to go back. But moan and groan as she might, nothing would change.

Between now and when she left, she would put on a happy face. No one else needed to suffer because she was miserable. If she was caught in a web of lies, it was of her own making.

She rose, went to her chamber door. Before she opened it, she set her smile in place.

It took only a moment to walk across the children's bedroom to Clement's door, even stopping to kiss foreheads and wonder what they were dreaming about.

Night by night it took nearly more fortitude than Vivienne could muster to join him at his desk.

She did it, though. Living her dream was the reason she had become a governess and she would not leave her post before her time was up.

Even though Clement's door was open, she knocked.

He stood at his desk, bent at the waist while he peered at a specimen.

Adjusting his glasses, he waved her in without looking up.

It was just as well that he was standing since she did not think it wise to watch over his shoulder tonight.

'Here, have a look,' he said, standing to the side. 'I found this in the meadow today. I would have enjoyed seeing it flutter about, but it was dead when I came across it.'

'What is it?'

'Garden Tiger…a moth. I spread the wings so you can see the orange it displays when it is frightened.'

'How beautiful. I hate to think of it being frightened.'

'Do you?' She had to catch her heart when he gave her that flat, turned-up-at-the-corners smile. 'At the beginning of the summer, you would have squashed it. You've come a long way. I am proud of you, Vivie.'

Was he…truly?

At this point there was no use in asking him not to call her Vivie. Bringing it to his attention would only serve to emphasise the endearment. She was trying so hard not to look too closely at the affection they withheld from one another.

'No, I would not have squashed it!' she protested, but he was likely correct, she would have.

'Do you recall the Speckled Bush cricket when we first met? You would have done the poor girl in if you could.'

But he had stopped her from harming it and they'd

ended up on the floor together. And she had become employed.

'Yes, well... I would not do it now.'

He arched a brow, looking playful. This felt right. Like who they were supposed to be. Neither of them was typically full of anxiety.

He was quiet for a second, watching her smile. His attention clearly focused on her lips. Then he blinked, the intensity in his gaze vanishing. The tingle on her mouth remained.

'This is the last one we needed to complete our book.' He tapped his finger next to the moth. 'Once you take your photograph all our information will be gathered. We only need to put it in a sensible order.'

'Here, then. I will take her photograph now. Would you like to come and watch it develop?'

'I'll wait here. But bring it up when you've finished. I'm anxious to see how she photographs. Her colours will not show, but still, she should be magnificent.'

'I wonder if moving images will ever be caught on glass. It would be magical to watch her fluttering about long after her short lifespan ends,' she said.

'Wondrous things are being invented every day. Who knows what a clever mind might come up with?'

They carried on talking about wondrous scientific things for a few moments in the easy way they had.

If only her memory could be like a moving photograph. She hated to think that once she went home and returned to her old life…began a new one…that her remembrance of this time would fade.

She would hold on to it for all she was worth, but it was the way of things for memories to fade.

For the two weeks remaining of their stay on the Isle of Wight, she meant to live each moment fully.

Clement stood up from his desk, stretched. He hated to step away from his work because as soon as he did, he would begin to worry.

With such a short time until his daughters must face the possibility of being taken to London by his brother, he feared they were not ready.

Dash it. Why should they be at ten years old? It was only a prideful baroness, wishing for it.

In his opinion his sister-in-law's motives were selfish. Presenting two accomplished players to the marriage mart would make her more respected and cause her own children to be looked at in a positive light.

Clement had reason to fear for their happiness. He had reason to fear for his own happiness. It was hard to imagine life without their bright spirits in his home.

The prospect preyed upon him.

What he needed was a visit to the classroom to reassure himself that their lessons in ladylike comportment were going well. He was not certain that Alice and Jayne were giving the matter the attention they ought to be.

He was certain that Vivie would teach them all she knew...but please let it be enough.

Coming to the bottom of the stairs, he turned right, then went down the hallway leading towards a room which he thought must have been used as a school-room when the Prentis children were young.

Before he went into the classroom, he heard Vivie's voice. It sounded as if she was reading.

Going inside, he found all three of them sitting atop pillows on the floor. Sunshine streamed through a lace window curtain and cast them in dappled light.

If only he could capture the image on one of Vivie's glass plates. He could look at the memory whenever he wished to. Pull it out and cherish it...live the moment again and again.

Come this time next year, would he have any of them? Alice, Jayne, Vivie?

The thought was too grim to dwell on, which did not mean that the fear went away even when he tried to think of something else.

Dread was the shadow which followed him each day.

'Hello, Papa.' Alice scrambled up from the floor. She gave him a hug. He tugged the bow in her hair.

'What are you reading?'

'Alice's Adventures in Wonderland.'

Wonderland? He was aware of the book, it was famous. He had not read it, though, and was not certain his daughters should be doing so either.

The title alone sounded too fanciful. They ought to be reading something that would help them with proper decorum. They could read about Alice's adventures once they were allowed to be children again.

'It sounds interesting,' he said. 'But tell me, what have you learned today? Proper speech? Ladylike posture?'

Jayne came up, stood on his feet and gave him a hug. 'Nothing as dull as that, Papa. We learned that Alice fell down, down, down a hole where she encountered strange creatures. There was a talking caterpillar.'

'A word, Miss Curtis?'

After instructing the girls to read to one another, Vivie joined him in the hallway.

'You look troubled, Clement,' she said. 'Is there something you need?'

Something besides her? Well, yes, there was.

'We are nearly out of time until the girls must show off their manners. Have you run out of what you are able to teach them?'

She frowned and he thought he caught affront flash in her expression, although he could not imagine why. It was a reasonable question.

'It is not as if I expect you to know every nuance of society,' he tried to explain. 'But have they learned enough to appear all they should?'

'I will continue to press the importance of impeccable comportment, but they are children and do not take it seriously.'

'They must, though.' He scrubbed his hand through his thatch of thick curls, frustrated.

'Unless you wish to advise them of the consequences, they will not. To your daughters, life is playful. At their age it is how it ought to be.'

'What ought to be and what is, are not always the same thing.' He spoke more sharply than he should have. 'Sorry, Vivie, I am on edge.'

'But who would not be? I think that when the time comes, Alice and Jayne will do well. I have approached this as a game for them so that they will—'

'A game!' He had to remind himself that none of this was her fault. She had been hired to keep them safe, entertained, and advancing in their studies. She had been doing exactly that when his brother and his wife had paid their visit.

'I know you are worried, Clement.' She touched his arm, softly, soothingly. 'But this must be presented to them as an amusement. If they are forced to perform, they will not do it. You of all people know this to be true. But they might play a game.'

'I apologise for being sharp, Vivie. But I cannot imagine them not being in my life every day. Please... focus more time on teaching them their social graces.'

'Very well, as you wish.' She nodded, seeming distant all of a sudden. He did not like that she suddenly felt more like his employee than his friend. Perhaps it was for the best. One day he would have to live without her, too.

At one point, he had come close to telling Vivie he was in love with her. Now he wondered if he should have gone ahead and done it. Perhaps if he carried through with it, she would change her mind about leaving. A marriage proposal could change everything. If she no longer needed to earn a wage, wouldn't she be free to cancel her next commitment?

Marriage would be a boon to him as well. If the girls had a mother, Mildred might not see it as her place to guide their debut into society. His attitude brightened considerably at the thought.

There was no doubt about who their mother should be...who he wanted for his wife. When he proposed he would not be asking for a marriage of convenience. He would make it clear that it was coming from the depths of his heart.

Tonight, he would press his suit. If she argued, he would kiss her. Nothing proved they were intended to be together more than their kisses did. Surely she felt it in her soul the same as he did?

This time he would not let her run away from what was meant to be. They were meant to be. He might be the only one to realise it right now, but it was true none the less.

He grinned inside imagining how, later, he would take her for a walk on the beach. There, under the stars and with the blessing of the moon, he would convince her they were destined for one another.

It was a romantic plan for a man who had never been romantic.

He liked it.

After Clement left the classroom, Vivienne considered teaching the girls one of the more frustrating lessons about being a lady of society. Oh, how it chafed that there were matters which a lady must not discuss in the presence of gentlemen. Politics and money were not proper for a lady to talk about, no matter how strong an opinion she had on the subjects.

She considered the lesson and then rejected it. It was nonsense which she would have no part in perpetuating. If in the unlikely event she had a daughter, she would be raised to believe her opinions mattered.

Here she was, though, and Alice and Jayne were not her daughters.

'Well, my dears, I believe we are finished with Wonderland adventures for the day. Which game would you prefer to play? Manners or swinging?'

They laughed, as she knew they would, then dashed out of the classroom.

Jayne ran ahead of Alice. She hopped on the swing before Vivienne was halfway down the steps. Up she went and then down, laughing.

At the highest point of up, she let go of the ropes, lifting her arms high.

'I'm Alice falling down the hole!' she cried.

'Hold on with both hands!' Vivienne shouted, rushing towards the tree.

Jayne was at the bottom of the sweep when she slipped off. She caught her fall with one hand under her.

Vivienne knelt beside her. 'Have you been injured?'

Jayne's bottom lip quivered. She nodded, then lifted her hand. Then she screeched.

Her arm was not straight. It sagged a few inches from her wrist.

Somehow, Clement was kneeling beside them. Where had he come from? Oh, but she was so grateful that he was here.

'There now, little one,' he crooned. 'It is not so bad.'

It was bad…one of the worst things Vivienne had ever seen. Her stomach twisted just looking at the injury.

'Run to the classroom, get that book you were reading,' he told her.

Lifting the hem of her skirts high, she ran. Not so fast that she did not hear Jayne whimpering, and Clement comforting her.

Reaching the front door, she glanced back. Clement had his shirt off and was ripping one sleeve off the shoulder.

By the time she returned, he had the sleeve separated from the shirt. He snatched the book from her without giving her a glance.

She was glad he hadn't. The reproach she would see in his eyes would be unbearable.

'I'm going put your arm on the book to hold it straight, sweetheart, then I'll wrap it up to hold it secure. It will hurt but I need you to be brave. Do not jerk it away.'

Jayne nodded. 'I'm sorry, Papa.'

'Show me how brave you are, sweetheart.'

Still, he did not look at Vivienne. He did not need to for Vivienne to know what she would have seen if he had.

This was all her fault. Clement had been against having a swing in the tree from the beginning, yet she had allowed the girls to use it.

'In Wonderland, Alice did not break her arm when she fell down the hole.' Jayne sniffled.

Clement did look at her then. The resentment in his eyes cut her to the quick. She deserved it. She was not a governess, had never been qualified to act as one and now an innocent child was paying the price.

If only she could run away from this moment, back up time and change it. Now that was a foolish thought. Adding cowardice to negligence was the last thing she was going to do.

Since she did not dare approach Jayne and have the child look at her the way Clement had, she went to Alice who was sitting several feet from the swing.

The child was weeping, but in all that was happening, her distress had gone unnoticed.

Alice latched on to her, sniffling into Vivienne's sleeve.

'Don't worry, my dear. You see Mr Prentis is already on his way to get the doctor.' She pointed to the road where the wagon bounced quickly over the road.

'He has made the trip before,' Mrs Prentis said, her voice reassuring.

So absorbed in her own guilt, Vivienne had not noticed her approach.

'I know you feel horrid, my dear,' she murmured, patting Vivienne's shoulder. 'I was standing right beside my Mary when she fell out of the swing. She was pretending to be a bird. It makes you feel to blame, but these things happen.'

They did not happen to Vivienne.

No one could be more to blame than a false governess.

Vivienne stood in the hallway outside the door of the room where the doctor was tending Jayne. Clement had not asked her to come inside and she did not blame him. No doubt he regretted hiring her. Regretted the time they had spent together, the friendship which had been deepening between them.

How selfish of her to have sought her own adventure when there were children involved. It was just as well she would not be a mother if this was an example of the care she gave them.

A yelp came from the other side of the door, sharp, painful, but quickly over. She heard the doctor's voice murmuring encouragement.

Moments later, Clement opened the door and came into the hallway. He took a deep breath, set his shoulders as if he was gathering the courage to go back into the room.

'Will she be all right?' Vivienne asked.

He slid his gaze towards her, then nodded. 'The doctor said it is a clean break and will heal with no lasting damage.'

'I'm sorry, Clement, I never meant for—'

'How could you have let this happen? If you had been teaching them what you ought to have been, she would not have been on the blasted swing in the first place.'

She opened her mouth in an attempt to explain, but what could she say?

'I apologise.' She blinked back tears and then ran away.

'Wait, I—' She heard him call out, but did not turn back.

She knew what she must do. As soon as she was assured Jayne would indeed, recover, she would go home.

Jayne and Alice deserved a governess who really was one. Not a dragon like the one Mildred wanted to hire, but a kind, caring lady who would not put them in danger because of her inexperience.

She dashed outside to the porch, sat in a chair and stared at the dunes between the house and the shore. Butterflies flitted in the sunshine but seeing their care-free rambling only made her feel worse.

'Oh, there you are, dearie.' Mrs Prentis crossed the porch, then sat in the chair beside her. She pressed a cup of tea into her hand.

'Drink it up, now. Nothing like it to set one right.'

'I am not certain this can be set right.' She had injured a child and there was no undoing it.

'Of course it can. I have been a mother for more years than you have been alive. I promise you, it will be all right. Give it time. Once Jayne is acting herself again, you will see matters in a proper light and feel better. Believe me, accidents and children go hand in hand. You are not to blame. Oh, I know it feels like it right now, but some things are simply not within our control. I cannot tell you how many times I have sat on this porch feeling the way you do now.'

'Clement blames me.'

'Well, he's a man. On occasion they lash out without considering their words. It was fear for his child speaking, not good sense. Ask Mr Prentis how many times he has been forced to beg my forgiveness over the years. I'm sure your young man will do the same.'

'Mr Marston is not my young man.'

Of all the things, Mrs Prentis smiled, winking at her. 'I see the way he looks at you. It is the very way Mr Prentis used to look at me.'

'He still does,' Vivienne said.

While this was wonderful for her hostess, it was horrible for Vivienne.

She did not want Clement to be in love with her. Nearly as much as she wanted him to be.

Clement was an ass. The second after he'd blamed Vivie for what happened he regretted it.

He had just watched Jayne go through a great deal of pain. Lashing out had been a release and Vivie had been his innocent target.

His behaviour was unmanly…inexcusable.

In an attempt to make amends he had followed her, but then found her sitting on the porch with Mrs Prentis.

What he had to say to her must be spoken in private so he went back to sit with his daughters.

Now, hours later, with dinner finished, and Alice and Jayne sleeping peacefully, where was Vivie?

Probably somewhere hating him for what he'd said. It was no wonder she wished to avoid him.

What a first-rate dunce he was, meaning to declare his love, intending to ask for her hand…and then to insult her?

He had meant to go down on one knee tonight, but to propose, not beg her forgiveness.

It would be his fault if she packed her camera equipment and went to her next assignment early.

No one would blame her.

'Ah, there you are, Clement.' Mr Prentis nearly ran into him coming around the corner. 'I assume you are looking for your young lady.'

'You have spoken to your wife? You know what I did?'

He grimaced, nodding. 'I've been in your shoes too many times. Last I saw of Miss Vivienne she was walking towards the beach.'

'Wish me luck, then.'

Moments later Clement left the house in search of his future.

There was a good chance it would not be the one he hoped for. Still he strode across the sand determined to do what he could to win his lady as well as a mother for his children.

Chapter Twelve

Vivienne sat on the sand, watching moonlight sparkle on the crests of waves.

The hypnotic roll of water rushing onshore did not soothe her, nor did the song of a night bird.

Hopefully what Mrs Prentis told her was correct. That once she saw Jayne recovering she would have a better perspective on what had happened. Right now she did not. She was haunted by the sight of a mis-shapen arm, by a scream of pain when the bone was set.

Of the accusation in Clement's eyes.

All at once she needed to walk. There was too much emotion rumbling through her to sit still.

She unbuttoned her shoes, rolled off her stockings, then walked towards the lapping waves.

Bunching up her skirt, she tucked the hem into the waistband. She stepped into the water, watched while froth tickled her toes.

Her chest ached. Her throat cramped. Tears which had threatened all afternoon dribbled down her cheeks.

Now that she was alone, she would finally allow herself to weep. If she did not release the tension squeezing her soul, she would not be able to fulfil her duties tomorrow.

Although she was a false governess, Alice and Jayne counted on her. Especially Jayne. She was bound to need a great deal of care. Care which a genuine governess would know how to give.

The imposter would be figuring it out as she went along. Why, oh, why had she believed she could step out of her station in life...outrun her destiny even for one short summer?

If she could go home now, she would do it. That, though, would make her a coward. Any suffering she was going through in this moment was of her own making.

She had only a short time left to try to make this up to Jayne.

And to Clement. It wasn't as if she would ever forget how stricken he'd looked coming out of the room after the doctor set Jayne's arm.

It was fair to say she had never met a braver man. All through the ordeal Clement had given his child reassuring smiles, as if to tell her this sort of thing happened on occasion, but there was nothing at all to be afraid of.

No doubt he was sitting at her bedside right now while Vivienne indulged in her weeping fit.

She was simply pathetic...and would be for a few more minutes. Then she would go back to the house and pretend she was a responsible person.

Sitting down with a plunk, she did not care that the waves lapped at her hips. So what if the water was cold and her skirt was getting soaked?

She would try to cry out her guilt. Not that it was likely to go away, but it must at least be released or she would explode. It only took a moment for her face to become as drenched as her skirt.

'Vivie!'

Oh, no!

Instead of turning her face to look, she buried her head in her arms.

'Go away,' she whispered even though Clement was still a distance away.

Clement was the last person she wished to see. Or worse, to be seen by.

Coming to the top of the dune, Clement could not believe what he was seeing.

Vivienne sitting at the waterline...with waves lapping her skirt. Luckily the surf was gentle tonight... but what was she doing?

Surely his unguarded and inappropriate comment could not have caused her this much distress? He'd been wrong to say what he had, but she seemed too overwrought for it to have been only that.

'Vivie!' he shouted and started to run.

It was rough going in the sand. By the time he reached her he was a little winded.

'What is it, Vivie? Is it what I said?'

Arms crossed over bent knees, she cradled her head in them. Without looking up, she nodded, then shook her head.

'Go away.' The quiver in her voice cut him to the quick.

But go away? No chance of him doing that. He knelt beside her. The water was awfully cold. 'How long have you been sitting here?'

'Not long enough.'

'Yes, long enough!'

'Can't...' she sniffled '...a person have a moment of privacy?'

'To weep?'

Although she was not doing so now, it was clear that she had been.

'Forgive me, Vivie. I should not have said what I did. I didn't mean it.'

'But of course you meant it. Words do not come out of one's mouth with no thought...' she hiccupped '...behind them.'

Still she did not peek up from her folded arms.

'Jayne might have broken her neck and not her arm... did you think of that?'

Yes, he had. Unreasonable worry had assaulted him. Although the last thing he was going to do was admit it. Now, with the emergency over and the doctor's reassurance that Jayne would fully recover, he saw the event in a more sensible light.

'I was wrong to say it. Jayne's fall was more my fault than yours. I should have insisted on having the swing taken down on the first day.'

Again, she shook her head, then nodded.

'Won't you look at me, Vivie?'

She did. He wished all of sudden that she had not. Even in the dark he saw how puffy her eyes were.

He wrapped his arms around her shoulders. Each foamy wave gliding around them seemed colder.

'Neither of us ought to blame ourselves or each other. What do you say, Vivie? Shall we call a truce?'

She nodded.

'Now, tell me why you are really crying.'

'Perhaps I turned my ankle.'

'Perhaps you are turning the truth.'

'Really, Clement. A lady is permitted to have her secrets.'

'You are shivering. No secret in that.'

'Yes, I will go back to the house.'

He stood, reached a hand down and then helped her up.

She dropped his hand, then turned as if she would walk away, her bare feet crusted with sand.

Now that his apology had been offered and probably accepted…one could only put so much faith in a nod…he had more to say.

Dash it, though. A true gentleman would not make a woman weep one moment and then profess his love in the next. It nearly seemed as if he should wait. Nearly, but no. Summer was almost over, after all. She meant to leave him. He meant to keep her.

'Wait. There is something I want to discuss.'

Discuss? That was a clumsy word.

Clearly he did not have the skill to sweep a woman off her feet with suave declarations.

Kisses though…that was a language neither of them misinterpreted. They might have denied it…but not misunderstood.

'May we discuss it inside?' she asked.

Fair enough. He did not wish for her to become ill from being cold and wet.

'This won't take long—' That was wrong. If this went the way he hoped, it would take a long, intimate time.

'Clement, if you wish to terminate my employment, do it quickly. The wind is rising. You must be as cold as I am.'

'Come with me.'

He caught her hand again. This time he did not let go, even when he bent to snatch up her shoes.

Here was a dilemma. Her feet were too wet and sandy to be put back into her shoes. At the same time she could not go barefoot. Splinters and thorns would prick her feet.

Stooping, he indicated for her to climb on his back.

She shook her head, her puffy eyes wide.

'Hold your shoes.' He handed them to her. 'I won't drop you.'

To his surprise, she took them and then did as he asked.

He settled her weight across his back, adjusted her legs in the crook of his arms.

Her arms went around his shoulders, holding tight. Her breath skimmed across his ear, warm and sweetly scented.

He had never carried a woman piggy-back before. One sensation led to another and left him wondering how this had come to be called piggy-back.

If there was one thing Vivienne Curtis did not feel like, it was a pig. Curvaceous-woman-back would be a better term for it. For his part, he felt like he could walk this way for ever.

Rather, he carried her towards the inn, but then walked past it and went to the carriage house.

Once inside, he let go of her legs. She slid off his back.

Interesting sensation, that.

Moonlight streaming inside illuminated a lantern hanging on a wall. He lit it and then closed the door.

Without the wind, it did not seem quite so cold. Cold enough, though, with no stove to light.

He spotted a pair of blankets hanging on the wall and plucked them off the hook.

There were two spots where romance might bloom. A wagon bed or that clean pile of straw in a vacant stall.

The choice was clear.

He spread one blanket on the straw, then punched and fluffed it. He stripped down to his small clothes which were damp, but not as soggy as his trousers. He sat down and covered himself with the blanket.

'Take off your skirt and sit with me.'

'I shouldn't.' She crossed her arms over her middle while shaking her head. 'No.'

'I will look away. Really, Vivie, you can be covered by a wet skirt or a dry blanket. Either way you are covered and the blanket is far more sensible.'

Still she hesitated.

'It's nearly warm under here,' he commented, giving her an encouraging grin.

She glanced between him and the carriage-house door as if deciding what to do.

Stay, go?

Love him…leave him? She was probably not thinking that.

Leave her post now or at the end of summer was more likely the decision she was weighing up.

A great gust of wind blew, rattling the door on its iron hinges. Vivie glanced back at him, a delicate frown wrinkling her brow.

He lifted the corner of the blanket. Love me, Vivie, love me was what he meant by it.

'It will be easier to speak if we are not across the stable from one another. And it really is getting warmer under here.'

Not much warmer, but once she joined him it would be. He hoped. If he could only manage to kiss her once, it would become heated in no time at all.

'Come now, your toes look white to the bone.'

'Oh, very well. Turn your head.'

He heard wet fabric thump on the floor.

A second later she scrambled under the blanket, but not close enough for him to coax a kiss out of her. Which he needed to do since it was the best way he knew of to express his feelings.

'Pivot this way.' He motioned for her to turn her feet towards him.

It surprised him when she did.

Surprised him even more that she did not kick him when he took her foot, held it between his palms.

What she did was close her eyes...and sigh.

'Icy,' he murmured while brushing sand off her toes.

Once her foot was clean he held, pressed and caressed it in the name of warming it.

'Nice,' he murmured, feeling her smooth skin and her fine bones. Her soft sighs of pleasure nearly made him sigh, too.

Ah, just there, her frown relaxed. That was encouraging. He picked up her other foot, cleaned and warmed it, too. Being under the blanket, her foot was hidden from his gaze, but his fingers learned as much as his eyes would have. Moving his thumb from her heel up her ankle, he felt how slim it was and smooth... strong.

With her foot properly warm, he was about to let go, but then she gave a long, delighted moan. Probably her calf was cold, too. No doubt it was as fine and smooth as her ankle was.

Did he dare find out?

Touching her would be an act of seduction and no mistaking it for anything else. If she allowed it, he would press for a kiss. If she did not, he would— Not give up! He'd brought her here to profess his love and then ask for her hand in marriage. He would not accept defeat until he had her answer.

'It's nice here, just the two of us.' He waited, praying she would return the sentiment.

'You said you wished to speak about something.'

'Yes, I do...' All at once his heart did not feel right. It galloped so hard he thought it might bruise his ribs.

But bruised ribs did not amount to much when compared to a bruised heart.

'First, there is something I must show you...' He shifted closer, all the while stroking the back of her calf with his thumb.

'What?' She leaned away from him, but her expression softened. Her brown eyes looked like simmering whisky...so intoxicating that he felt woozy and yet, at the same time, determined.

He slipped his hand from her calf to the small of her back, drew her slowly closer. 'This will make what I want to talk to you about make sense.'

'You are ever logical.' Wonder of wonders, she leaned back towards him.

Her breathing came so quick and fast he could see her chest rising...falling. She touched his undershirt with her fingertips, probably noticing how the fabric pulsed with his heartbeat. He would kiss her and make no excuse for it. He was going to act on what was in his heart and then...and then he was going to place that heart in her hands.

'Sweet Vivie,' he murmured the whisper on her lips.

And then she closed that last gap and kissed him. She wrapped her arms around his neck, drawing him in. Into her heart, into her soul and into the rest of her life. Surely he was not mistaken.

'Vivie...' he murmured again, as if somehow in saying her name he claimed her.

He lifted away, but only far enough so that he could gaze into her eyes…and see his love returned. Because how could it not be? The kiss held the promise of their future.

He rose to one knee, cupping her face in his palms. Felt cool air pebble his skin when the blanket slid off his thigh. Then he kissed her again. Being able to kiss this woman whenever he wished to for the rest of his life was going to be a sort of bliss he could have never imagined.

'I love you, Vivie.'

He waited a heartbeat, then two, and then he could not breathe. She ought to have said she loved him, too, by now. Dim lantern light revealed tears welling in her eyes.

'If you say you don't love me, I'm afraid I will not believe you.'

She pressed her mouth with pale fingertips. Wind rattled the door. Loose bits of straw blew across the stone floor.

Surely she couldn't deny what was happening between them. He would not let her! On one knee, he hugged her tightly to him, not willing to let her say anything to douse the hope flickering in his heart.

'If…' The word tickled his ear. Please let what she was about to whisper be of a forever love. 'If I say I do not love you, it will be a lie.'

Her words were what he longed to hear, but the tone…it was all wrong. He'd better finish before she said something to prevent his proposal. Already on bended knee, he took her hand, pressing it to his heart.

'Vivienne Curtis, I love you with my whole life. Will you—?'

'Don't say it, Clement. Please do not!' She pulled her hand from his grip. 'Do not break both our hearts.'

'Loving me breaks your heart?'

'Yes.' She swiped at tears with the back of her hands. 'I tried not to love you. But you...you are—'

She'd tried not to love him! Why?

His heart split open, cleaved right down the middle. Pain unlike any he had ever known bled out of the wound.

'What am I, Vivie? If you love me, why won't you have me?'

She touched his lips with her fingertips. He did not kiss them because her eyes were filled with sorrow... sorrow for loving him.

'Because you are as forbidden to me as the moon is to the sun.'

As if that explained it, which it did not, she leapt up. With a yank she snatched the blanket, wrapped it around herself, then ran for the door. She did not close it. Dumbfounded, he watched darkness swallow her fleeing figure. The awful silence was cut only by wind banging the door against the wall.

While he stared after her, not quite believing what had just happened, he noticed her shoes on the floor. The pointed little toes facing him gave him the oddest sensation. It felt as if the woman he loved, the one who had only just said she loved him, had simply vanished.

Well, she had, he decided. She was as lost to him as if she did not exist. What did exist was the ache in his soul and the confusion making him dark inside.

He sat down on the pile of straw, drew the other blanket around his legs while he struggled to make sense of what had just happened.

The reality was, Vivienne was not gone. He would see her tomorrow in her role as governess. Dash it, he would see her and, every time he did, his heart would break all over again.

Vivienne raced up the stairs, red plaid blanket tucked under her chin and dragging on the floor behind. It smelled a little bit like a horse, but also a great deal like Clement.

The wonder was that she could smell anything given how stuffy her nose was. She should never have allowed herself to share such an intimate moment with him. Should not have…and yet, it had been too beautiful to resist. The man too enticing to refuse. The temptation to reveal her heart to him had been overwhelming and in the end she'd been helpless to resist his draw.

Now she must pay the price…worse, Clement must, too.

Reaching her bedroom, she went inside, closing the

door without a sound. Pure providence kept her from being spotted while she'd dashed through the house.

Who had she become, believing it was acceptable to remove her skirt in the presence of a man…to let him caress her bare feet…her ankle and her calf…? She was not a woman who was mindful that she was promised to someone else!

'Clement,' she whispered, leaning her head back against the door. 'I would marry you if I could.'

He had not asked, but only because she'd prevented him. An incredible man had offered her his heart, his whole future and she had all but slapped it away. What a heartless wretch she was.

Walking over to the window, she looked out at blowing grass and sand. From here she could see the corner of the house and the big tree where the swing went up and down as if it entertained an invisible passenger.

There in the distance was Clement trudging along the path leading from the carriage house to the inn. He was bent forward against a strong gust of wind, carrying her skirt under one arm and her shoes under the other.

And her heart. He carried that, too.

She actually kissed the window, pretending nothing blocked the distance between them. How wickedly sorrowful it was that this was the last kiss she would ever give him. The glass was cold, like her future was sure to be.

Choking back a sob of self-pity, she went to the wardrobe and withdrew a gown. She did not even notice which one, but put it on unseeing. The time had come for her to tell him the truth. Clement had confessed his love to a woman he did not even know. Going on as they had been was out of the question now.

Crossing to the desk, she opened the drawer and withdrew a sheet of paper and a pencil. Writing her confession was the only way to tell him what she must. How else was she to make sense of things which made no sense?

Speaking with him face to face would surely end with her stumbling over her words. Her mind would be preoccupied with kissing him. She did not dare to indulge in it again. The temptation to take a different path than her family wanted was too great. With only a little push she would be a mother to the children she adored...a wife to the man she loved.

And it would be the shame of her family. Clement and his daughters were not the only people she loved. She loved her parents. They were the dearest people in the world and had indulged her desire for independence longer than most parents would have.

There was also Great-Aunt Anne to be considered. Vivienne had it within her power to make her aunt's last years contented ones, with everyone she loved united in one family.

She set the tip of the pencil on the paper, stared at it while listening to the wind racing under the eaves and grains of sand pinging the window.

'Dear Clement,' she wrote, mouthing the words while she wrote. 'I am not who you believe I am...'

Well, she was...but she was not. She pressed the pencil tip to her lips at a loss as how to proceed.

'Clement, I regret to inform you of who I really am...who I am not...'

She wadded the paper, tossed it on the floor then took another.

'My friend, I have something I must tell you... You cannot ask me to marry you. I am promised to another.' She gripped the pencil hard, causing her usually smooth writing to be jerky. 'I regret that... I sincerely regret that...but perhaps you are acquainted with him.'

The letter sounded so cold. It would seem to Clement as if a stranger had written it. But it must be so. She, the real Vivienne was a stranger...she was not his Vivie any more.

'I hope that you will find a woman who will give you the love you are worthy of, but she cannot be me. With greatest affection, Lady Vivienne Curtis, daughter of the Marquess of Helmond...a lady shackled by expectation and yet bound by love. Doomed to sorrow.' Harsh, but the truth.

This time she did not wad the letter and toss it away. No, indeed, she ripped it into dozens of pieces, opened the window and let the wind take the scraps. A letter was a coward's weapon. Clement deserved to hear the truth from her own lips.

When she thought about it, there really was no danger of him trying to win her back with a kiss or a proposal. After the first few words of her confession, he was bound to hate her and be glad to see the last of her.

Leaning out the window, she let wind blow on her face while taking several fortifying breaths. She must be strong for what she needed to do, or at least look as if she were. What she must not look was pale and lovelorn. She patted her cheeks to give them colour and then closed the window, crossing the room to the mirror.

There was nothing to be done about her swollen eyes, but her hair could do with being put into some kind of order.

That done, she stared at her image. Interesting how she looked calm and not desperate with grief.

Why wouldn't she, though, when all her life she had been trained to disguise her emotions? How horrible that Alice and Jayne would be forced to learn the same. Thinking of the girls nearly made her weep, but she caught her heart in time.

Not for long, though.

After leaving her bedroom, she stopped at Jayne's bed. For having endured a broken arm she did not look so bad. Rather, she seemed peaceful. Just there, she smiled briefly, then relaxed back into her dream.

Vivienne did not touch her hair tonight, but she did bend to kiss her brow. 'I wish you could be my daughter,' she whispered.

Then she turned to Alice. Bent and kissed her, too. 'I would be your mother if I could.'

Vivienne paused for a moment, placing one hand on each child's head. She lifted her face, prayed that they would find a mother who loved them. Also for courage to get through the next few moments.

It was selfish, she knew, but she could not bring herself to pray that Clement would find a wife to love him. It hurt too much to think about.

She wished she had never admitted she loved him. Very soon he would know that, in spite of the fact that he had her heart, she would give herself to another. It wasn't as if she could take back her confession of love. All she could do was not repeat the mistake.

She lifted her hand to his door.

Let guilt be her guiding light. Shame would keep her aloof when all she wanted to do was wrap her arms around Clement's neck and feel him fold her close to his heart. A heart that would turn brittle and break within the next few moments. One day he would give his love to someone, only it would not be her.

Breathe in, she reminded herself, breathe out. Stand tall and do not weep. Although she went through her mental list of admonitions, she could not manage to rap her fingers on the wood.

How would she begin? She had not been able to write the words, so what made her think she could speak them?

Taking a steadying breath, she knocked, but softly so she would not wake Alice and Jayne.

Hopefully something inspired would come to her before the door opened.

Nothing did.

Seeing Clement's face was nearly too much. His lips were drawn tight and turned slightly down at the corners and his eyes held no spark of humour in them.

She could not bear it. Her brain went utterly blank.

He looked down at her with one brow arched in question. 'What is it, Vivienne?'

Not Vivie...and it hurt dreadfully knowing she would never hear the endearment again. She had made a mistake in allowing it to soften her heart in the first place. One mistake among many and all of them her fault. Here was her chance to begin her confession and all she could say was...nothing.

'I suppose you have come for your clothing.'

'Yes, of course.'

He did not invite her inside, but came back a moment later and placed her skirt and her shoes in her arms. They were damp, scented with the sea. Grains of sand rubbed her palms.

Giving her a dispirited glance, he started to close the door.

'Wait! I need to speak with you.'

'Tomorrow, perhaps.'

He continued to close the door. She wedged herself between the door and the frame, then wriggled past him. Once inside his room she walked to the desk which she had come to think of as her spot.

There were no jars containing insects, no crisp white pages waiting to be drawn on…no pencils sharpened and ready.

'You should not be here,' he said bluntly.

No, she should not. She never should have been. Her place was in London announcing her engagement.

'There is something I must tell you, Clement.'

Chapter Thirteen

In spite of her red-rimmed eyes, Vivienne looked composed. Clement believed it was a false front. She could not possibly be unruffled after what had happened between them only an hour ago.

It was as if she was drawing a mask over her feelings, closing herself off in a way she had not done before.

No surprise since he was doing the same. In the name of protecting his heart he was making it appear as if he did not have one...that it was not aching to hold her and love her.

The blame for what had happened was all on him. Had he not suggested Jayne's fall was due to Vivienne's neglect, matters would be much different between them.

He had seen how she'd been consumed with guilt over the accident and what had he done? Bungled things and pressed her for a commitment. A commitment she had refused in the past. It had been the worst sort of judgement to try to hold her with a proposal.

What he had mistakenly believed was that, if she knew he loved her, it would make a difference. The frustration of it all was that she returned his love and yet had stopped him from proposing. Surely she understood it was what he had been doing?

'I find that I must apologise, once again,' he said.

A moment ago he'd wanted her to leave him alone, but now, with a flick of his hand, he indicated that she should sit on one of the chairs beside the window.

The gesture came off harsher than he meant it to, revealing how confused he was.

The tall curtain over the window stirred. It must be cracked open and the wind seeping inside. He would deal with it tomorrow. Now he needed to rectify the division separating him from Vivienne.

How, though…when the puzzle pieces would not knit together in his mind? There was her next engagement and something to do with the moon and the sun being forbidden to one another. Which made no sense.

Now that they had admitted their love for one another, nothing was the same. Life's expectations had changed. Surely she must recognise the fact that they should remain together…that they were meant to be a family?

'Won't you sit down so we can discuss this?'

It would be best to let her begin, given that he had

no idea how to. Clearly, telling her he loved her and beginning to propose marriage had been all wrong.

Perhaps her hesitation, refusal to be honest, had to do with him belonging to a ranking family and her being a governess.

If it was as simple as that, he could put her concern to rest.

Some in society might expect him to wed higher, but he had brothers to do that. It was unlikely that anyone would care who he married.

'No. I have something I must say to you. It will not take long.'

It would if she continued to stare silently at him, wringing her fingers.

'May I ask you something?' He would speak first after all since she seemed unable to.

'Very well.' Why the blazes was she staring at the floor instead of looking at him?

'I do not care about social rank, if that is the reason you turned me down.'

'It has something to do with it.' She looked up sharply, her face pale. Her pulse tapped hard in the tender spot under her jaw.

Only by the greatest restraint did he keep from reaching across and soothing it with his thumb...or a kiss.

'Let my brothers have their heiresses, Vivie. I desire a love match.'

'And I hope you have it one day. But it cannot be with me.'

He tamped down the urge to make a sharp retort because why on earth could it not be with her?

'You must give me a reason why not,' he said, using the most sensible tone he could muster. The facts all pointed to one conclusion. 'I have told you I love you and you have admitted the same. That confirms we already have our love match.'

She had not confessed her love with joy, he had to admit. But she had spoken the words.

'There are things you do not know about me, Clement.'

'No one can know everything about another person, but I do know you…your heart. What I do not know cannot matter so much in comparison.'

She blinked and he thought that she might weep. But, no, she shook her head, bit her bottom lip. She did not cry in the end.

'It matters. The engagement I mentioned I was going to…it is exactly that. It is a betrothal. My betrothal. The formal announcement is to be made in a few weeks.'

What was this? No…it could not be true. And yet he had not misunderstood the words. Her lips had moved, his ears had heard. Now his heart lay at her feet, cleaved in half, gutted…slain.

'But you will not go through with it?' How could

she? Not after what they had confessed to one another. 'Not now?'

'I am to wed the Marquess of Winterfeld.'

A governess marrying a marquess? It did not happen.

'Who are you really, Miss Curtis?'

No longer was she his Vivie for certain. Or perhaps she never had been.

More fool was he for not pressing her about her past. The secrets she kept did affect him and his children, after all. What a foolish thing to give his heart to her, not even knowing who she was.

'I am Lady Vivienne Louise Curtis. My father is Thomas Curtis, Marquess of Helmond.'

If a chrysalis had hatched a frog, he could not be more stunned. His governess, this woman he loved, was not just any stranger, but a lady of high rank!

Stunned, he felt like plunging headlong into misery. Instead, he set his shoulders, stood straight-backed... stiff.

'I deserve an explanation. Why have you have done this to us? How do you expect me to explain who you are to Jayne and Alice?'

'I never meant for this to happen. Please believe that I had every intention of doing my duty towards them. Surely you know I love your girls no matter what position I was born to.'

'Something occurs to me,' he said, wishing it had

not. 'As the daughter of a marquess, and soon to be a marchioness, you far outrank my sister-in-law. I wonder—why is it that you did not admit who you were when Mildred threatened a more highly qualified governess? You are far more qualified to teach them than she is. If you had spoken up—'

But, no, she could not have. The scandal of having a lady of such high rank working for him...living with him...would have been ruinous to them all. A fact which did not keep him from feeling bitter, betrayed to his soul.

'What a fool you must think me, Lady Vivienne.' He knew his voice had a bite to it. The emotion was too raw to disguise.

She looked down. When she spoke, he barely heard the words. 'No, Clement, I would never think that.'

'A moment ago I thought you might not want me because my rank was above yours, that you might worry about feeling socially inferior, in society's eyes. And all the while—'

He had to breathe long and slow in order to not shout, or growl, or stamp out of his own chamber.

'All the while you were so far above me, that there was never any hope for us. You must have thought my proposal rather pitiful.'

'It's not true! That was the most touching moment of my life. I will never have another like it.' She blinked rapidly. He wondered if there was any truth to what she said. 'You must understand, my engagement is an arrangement of convenience. From the day I was born I was…but you know how it works. I have little control over whom I wed.'

Well, dash it all, he did know that. What he also knew, vowed in this moment, was that his daughters would never be forced to marry against their wishes.

If he had one thing to thank the governess for, it was pointing out the need for a woman to have a choice in the direction her life would take. He would never see Alice or Jayne forced to choose duty over love.

If that was all there was to what had happened, he might feel more charitable towards Lady Vivienne Curtis. To a great degree she was a victim of her birth.

There was more, though.

What she had failed to explain was why she was here acting the part of a governess when she ought to be at home planning her grand society wedding. What could she want from him and his family?

She must have a reason for what she'd done. Something that seemed reasonable in her eyes. But surely it was not worth the cost of breaking his daughters' hearts? He might eventually learn to live with his own misery, but not theirs, not again.

'May I offer you my congratulations?' he stated formally, his heart as far from the sentiment as it could be.

'I would rather that you did not. I will fulfil my duty. There is nothing to be congratulated or celebrated.'

Indeed. Only mourned.

'Goodnight, Clement.' She turned towards the door and so did not see him reach for her. He had not meant to, was not even certain why he had done it. Wishing, perhaps, that life would turn back to what it was yesterday.

'Why?' he asked, watching her fingers grip the doorknob and turn it. 'What was worth the cost of this deception?'

To save a life, perhaps, or for the betterment of… of something…anything. He might understand it, if it was.

The knowledge would not help when he was alone in the night and missing her…imagining her married to someone who was not him. But understanding might ease the ache. Or make it worse. Whichever it was, he needed to know.

She opened the door and stepped into the dim light of the girls' bedroom. It seemed as if she would not answer, but then she stopped between the beds, turned.

'I wanted one last adventure before I wed.'

'And I was it? I was your adventure?'

'No, you were my love.'

With that, she spun about, went to her bedroom and closed the door. The quiet click sounded like an explosion in his heart. She was not gone and yet she was. He had never felt so bereft.

He left his door open in case Jayne awoke and

needed him. It wasn't as if he could expect Lady Vivienne to rise in the night and do it.

It was fair to say he ached for the governess...perhaps for the lady, too. He could not say for certain since he did not know who she was.

Only that he ached.

Sitting at his desk, he stared at the stacked pages of his book, their book. Without Vivienne he would have been only one among dozens of authors hoping for publication. Now he had great hopes his work would be seen.

If they had nothing else between them, they at least had this.

And memories. He did at any rate. Vivienne would go on to make memories with another man...have his children, be the love of his life.

One thing was for certain—he would never attend another society ball. Not that, in the past, he had attended all that many of them. If he had, he might have encountered the Marquess's daughter and recognised her that first day on the drive.

Now his visits to London would be even fewer than before. If he happened to encounter the new Marchioness Winterfeld at some elegant event, he was not certain he would recover.

Getting through the next several days until her time was up would be a trial of its own kind.

An adventure was all this had been to her? All he

had been to her? No, not all…she'd also said he was her love. It would be better not to have heard her say that. Knowing she loved him, but would marry another anyway…how was he to get over that?

He picked up a page, the one with the illustration of the White Plume moth. He clenched his fist around it, remembering Vivienne's interest in it. He let go, watching the illustration flutter, crumpled, to the desk.

Clement did not expect to sleep, but he had and so deeply it felt as if he had been knocked out.

His limbs were heavy, his eyelids seemed glued together. This was the sleep of grief; he recognised it, having felt this way when his parents had left this earth. At least this time no one had died. Only a beautiful hope for his future.

Sun shone brightly through his window. He was late rising.

But what was that on the floor? An envelope. It appeared to have been slipped under his door. Although there was no name on it, he could only assume it was meant for him. Drawing a note from the envelope, he frowned.

'Dear Clement, if you wish, I will sponsor Alice and Jayne into society when the time is appropriate. Do not allow them to be sent to London.'

'It is not my intention,' he grumbled, but his intentions seemed to have mattered very little lately. However, he would accept what help she was willing to give. If her rank would keep them with him, he would accept it.

Rank, what a fickle thing it was. While Vivienne's might benefit him, allowing him to keep his girls, it would also separate him from her.

As a member of society he knew the rules. He understood that the higher the rank, the less a woman had to say about her own future. He could accept that, could forgive her in so far as that went. But to use him in her quest for adventure...worse, to use Alice and Jayne...

He ought to let her be the one to explain to them why she must leave...that, although they wished for her to be their mother, she would not be staying. True love would not win the day.

Dressing, he went downstairs. He would be late for breakfast, but he might beg something from the kitchen.

At this hour, the lady governess would be in the classroom with the children, which was just as well. He was not ready to face her, to paste on a smile for Alice's and Jayne's sake.

He was in luck in the kitchen. After a bite to eat, he felt somewhat revived, able to rise to the challenges this day was bound to present.

As much as he did not wish to, he would speak with Vivienne about her offer. Whatever the cost to him–

self, he must see his girls protected from Mildred's visions for their future.

If she got her way, they would have no choice in who they wed. Recent heartbreaking events had taught him just how important it was for them to have one.

Lady Vivienne was someone he did not know, but he did know the governess. Vivie would do her best for Alice and Jayne and do it out of affection for them, not because it would enhance her social standing… which needed no enhancing, being already so elevated.

Clement knew of her father, but hadn't ever met him. The man had a sterling reputation…and a daughter who had stolen his heart. The future Marchioness was a thief. In spite of it, he did trust her with his children.

What he needed right now was a breath of late summer air, something fresh to help set him right before he spoke with Vivienne about her offer.

Going on to the porch he found Mrs Prentis standing at the porch rail, looking towards the shore. He joined her.

'Good morning,' he said.

'Good morning, my dear.' She patted his hand, gave him a consoling look. That was odd since there was no reason for her to. She would not be aware of all that had happened between him and Vivienne.

Before he could give the matter more thought, he heard laughter coming from the direction of the shore.

'Miss Curtis must have taken their lessons outside this morning,' he said.

'Morning? It's just shy of noon by now.' This time she squeezed his hand. 'Mr Prentis has taken the girls on a walk.'

'Has he? Is their governess ill?' Worry gave his insides a tumble. Perhaps the drama of last night had got the best of her.

'I do not believe so. She was terribly distressed last time I saw her. Not ill though.'

'When was that?' Regardless of Vivienne's emotional state, he did need to speak with her. No matter what misgivings were between the two of them, his daughters' well-being must come first.

'But perhaps you would like to sit?'

'Mrs Prentis, you are giving me odd looks. Is there something you need to tell me that you think I will need to sit down for?'

She sighed, considered him up and down. She nodded. 'I believe you will do standing.'

Clearly the children were safe and enjoying their break from study, so what could be so dire?

'Miss Curtis has gone home…to London.'

Chapter Fourteen

The ferry crossing was not as turbulent as the first time Vivienne had made the trip, which did not keep her from gripping the rail and feeling ill.

She watched the Isle of Wight growing ever distant. Felt her heart grow tight and her soul…grey. Indeed, that was the very word. Grey like storm clouds, or perhaps it was grey like depressing fog.

How ever one described it, she disliked it. Disliked herself. She was miserable for more reasons than she could keep track of. The latest was leaving without a word.

She ought to have given Alice and Jayne some sort of reason as to why she had to go. Only, she could not look into their sweet grinning faces and tell them she could not be their mother because she must marry someone who was not their father.

How was she to say that, while she wished for nothing more than to become a part of their family, she was obligated elsewhere?

She would not be able to say anything of the sort without weeping because, unless Clement managed to prevent it, Alice and Jayne would one day stand in her shoes. At their tender ages, those sweet girls had no idea what was in store for them.

Vivienne squeezed her fingers around the rail. Please, oh, please let Clement accept her offer to take the girls under her wing. She would do her best to ensure they were not forced into a marriage not of their choosing.

As a marchioness, she would be supremely qualified to present them to society. Mildred would be agreeable to the arrangement since a close association with Lady Winterfeld would greatly advance her in society, too.

It was all a heap of nonsense, of course. Vivienne was the same person, governess or lady.

All of a sudden wind swirled over the deck. A wave rocked the ferry. She drew the hood of the cloak over her head.

Heavy wool covered half of her face. She could weep if she wished to and no one would know. Except for herself. She would know.

Over the past few days she had done far too much weeping. Her eyes ached. At the end of the day, life was what it was and she must accept it.

Now that she had admitted the truth to Clement, she must also admit it to her parents. Although she would keep the condition of her heart to herself. They would question why she had arrived home without her sister. While she could invent another lie, she would not.

One thing she had learned was that a great deal of harm came from twisting the truth. It did not matter how justified one felt.

What, she wondered, would her parents think of her being a governess and receiving a wage? Distressed, no doubt.

Yet she was going to miss the sense of worth it gave her. Doing a job and being recompensed for it had been fulfilling. All things considered, she knew she would have been happy as a governess had she been born to it.

The deck rolled and hitched. She had to adjust her weight, leaning left, then listing right in order to keep her balance. Funny, but the movement was a reflection of her life right now. Up, down, tossed this way and that.

Clearly, it was time to go below deck. When she turned she spotted a young couple at the rail. The man held his lady close. Cheek to cheek they gazed out at the water. She thought they were laughing at some small thing.

She and Clement used to do that. Not with the intimacy that the couple at the rail had, of course.

Oh, but there had been moments when she'd known how strong and lean his form was...how wonderful he smelled. How it felt to be pressed against him while under the spell of his kiss. Those moments had been intimate. But no more of that. She would gather her composure and move on.

Moving on proved to be more challenging than she would have wished. No more than a dozen paces along the way she encountered another couple, an elderly pair. The same as the younger couple, they held one another. Like them, they, too, were chuckling over something. No doubt their lives were bursting with memories to reminisce over. It would be best not to look too closely at them or her heart would break anew.

Vivienne's stomach turned. It was hard to know if it was from the turbulent crossing or her upside-down emotions.

When she looked back over the rail at the sea, the Isle of Wight was no longer visible. With an awful sense of loneliness, she continued on her way across the deck. A movement caught her eye. Something dashed in front of her hem. A tiny many-legged creature scuttled this way and that.

She stooped to peer more closely at it. My word, it was a Speckled Bush cricket.

'And how did you manage to get aboard, my little friend?' Who had she become, speaking to an insect as if it were a confidant? 'Clearly you are as lost as I am.'

It had been three weeks since Vivienne went away, each one longer than the next.

Clement sat at his desk, still at the inn, looking at book pages and photographs. He shuffled them top to bottom, bottom to top. He could not even feign an interest in the project. Insects used to be exciting, but now? A fifteen-legged beetle might crawl across the toe of his foot and he would barely give it a glance.

Who was he these days? Barely a researcher. No longer an employer. Not an engaged man. A miserable, grumbling pillbug all rolled up in misery was who he was.

On the first day after Vivienne went home to London he had walked about angry, probably with steam coming out of his ears. He could scarcely believe that on top of everything else, Vivienne had simply left. Bad enough she had come into their lives under false pretences, but to have run away like she had…

It was unforgivable. Until it wasn't.

Under the guidance of Mrs Prentis, he came to see matters in a truer light. It took more than a week of her reminding him that Vivienne had never deceived him and that she had been upfront from the beginning about not being able to stay.

She had, in fact, stated plainly that she had another engagement. He had been the one not to recognise the nature of the commitment. He had assumed it was another governess position which, Mrs Prentis had informed him, was assuming too much.

The good lady had pointed out another truth regarding Alice and Jayne. It was hardly Vivienne's fault that they had become so attached to her. She was a doting governess who adored her charges. And isn't that what he'd wished for when he hired her?

During the second week he'd tried convincing himself that life could go on as it always had. He could get past this.

What had changed, really? He had his daughters and his studies. It had been an interesting summer of exploration, just as he had planned it to be. If one did not count chickenpox and a broken arm. Or a shattered heart.

Yes, life would go on as it had. Perhaps it would. Although Mildred's plan for his girls was still a cloud on his horizon.

Now, here he found himself in the middle of the third week and missing Vivienne more than he had in the beginning.

Very clearly, life was never going to be as it was. The governess, or Lady Vivienne rather, had left her mark.

It did not matter how much he loved his Vivie. She had chosen someone else. There was no undoing it, so he must find a way of living with a burdened heart.

'Here you are, my dear,' Mrs Prentis slid a cup of tea across the desk, jarring him from his indulgent misery. 'Drink it up.'

'Ah, thank you. You always show up with aid when I need it most.' Also when she had something to discuss.

Mrs Prentis sat down in Vivie's chair. She patted his hand in the motherly way she had.

'Do you know where my girls are?' They must be finished with the reading he had given them to do by now.

'Keeping Mr Prentis out of trouble, I imagine.' She smiled kindly. 'If you were my boy, I would tell you to go after your young lady.'

'My young lady is about to become engaged to someone else.'

'As far as we know, she has not done it yet. I imagine we would hear the news even here on the Isle. Newspapers delight in society engagements. If you hurry, you might stop it in time.'

'Stop it?'

'You know you must try.'

'She has rejected me at every turn. I do not know why she would change her mind.' Or why he would hand his heart over to her to be crushed again.

How foolish could a man be?

'Vivienne loves you. I doubt she has changed her mind about that.'

'And yet she is in London, not here with me.'

'She did not reject you, you do understand that? All she did was accept her duty. In a sense, I find it admirable...yet also incredibly sad.'

'So, you are suggesting that I, the brother of a baron, present myself as a competing suitor to a marquess?'

'Not quite that. You will present yourself as a man who loves her, as opposed to one who does not.'

He did not drink the tea, which was not the point of her bringing it. The point was to listen to her advice. To hear what a woman with many years of experience in marriage and raising a family had to say... that was the point.

'It is a risk, my dear. I will not pretend it isn't. But if you don't try you will always wonder. Do not give up on Vivienne without a fight. For her sake if not for your own.'

Mrs Prentis might be wrong. Logically, there was a very slim chance of winning Vivie away from a respected marquess.

And yet, slim was not none.

Energy buzzed through him at the prospect of battling for Vivienne's hand. He had not felt such a rush of hope since she went away.

'Love is a risk, but it is also life's great reward.' Mrs Prentis rose, collecting her cup and his, although he had yet to take a sip. 'Give it some thought, but don't take long. Once the formal announcement is made, there will be a scandal getting out of it.'

Mrs Prentis had not made it to the doorway before he sprang from his chair.

'I will take the evening ferry if Mr Prentis is willing to give us a ride to the village.'

'He will be relieved to know you have come to your senses. After all these years he still has not recovered from me nearly wedding a neighbouring farmer, don't you know?'

'I did not know.'

'The farmer was already on one knee, it was that close. Now, go and tell Mr Prentis to hitch the horse while I pack your family's belongings.'

He dashed towards the stairway, then paused, looking back. 'My children and I will miss you. This has been the best summer of our lives.'

Mrs Prentis smiled, then made a shooing motion with her fingers.

'Go on with you now, you will be back next year or the one after...you and your bride.'

Tomorrow night Vivienne's engagement would be announced. Mother had a dinner party planned for the event.

She had not seen her future betrothed since her return, although she understood he was also in London. He had sent her some lovely yellow roses, though, as a token of his esteem.

Friendship was what the pretty buds represented. Lovely in their way, yet she found herself lost in a fantasy that Clement had sent them. If he had, they would be deep crimson, the colour of love.

She had not meant to sigh, but after tomorrow she would no longer be able to fantasise about Clement, not without being unfaithful to her fiancé. Right and wrong were what they were, no matter how her heart perceived the situation.

'What is it? Don't you like them?' her mother asked. 'They are a lovely gesture.'

'Yes, quite a lovely gesture.'

'Come, sweetheart, walk with me in the garden. Everything is such a bustle in here getting ready for tomorrow. It is difficult to have a proper conversation.'

The garden was at its best with hints of autumn in the air. This time of year used to be her favourite. Now, she thought she did not have one.

There was only one thing she liked best. The man and his children she'd left behind on the Isle of Wight. Being separated from them had not helped her move on and accept her future. She only longed to see them more acutely. Everything reminded her of them.

'Look, Mother.' Vivienne pointed to a bush they walked past. 'It's a Painted Lady butterfly.'

'You learned this from the young man you spent the summer with?'

'He was my employer, an entomologist, you know that.'

'Indeed, yes, but I wonder…was he perhaps a bit more than that? I get the feeling he may have been.'

'It does not matter. Summer is over and here I am, ready to accept Everett's proposal. It will make Great-Aunt Anne madly happy, I suppose.'

'Madly happy. She is a great one for matchmaking. You do know that your great-aunt wed for love, though?'

'I have heard her speak of how much she adored Everett's father.'

'It is understandable after her first marriage. She was extremely unhappy in it.' Mother brushed a lock of hair from Vivienne's cheek that the breeze had stuck there. 'She did not love her first husband a jot. To make it worse, there was another man she did love. But her father forbade it and she was given to a viscount who was as wealthy as a bank.'

'I am glad Great-Aunt Anne was happy in the end.'

'It is the most important thing. Give that some thought, won't you?'

'Did you love Father when you wed him?'

Funny how her mother never spoke of it and Vivienne had never asked. Perhaps because in the past, she'd spent so much time thinking of how to avoid marriage. In those days she considered vows a trap, not a blessing.

For all the good it had done her. Here she was only a day from being entrapped…rather, engaged.

'No, dear, I did not. It took a bit of time. I love your father now, though.'

A servant hurried across the garden. 'The flowers have arrived, my lady. Where shall I direct them to be put?'

'Thank you, Morgan. I will be along.' Mother kissed Vivienne's cheek. 'Do you understand what I am telling you?'

'Not to despair. Love can come from unlikely beginnings.'

'Yes, something of the sort. Now let me see your pretty smile. Everett is coming for dinner. Grace and George will be here, too. I'm certain you will want to know all about their trip.'

And later, Grace would want to know all about hers, too.

Even speaking Clement's name was bound to make her tear up. She had not spoken it more than was necessary in order to explain where she had spent her summer. And then she had called him nothing more personal than Mr Marston.

Her mother had been wonderfully forgiving of her escapade, once she'd recovered from being stunned. Father had not been. It had taken a week for him to stop glowering at her. Another after that for him to smile. It took a while, but once she'd convinced him she was ready to fulfil her duty to the family, matters were easier between them.

There was no point in wasting a lovely late afternoon inside the house so she sat on a bench, resting her chin on her open palm.

She would think dreamily of Clement one more time and then put him away, assign him and his children to the past.

Until tomorrow night, when fantasising about a man who was not her fiancé would be unacceptable, she would indulge. She would give herself up to Clement's funny, flat smile.

Sighing aloud would not hurt, this once, while she pictured him sitting at his desk with his black glasses low on his nose. The dedication he gave his research was endearing.

She nearly giggled, recalling how sometimes the top half of him would vanish into a bush while he chased a fleeing insect. His backside would shift the branches, then he would shout out in victory once he had his trophy.

Oh, and just there, her imagination watched him drawing, then writing. This one last time, she let him appear to her in the moonlight while he kissed her on the beach. Her imagination was vivid. It was as if she could hear the surf, smell salt air…feel his hands pressing her ribs in an embrace.

It was only a breeze stirring the hair at her temple, but it felt as warm as Clement's breath.

It was not only Clement she had to tuck away in her

heart...there was Alice and Jayne, too. How was she to forget being called Mama?

Rather than making her feel fulfilled, her fantasy left her aching. One thing was certain—Everett Parker would not be able to heal her heartache.

'What,' Mildred demanded, peering at Jayne with narrowed eyes, 'has happened to Alice?'

Alice shot Jayne a glance, Jayne shot it back.

The girls did not look alike. The fact that their aunt could not tell them apart showed how little she actually thought of them.

'I jumped through an enchanted hole,' Alice said.

'And,' Jayne added, 'she got attacked by a mad hare.'

Mildred turned her narrowed eye on Clement. 'This is not acceptable. You were to teach them proper behaviour and look at them! Making up outrageous stories.'

Indeed, look at them. In spite of everything that had happened, his daughters sparkled. Right now, it likely had to do with some mischief they were clearly brewing. But in part it had to do with him not being completely forthcoming about why their governess had left.

He had told them there was something Miss Curtis needed to do in London but they would see her again soon. Now that they were in London the girls were in high anticipation of a reunion.

'Papa, may we play in the garden?' Jayne asked.

He did not feel awkward giving permission since he had grown up in this house. It was still his family home even though Mildred was now its baroness.

'You may, but do not do anything I would disapprove of.'

'We won't,' Alice answered.

They would, he knew. It was the very reason they'd asked to go out.

Perhaps he ought to have taken rooms at an inn. It would have been wise to keep the girls away from Mildred.

However he meant to make his position of authority clear. He might be their uncle the same as Duncan was, but he was the man who'd raised Alice and Jayne. He was the one they considered their father.

Let Duncan and Mildred argue the point if they wished to. He was who he was, their father.

Hiding the children away would not serve any good purpose other than making him appear less than confident of his authority when it came to their futures.

'A word, Mildred,' he said when it looked as if she would leave the drawing room.

'I assume you have come to discuss which governess the girls should have. I will fetch Duncan. Clearly, they still need proper training.'

So far Alice and Jayne had done nothing to warrant that comment. There was nothing like criticism of one's children to make one cross. It was an effort to hold his temper, but he managed.

'You will not pass judgement on my daughters within my hearing or theirs. You will not malign them or denigrate them in any way to anyone.'

'But clearly they need guidance and I fear it will not come from you.'

'The reason for my visit is to tell you to forget your idea of the children living in London. They will remain with me until I decide otherwise.'

'Shall we see what Duncan has to say about that?'

'About what?' his brother asked striding into the drawing room at that very moment. 'Clement! Welcome home, Brother!'

Duncan clasped his shoulders in a hug.

He returned the greeting.

'Thank you. It's a short stay, only. After I tend to a matter here, we will return to my house in the country.'

'Not with your nieces, you will not! Wait until you see, Duncan, Clement has not improved their manners in the least.'

'I saw them when they dashed past me a moment ago. They did pause to offer very sweet curtsies. And then they hugged me! Imagine that.'

'Sweet curtsies will not see them placed in advantageous marriages. They must have intense training.'

'Which they will have,' Clement said. 'But it will

not be from you or from a martinet of an old-fashioned governess you wish to foist on them.'

'Foist on them? Do you hear that, Husband?' Mildred pretended to pout.

His brother nodded, looking thoughtful. 'I wonder if perhaps you have something else in mind, Clement?'

'Lady Vivienne, the daughter of the Marquess of Helmond, has offered to guide them in society when the time is appropriate.'

Silence followed this pronouncement, but only for half a minute.

'Your brother has lost his mind, Duncan. As if he has ever even met the lady.'

In that moment, running footsteps were heard in the hallway.

Alice and Jayne rushed into the room. Alice had both hands clasped behind her back.

'Auntie Millie, we have a gift for you.' Jayne announced. 'Because we are sorry Miss Curtis kept your nest and put it in a tree.'

'So we found you another to take its place.' Alice withdrew a mass of feathers and sticks, dried grass and who knew what sorts of fluff. It looked well used.

What Clement wondered was, what sort of insect the girls had stashed inside.

There was a time for discipline and there was a time for pranks. This was a time for pranks.

'You will call me Aunt Mildred, Jayne.'

'Yes, Ma'am,' Alice answered.

'Do not play games with me. You are Jayne. I will not tolerate your nonsense.'

'How do you expect to be responsible for them when you cannot tell them, one from another?' he asked exasperatedly.

'I don't mind, Papa,' Jayne said. 'But here is your nest, Aunt Mildred.'

Alice placed it in her hand before Mildred could snatch her fingers away. The grin his sweet daughters exchanged had him peering hard at the nest.

The insect turned out to be a grasshopper which blended in with the shade of the twigs. The marvellous creature made a leap. It alighted in Mildred's hair.

Mildred screeched, dancing about and batting her hair.

Heroically, Duncan plucked the grasshopper, carried it to the window and tossed it out.

'I am certain they did not know it was there.' Duncan soothed his wife with a pat on the shoulder.

An apology was in order, from someone to someone. Mildred ought to apologise for threatening to take his children away from him. Alice and Jayne should apologise for the grasshopper.

Weighing the sins, he decided, 'It was all but invisible, after all.' He could hardly censure his daughters when privately he applauded them.

'I suppose, so,' Mildred muttered, but her frown

expressed doubts. 'But back to what you just said… about the Marquess's daughter.'

'That she has offered to teach them?'

'Why would she? Truly, Duncan, do you think he has ever even met such a high-born lady? We certainly have not.'

'But you have met her,' he pointed out. 'There was a bit of a disagreement between the two of you over a hat?'

'You are mistaken. That was with your governess. I do not even recall the awful woman's name.'

'One and the same… Lady Vivienne Louise Curtis.' This conversation was taking up valuable moments. 'Duncan, will you watch these two for a while? I have a marriage proposal to make before the woman I love accepts one from someone else.'

Apparently dumbstruck, his brother managed one nod.

Mildred clasped her hand to her throat. 'Your brother's research has finally driven him out of his mind.'

Chapter Fifteen

Rather than wait for his brother's carriage to be brought around, Clement dashed down the steps and waved over the first hansom cab to come by.

Fearing he had no time to spare, he did not wait for the driver to come down but scrambled up beside him. It might be days before Vivie announced her engagement or it might be moments.

There was also a chance that he was already too late. While he had wasted time blaming her and feeling sorry for himself, Vivienne might have already become engaged.

Although clearly surprised to see Clement riding on the bench, the driver did not protest.

'I'm in a great hurry.' Clement told him where to go.

Even if the announcement was still some time off, he would act while his courage was high. He must reach Vivienne before he thought too closely about what he was doing.

Had it ever happened that the humble brother of a baron had charged in to unseat a marquess for a lady's hand?

Better not to give that too much thought. It was as Mrs Prentis pointed out, Clement was the one who loved her, the other man was the one who did not.

The banner he carried into battle was love. Now wasn't that a noble and romantic thought for a scientist?

'Something is happening at the Helmond mansion tonight. Can't help noticing the fancy carriages dropping off high society folks. Since you are going there in such a hurry, maybe you know what it is?'

'Did you see the conveyance of the Marquess of Winterfeld among them, by chance?'

'It's a hard one to miss, being even grander than the others. I did spot it, though, when I drove past with my last customer before you.'

'I might know what is happening. But how long ago was that?'

'Oh, an hour or more ago. So, what is happening, Sir?'

'I believe the Marquess of Helmond is about to announce the engagement of his daughter.'

'Why, that is grand news! Do you know who the gentleman is?'

'Me... I hope. If you can get me there fast enough.'

He was not dressed for the occasion and the driver's sceptical glance said as much. But then the fellow grinned. 'Very well, Sir. Hold on tight.'

The driver snapped his whip over the team's ears. The carriage jerked, then lurched. Clement leaned forward as if it would somehow make the conveyance go faster. He clamped his hat to his head to keep it from flying off.

Still, the wheels could not turn quickly enough. At this very moment the announcement might already be in progress. His future happiness and that of his daughters could be slipping away from him.

What, exactly, made him think Vivie would change her mind about him, he could not imagine. It was only that he felt something drawing him to her with great urgency. He had never had a feeling like it before. Her soul calling his…again, a romantic notion and far from scientific.

Love was not scientific, he was learning…it was far from logical. Yet it was the truest, most compelling thing he had ever known. And so, yes, he did feel Vivie calling to him, even if she might not be aware of it. Hopefully he would feel her presence strongly enough to lead him to wherever she was.

The estate was impressive, as vast and formal looking as any he had ever seen.

He tried not to dwell on what he was up against, what he was asking her to give up for love…of him.

He lifted his banner and raced through the streets of London.

* * *

Vivienne stood at the foot of the gallows, more commonly known as the grand hall steps. The room where her fate was to be announced was one floor up.

Rather than look that way, she plucked a chrysanthemum from an urn, taking what comfort she could from the tickle of the petals on her palm.

'Where is Everett?' Vivienne's father slid a pointed look at her mother, impatience evident in the tight lines creasing the edges of his mouth. 'Dinner will soon be announced.'

'He is here, my dear. I imagine he only wishes to have a bit of time to himself. After the announcement is made he will not have a moment's peace with all the congratulations he will receive.'

Nor would Vivienne. Oh, what wouldn't she give for a moment's peace, as well?

Given a choice, she would be walking on the beach with Clement. Since she did not have one she had spent the afternoon submitting to the ministrations of three maids who were set upon making her beautiful for a fiancé who did not even love her.

This was all a show for society. To demonstrate her father's wealth and position. It had little to do with her. Perhaps not so much to do with Everett either.

They were dancing to society's tune, no matter how either of them felt about it.

She had fought this moment for years and now that

it was upon her, it was worse than she'd ever feared. Dread cramped her stomach.

'Let's go to the dining room and make certain everything is in order.' Father extended his arm to Mother.

'I will meet you there in a moment, my dear.'

Once he was gone her mother touched Vivienne's chin, peering into her face.

'You look exceptionally beautiful, though pale. Are you feeling well?'

'I feel as if I will burst out of my skin.'

'I remember feeling the same way. You will get through the night, I promise.' Mother patted her cheek. 'And now I must join your father.'

Vivienne pressed her stomach. She wanted so badly to see Clement. To feel his arms holding her securely, to get lost in his kiss.

She ought to have let him propose that night. She ought to have accepted and then written her father a letter telling him she could not wed the man of his choice because she was marrying the man of her choice.

Mother paused where the grand hall met the imposing staircase.

'Everett is a good man. It is possible that you will come to love him. It was my experience. But you will recall what I told you about your Great-Aunt Anne. She could not love her first husband because her heart was with another. It is only a shame that she did not

speak to her father before her engagement was announced. He might have listened to her.'

With that her mother went on her way.

Was she giving her advice or telling a story? It had
been too vague to know for certain. Would her father
listen if she went to him? Probably not. Now that he
had her nearly betrothed, he would carry on with it.

Even if Vivienne picked up her elegant skirts and
ran away from all this, what then? Would Clement still
want her after what she had done?

The cramp in her belly crept to her throat.

Footsteps came from the grand hallway. A stranger
came around the corner, looking as miserable as Vivienne felt. The lady clasped her a hand over her mouth,
as if she were startled to see her. Then she dashed
down another hallway.

It was just as well the other woman had not said anything. If Vivienne had to speak to anyone, her throat
would clog and choke her.

She fled to the garden to gather herself.

Outside the air was cool, crisp on the brink of autumn. What, she wondered, was it like this afternoon
on the Isle of Wight? Were Alice and Jayne still romping after their father in search of insects, or had they
gone home to Cheshire?

Or perhaps he was working on his book. Was he,
maybe, thinking of her? Missing her? Probably not.
After the way she had left him without a word, he

could surely only resent her. But she'd had the oddest feeling all day. Even with the bustle going on around her, she had felt her heart reaching for him. Probably because she missed him so intensely.

Yesterday, she had meant to put memories of him to rest, delegate him to a place in her past. A precious episode of her life, lived and now gone. Clearly the attempt had not worked. It made no sense, but she had the oddest feeling that if she turned a corner, suddenly he would be there. He would open his arms and she would run into them. Once she was there, no one would prise her out of his embrace.

Father would not, society would not.

Guilt for what she had done to Clement and his children might keep her from him, though. Guilt held her to this pending engagement as much as anything else. Since she could not have her Clement, she might as well go through with marrying Everett. What did anything really matter without her entomologist?

But then...was that what Great-Aunt Anne had thought? How bitterly had she regretted not fighting for love?

'I love you, Clement Marston,' she said because there was no one nearby to hear.

And that was the last time she would ever speak those words.

Unless...

She stopped where she stood and closed her eyes,

listening to birds chirruping, to leaves shifting in the breeze...to her heart swelling with emotion.

'Should I fight for you?' Did she dare?

'Do it, Vivie. Fight for me as I am fighting for you.'

She went utterly still. This voice was not in her mind...not a dream. It was behind her.

Before she completely turned, Clement's arm stole around her waist. He spun her about, drew her tight to his heart. He tipped her chin.

'Tell me you will. If you love me as I love you, please, Vivie, fight for us.'

'I do love you. But...do you forgive me?'

'I was wrong to blame you. Do you forgive me?'

Before she could nod, he kissed her. For the first time she kissed him back not as a governess, not as an imposter. She, Lady Vivienne Curtis, gave herself completely and without regret to her love. There was one emotion behind this kiss and it was joy...celebration.

Clement had come to fight for her. And now she would fight for him.

Father was formidable, yes—but she was in love.

The last thing Clement was inclined to do was end this kiss. It was the first one that felt truly binding between them. The others had been taken, or surrendered, but this one promised for ever.

'How did you find me?'

By the guiding of Providence, he could only think.

'I crossed paths with a woman—your mother, it turned out to be. When I told her who I was she led me through the house and out to the garden.'

'Truly?'

'Yes, truly. She said something about not ending up like Great-Aunt Anne. I thanked her even though I have no idea what she meant by it. Then your mother shook her head and pointed to where you were.'

It was a lucky thing, too. He would never have found her on his own. The garden, like the house, was immense, with hedges, trees and paths leading in every direction.

'I will explain about Great-Aunt Anne later, but now... Clement, I have missed you so much. Come...'

Gripping his hand, she led him a short distance away to a secluded patio. A pair of doors opened to a room with bookshelves on every wall. It could only be a library.

Once inside, she leaned against the doors, drew him close. He felt her heart thumping, her chest rising and falling with her quick breathing.

'Is this truly real?' She touched his cheek as if to be certain. 'It seems like another dream.'

Hands around her waist, he held her hip to hip. He nipped her lips, kissed her deeply.

'Seems real enough to me.'

He kissed her for a long time, until his lungs ached for air. Partly because he wanted to and partly to be certain she wasn't right and this wasn't actually another dream. Since dreams did not require one to breathe, this was real.

'If this was a dream—mine, I mean—your hair would not look like that.' Seeing it piled in stiff curls on top of her head wasn't what he was used to. He'd only ever seen it wavy and loose.

'Once we have your father's blessing, I will free you from all this,' he said, meaning her rigid coif.

'You might not get it. But apparently you have my mother's.'

'I am glad for that, at least. But, Vivie, all I need is your blessing. All I need is you.' He did need her. Now, urgently, in every way a man needed a woman. But first things first. A formal commitment, a wedding, and then the pleasure of being her husband.

He went down on one knee. This time he would do it the right way. Last time, although he had also loved her then, his motive had been to keep her from leaving him. This time he was offering his heart and his life because he simply couldn't imagine life without her.

'My Vivie, I love you with everything that is in me. Will you marry me?' Ever-prepared fellow that he was, he'd come with a ring. He drew it from his pocket, where it caught the fading sunlight streaming through the window and gleamed.

He heard a sniffle. That was odd since Vivie was

grinning and waggling her hand for him to place the ring on her finger.

'Yes, I will marry you.'

He slipped the ring past her knuckle. A perfect fit. Just as she was a perfect fit for him and his daughters.

'It is the most beautiful thing I have ever seen, Clement. The tiny butterflies take my breath away— oh, and the diamond!' She turned her hand this way and that, clearly admiring it. 'It suits us, don't you think?'

'Love suits us.'

He rose from the floor, kissed her while backing her towards the couch. He eased her down to the cushion, then back. Half-reclined, he kissed her yet again. Somehow he could not get enough of tasting her. This time he felt a hint of her curves under all the clothes she wore. Even if he had intended to get them off her before the vows, which he did not, he would not be able to figure out how.

He contented himself with kisses. She was kept busy giving them back.

'We will be deliriously happy, Clement.'

'I am already delirious.' Getting lightheaded and out of breath. His good intentions were fast losing ground. 'I must speak with your father immediately before I lose control.'

He sat up, drawing her with him. 'Did you hear a noise?' he asked.

She shook her head. 'We must speak to someone else before we speak to Father,' she said, patting her hair although not a strand was out of place. 'Do not forget Everett is involved in this, too.'

So caught up in being with Vivie, winning her hand, he had all but forgotten there was another man believing her hand would be his.

'We do have challenges facing us,' he admitted.

'This won't be easy,' Vivie said while pressing her engagement ring to her heart. 'I do not even know where he is right now.'

All at once a door between the bookcases squeaked open. A woman stepped out.

'I know where he is,' the lady said through her sniffles. She swiped tears from her face with trembling fingers. 'And it might not be as difficult as you imagine.'

Vivienne remembered this woman from earlier. She was the very lady she had encountered in the hall.

Her name was Clara, they discovered while hurrying with her through the garden. What she breathlessly disclosed along the way was stunning.

The stuff of fairytales was what it was turning out to be.

They came upon Everett sitting on a bench beside the south-reflecting pool, head in hand and looking as miserable as she had felt not an hour ago.

And no wonder. He had just bidden a heart-wrenching farewell to the woman he'd fallen in love with over the summer.

Wonder of wonders, while Vivienne had been falling in love with Clement, Everett had been falling in love with Clara.

If he was as devoted to Clara as he'd been to his first wife, she would be a lucky woman.

'Everett.' Clara rushed to him, knelt and spread his hands away from his face. 'There is someone who wishes to speak with you.'

The Marquess stood suddenly when he spotted Vivienne, bringing Clara to her feet along with him.

Casting Everett a tremulous smile, Clara went to stand beside Clement.

'You have met Mrs Newport, I see,' Everett said heavily.

Mrs Newport? A widow, then. No wonder she and Everett had bonded so deeply and so quickly.

'Oh, yes, and quite by surprise,' Vivienne said with a twinkle.

'Then you must surely guess that… At any rate, the lady and I have just said our goodbyes. I intend to honour the agreement I made with your father.'

'That is upstanding of you, Everett, and I appreciate it. But you see, I will not honour it.'

Lines creased the corners of his eyes, showing his

strain when he glanced at Clara and then back at Vivienne.

His pensive gaze reminded her that there was a generation between them.

'You would go against your father's wishes? Are you certain? Walk with me for a moment, my dear. We must discuss this.'

They did not go far, only around a rosebush and an alder.

'There will be consequences to you refusing my suit. Your father will not take it well.'

'He will not die of his disappointment. I do not see why all four of us should suffer broken hearts just to spare his pride.'

'I suppose pride does have something to do with it. The aristocracy does tend to suffer that flaw at times.'

'It can certainly be a trial for their daughters. But, Everett, I am so pleased you found your lady. Please accept my congratulations. Mine and Clement's.'

'Ah, the young man with the broad grin on his face? I assume by the ring on your finger that he has proposed.'

'It took a while, but here we are.'

'I envy you, Vivienne. Being young and in love is a wonderful thing. My best wishes to you both.'

'Thank you. And now that we are not to become engaged, you are at liberty to propose to Clara.'

'I intend to, just as soon as I am able.' He started to

lift his hand, but let it drop. She wondered if he'd meant to pat her on the head. 'I admit I did struggle with your youth as you must have struggled with my age. But we would have made an adequate match, I think.'

'Not a happy one, though. Not with me weeping for Clement and you pining for Clara.'

'Indeed, not a happy one. Since I did not expect to fall in love again, I agreed to marry you in order to secure the future of the title. And if I could please my stepmother at the same time, all the better. I suppose your reason was much the same.'

'Yes, I did wish to make Great-Aunt Anne happy. I hope she does not take this too badly.'

'She is resilient. And don't forget she has a soft spot for love matches.'

'No point in putting this off, is there? I shall find my father right away and give him the news.'

'No, my dear, it must come from me. If I back out of our arrangement there is nothing he can do about it. I am afraid it would not go as well for you.'

'You are a gallant man, Everett. I shall make certain Father understands I am completely in agreement with you.'

'Shall we get on with it, then? I have a lady to propose to.'

A lucky lady, Vivienne thought. She was happy to have the Marquess as a friend. And grateful for ever that he would not be her husband.

* * *

'I rather doubt that they have eloped, Thomas,' Vivienne heard her mother say as she and Everett approached the doorway leading to the grand hall. 'Take a breath and calm yourself.'

Clement and Clara followed a few steps behind.

'My boy would not do such a thing, you know that, or you would not have agreed to let him have our Vivienne,' said Great-Aunt Anne.

'Good, my stepmother is with them,' Everett whispered while they paused out of sight. 'Better to get this said with all of them together.'

Vivienne peered around the corner. 'It is only the three of them.'

'The guests will be in the dining room by now, waiting for us to make our grand appearance.'

Everyone would suspect the reason for the gathering. Anticipation would be running high. What high-ranking gentleman would finally win the hand of the reluctant Lady Vivienne? they would be wondering.

Vivienne glanced back at Clement who in her eyes was the highest ranking of them all. He did not notice since he was busy murmuring reassurances to Clara that all would be well.

Clement walked into the hall in step with Lord Winterfeld, even though it was the Marquess who would be delivering the news. Perhaps it was presumptuous to take this position when he had no rank other than the brother of a baron.

He might be the Honourable Clement Marston, but all he had to present himself as was a man in love. A stubborn one who would not leave this grand mansion without being granted the hand of the Marquess of Helmond's daughter.

One thing went in his favour. It was easier to capture an insect when it was stunned and although Vivienne's father was not an insect, he would be stunned to his core.

The principle might hold.

He matched the Marquess of Winterfeld's strides, his shoulders set as firm as his determination.

'Ah!' Lord Helmond declared. 'There you are. We are ready to begin.'

'Before we do, Thomas, I would like a word.'

Clement knew the Marquess must notice him standing beside them, but Vivie's father's attention was focused on Everett.

'A quick word, I hope. Our guests are anticipating the announcement.'

Vivienne's mother took a spot on one side of her husband, then nodded for the lady who must be Great-Aunt Anne to take his arm on the other side. In his mind he saw them flanking the fellow in support of

Vivienne. It might not be true, but it was comforting thinking they did.

Lady Helmond had pointed him toward her daughter in the garden so perhaps he already had her support.

While her endorsement would be welcome, if he did not have it he would still leave here being granted Vivie's hand...somehow.

'I see that you found her.' Vivienne's mother spoke to him, but it was her daughter she smiled at.

'My deep thanks, Marchioness. I would never have managed on my own.'

'Found her?' Vivienne's father arched a brow at his wife, then lowered it at Clement. 'What is this about?'

Great-Aunt Anne spotted Clara standing beside Vivie near a potted palm several paces back. She crossed the foyer, took both of Clara's hands and gave them a squeeze.

'My dear, I am so pleased to see you out of mourning. You look...' She tipped her head this way and that. Then with a glance at her stepson, she smiled. 'Oh, I see.

'What does everyone in this room see that I do not?' the Marquess of Helmond asked.

'I'm afraid I must back out of our agreement, Thomas. Over the course of the summer, matters have changed.'

Lord Helmond's complexion went through a few shades, but settled on pulsing crimson.

'You would insult my daughter? Tonight, when we have guests anticipating a betrothal announcement? I would not have expected this of you, Everett.'

'But, Father, I am not at all insulted. Truly.' Vivienne hurried forward, standing next to Clement rather than either marquess.

'Yes, dear.' Vivie's mother patted her husband's arm. 'Our Vivienne is in love.'

'With this fellow?' Lord Helmond seemed a formidable man, but Clement had no intention of being cowed. 'I do not even know who he is. Why have I not met him before?'

'I believe he has obligations which keep him in the country most of the time,' Lady Helmond pointed out.

'I am an entomologist. And I am in love with your daughter.'

He could point out that his brother was Baron Granville, but the connection was unlikely to impress a marquess.

More, he was who he was and would stand on that.

'Love? What has love got to do with it?' Vivie's father looked like a storm ready to burst.

'Love has everything to do with it. Open your eyes, Thomas. You will see that my boy is completely smitten with our friend Clara.' Great-Aunt Anne beamed at them all.

'I am in love with her,' the Marquess of Winterfeld declared.

'You see, no one wishes for this engagement, Thomas, only you.' Great-Aunt Anne was smiling at Clara when she said so.

'Perhaps because I have houseful of guests and no announcement to make.'

Ah, Thomas Curtis was properly stunned. This was Clement's moment.

'May I have a private word, Lord Helmond?'

'Private does not seem to be the order of the hour. You may speak to me in company. And if it is not an inconvenience, may I have your name?'

'No inconvenience at all, my lord. I am Clement Marston. I have been eager to meet you.'

'Ah, Marston, my daughter's former employer.' Quite clearly, Vivienne's father did not look pleased to meet the man his daughter had spent the summer with.

'Mr Marston is the brother of Baron Granville,' Vivienne pointed out.

The name must not be one the Marquess recognised immediately for he pursed his mouth.

'I believe you have met the Baron once before, my dear,' Lady Helmond murmured. 'The family is well respected...and the baronetcy is a prosperous one, I believe.'

'Indeed? Perhaps I did then. I meet a great many people.'

Lord Helmond stared at him, the silence strained, but Clement did make the observation that the corner of the man's mouth twitched.

In humour or anger, he had no way of knowing. What he did know was that it made no difference to what he intended to do.

'I stand before you, my lord, to request the very great honour of your daughter's hand in marriage.'

The Marquess responded with an ungentlemanly grunt. Understandable, given that the man was being asked to hand over his daughter to a complete stranger and an untitled one at that.

'Tell me, Mr Marston, why would I not seek a fellow of higher rank than you?'

'Because no man will be more devoted to your daughter than I will be.'

The man looked back and forth between him and Vivie, probably torn between what he wanted for his daughter and what she wanted for herself.

All of a sudden his heart softened and he understood Lord Helmond's dilemma. There was every chance that Clement would one day stand in the fellow's shoes...twice.

'I understand your hesitation, my lord. But I will not leave here without having your blessing.'

'And you love this man, Vivienne? You will not consider another?'

'No, Father. There is no other man in the world I would touch a beetle for,' she said firmly.

'Touch a beetle? You did that?' Vivie's father tipped his head, narrowed his gaze as if judging the truth of what she said. He shrugged, then looked back at Clement. 'I have been rescuing her from insects ever since she was two years old.'

'You will always be my hero, Father, but now...'

She displayed her hand to her mother, then her father. 'This is my engagement ring. You see the sweet little butterflies. I am no longer afraid.'

'Oh, my dear, it is lovely.' Lady Helmond hugged her daughter while Great-Aunt Anne hurried over to have a look at the unusual ring.

'Well, Mr Marston, clearly you have won my daughter's heart.' The Marquess's expression was too stern for Clement to believe he was overly pleased. Which in no way put him off his purpose. 'I'd have preferred that you had asked me for her hand before you gave her the ring.'

Then the oddest thing happened.

Lord Helmond grinned and slapped Clement on the back. 'You have my consent and my blessing. Welcome to the family, my boy. I was losing all hope that any man would catch Vivienne. You should be warned, though, my daughter is stubbornly independent.'

'It is only one of the qualities I admire about her, Sir.'

'We've done it, Eleanor.' Lord Helmond turned his

triumphant grin on Lady Helmond. 'We've finally got her settled.'

'She gave us a good struggle over the years, didn't she?'

'We will announce your engagement as intended, young lady. Your guests are waiting.'

That said, the Marquess enfolded his child in a hug.

'Thomas,' Everett, who had been standing in the background through it all, said. 'Since this was to be an event to announce my engagement as well, would you mind carrying through with it? As long as Clara will have me.'

Everett went down on one knee, took her hand and kissed it tenderly.

Clara gasped and accepted his proposal.

'Two announcements! We shall be the talk of society.' Lady Helmond waved to the butler who had been standing near the door.

'Smith, please take Mr Marston to my husband's chamber and find him something appropriate to wear. They are of a size.'

'This is all so romantic.' Great-Aunt Anne hugged Clara.

Then she hugged Vivienne. 'You are a far bolder girl than I was, my darling. I admire you for not making my mistake.'

No more than Clement did. After meeting the Marquess, one of society's loftiest men, he understood how hard this all must have been for Vivie.

'Can you imagine, Thomas?' Lady Helmond glowed in pure happiness. 'A son-in-law and a… Oh, well I do not quite know what Clara will be to us, but some sort of family relation, to be sure. Isn't it wonderful to see our family growing at last?'

Clement was halfway up the grand stairway when he heard Vivie say, 'More than you know. I am to be a mother.'

Everyone went still. Had an insect been creeping across the floor they would have heard its scratchy feet.

'Alice and Jayne,' she explained hastily. 'Clement's daughters. I told you about them, Mother. You have granddaughters!'

'You did tell me, darling. From all you had to say about them, they remind me of you.'

'Heaven help us, then,' Vivie's father said with a smile.

Heaven had and that was a fact.

Clement grinned down at his intended. He would no longer need to schedule a trip to find adventure.

Simply waking each day with Lady Vivie Marston would be the adventure of his lifetime.

Vivienne's parents had spared no expense for her engagement announcement.

There was a feast for their hundred closest friends, an orchestra and dancing.

It was lovely. But the truth was she would have been just as happy celebrating on the beach with only breaking surf and moonlight to wish them well.

'We are engaged,' she murmured to her fiancé while he danced her out of the open ballroom doors and into the garden. 'Can you believe it?'

'It depends.'

'Depends on what?' He twirled her down the patio stairs and it felt as light as flying.

'If one looks at the facts, how often does a lady meant to be a marchioness end up the wife of an entomologist?' he asked. 'Statistically it is beyond unlikely. It may never have happened in the history of England.'

At the bottom of the steps he simply held her, swaying as if they were still dancing. How delightful to live in a musical embrace.

'But then there is love. If you base it on how much I love you... Vivie, it was destined to be.'

'Destined.' She slipped her arms about his neck, swaying ever closer to him.

Then he kissed her for a long time. She kissed him back even longer. During it, he tried to pluck a pin from her hair.

'It's no use,' she said against his lips. 'I think my maid used paste. I will not have to arrange my hair again until our wedding.'

'Please say it will be a short engagement.'

'I would say so, but I cannot. My parents have been so accepting of us. We must give them a proper engagement.'

'It will be a grand event, won't it?'

'The talk of London.'

'I suppose I shall survive the ordeal, but only out of love for you.' More kisses, closer swaying. 'The worst of it will be missing you.'

'But why will you miss me?'

'Because you live in London. I live in Cheshire.' He breathed on her ear, nipping the lobe which gave her a shiver.

Feathers, why did society engagements have to be so long?

'Have you dismissed me as your governess?'

'Now that we are engaged I do not see how you can work for me. We can no longer live in the same house until we are married.'

'One would think a researcher would be more logical. See the obvious answer to the challenge.'

'Right now, the researcher is being kissed and he is not thinking clearly.'

'Let me help you then.' She traced his lips with the tip of her finger, watching the torch glow glimmer on her engagement ring. Even now she could not believe the past several hours had happened.

Clement twirled her about, probably in an attempt

to keep up the pretence of dancing in case anyone was out walking in the garden. Glancing about she did spot two couples. Everett and Clara vanished behind a curve in the garden path. Grace and George were coming around the same curve, but returning from one of the secluded alcoves.

Spotting her and Clement, Grace waved her hand. George nodded and grinned.

'We cannot be wed soon enough,' she said with a great deal of envy that her sister and her husband could...well, better to leave that a thought for another time. Dwelling on it would make her as unfocused as Clement was.

Until she explained the solution to their dilemma, she needed to keep her mind clear and not muddled with intimate imaginings.

'You know I will not let another governess take my place with Alice and Jayne.'

'I pity the woman who tries to.'

'Quite. And so I will be Alice's and Jayne's governess until I am their mother.'

'Hmmm,' he whispered into the stiff hair near her ear. 'Shall we move to London then?'

'I could not be a governess here. It would be a great scandal. What I shall do is live with Great-Aunt Anne in Cheshire. During the day I will be your governess and then each night I will return and dream of you as I lie alone in bed.'

'I don't know why I didn't think of that.'

'You were not thinking with your logical mind, that's what you said.'

'I wonder if researchers place too much importance on logic.'

'Oh, well, I suppose it depends upon what they are researching.'

Several kisses later they stopped to breathe.

'In some cases research is all one wants to do…a fellow could work all night long on it.'

'And his assistant along with him.'

A moth flapped around their heads.

'Ah, to see a moth on one's engagement night is good luck,' he declared.

Vivienne touched the grin she adored, tracing the flat line, then the upward curve.

'Even if you are making that up, I shall believe it's true.'

'Our love is true, that's all that needs to be believed.'

The moth circled their heads, then fluttered towards the stars where, she suspected, wonders and miracles came from.

London—one year later

Clement decided he was a saint. During the year between his engagement party and his wedding reception, he had been the soul of discretion when it came to his fiancée. Working side by side with her on their new project had been a daily temptation. It hadn't helped that the subject they were exploring was the mating rituals of insects.

Now, with their vows spoken and the wedding breakfast eaten, he was finished with being discreet. It was time to explore the mating rituals of Mr and Mrs Clement Marston.

'Come, Wife,' he said after a well-wisher moved on from the ornately decorated table where they had just finished a magnificent feast. 'I believe that is the last of them. I have something special for you…in our chamber.'

His bride touched the corner of his grin as she was fond of doing. 'Do you? What could it be?'

Their chamber was actually a suite of rooms reserved in the Helmond mansion for him, Vivie and the girls. His mother and father-in-law had made sure to design the suite with a room included as a nursery.

His bride slid her fingertip across his mouth. Ah, then, let the mating ritual begin.

'I like it when you touch me that way.'

'If you like that,' she said while rising from her chair, 'you will love it when I touch the special thing you have for me in our chamber.'

He bolted out of his chair, her hand tightly held in his.

Across the room, he saw Mrs Prentis laugh and nudge Mr Prentis in the side.

It would be proper to bid each of their guests an individual farewell, but it would take too much time. He had already waited a year as it was.

Alice and Jayne would not notice they were gone. That very moment they were romping in the garden with a few other children. When the breakfast ended and the guests went home, they were to be taken somewhere for the night by their new grandparents. Exactly where they were going escaped him right now.

The main thing was that they would be occupied so that he and his bride could also be…occupied.

Taking the stairs to their suite, arms entwined, he was completely focused on being alone with Vivienne. Alone in a way which had been forbidden to them until a couple of hours ago.

The past year had been a good one and he would not have traded a moment of it. However, he was relieved it was finally over and the waiting was done. At last Vivienne Marston was his to have and to hold… especially to hold.

'Give me a hint about my surprise,' she urged.

'It is large.'

'Oh, my…tell me more.' His bride had an inquisitive mind and a pretty blush to go with it.

'Ah, well, it is hard until it is unveiled. After that it is more bendable.'

'Bendable?' Vivie's eyes went wide. She blinked.

'Malleable, if you wish… Perhaps even pliant?'

Her jaw dropped.

Perhaps he should not tease her this way. Any more of it and he would laugh out loud, spoil everything before he got her alone.

Better to have rooms here than at the Granville town house. The Helmond mansion was huge, the grounds were lovely and, most importantly, Mildred lived miles away. While his sister-in-law no longer tried to interfere with his family, she was still an unpleasant relative.

Still, they would spend most of their time in Cheshire where life was fresh and healthy for the children...for the ones they already had and the ones still to come.

Coming to the doors of their suite, he did not open them at first, but pressed her between the wood and his body.

'You, Vivienne Marston, are the most beautiful woman I have ever seen. I cannot believe you are my bride. Are you ready for your surprise?'

'I am and I might have a surprise or two of my own for you.'

'You fascinate me, my bride. I can scarcely think a clear thought wondering what your surprise...or two might be.'

He kissed her while he turned the knob, slowly opening the door.

Without letting go of her mouth, he shut the door

with his boot heel. He backed her across the small drawing room.

Afternoon light filtered inside, but heavy curtains blocked most of it. The room had a soft romantic aura that even firelight could not match for romance. Besides, there would be no firelight until later tonight. He had no patience to wait for it. To his delight, it did not seem that Vivie had the patience to wait either.

When he figured they were near the desk, he broke the kiss, but covered her eyes with his fingers. One finger slipped and he felt his bride give it a nip, a kiss.

He turned her about, then dropped his hand. 'There, you have your surprise.'

She stared for a moment, probably not believing what she was seeing. 'Our book!' She dashed forward, picked it up and hugged it to her chest. With a squeal of delight, she twirled. Her skirts flared around her as if they also expressed happiness.

'Fresh from the publisher. My wedding gift to you.'

She slid her fingers along the binding. 'Hard, just like you said.' The glance she gave him was long, simmering and slipping slowly down the front of him.

After a moment, she set the book down on the desk, opened it and turned the pages, sighing over each photograph and drawing. 'Bendable, just like you said… pliable…quite malleable.' Finished, she closed the book, set it back down. 'We ought to do something about that.'

'I think you already have.' He shifted his weight from one foot to the other.

She took him by the hand, drew him towards their bedchamber.

Crossing the rug, he plucked pins from her hair, tugged stiff loops, sifting them though with his fingers until they were silky again.

'Thank you,' he whispered, then went to work on dress buttons that were too small for his fingers to undo quickly. Luckily he was a diligent man.

'For what, Husband? I have barely begun act like a proper bride.'

'The thanks were going to the Good Lord for the turn our lives have taken. And now...' With the wicked buttons finally conquered, the dress fell away. 'And now I am only yards of lace away from being a proper groom.'

She gave a low, throaty laugh. 'We shall free me together. We have always done brilliant work while exploring shoulder to shoulder.'

If there was one thing he appreciated, it was the thrill of exploration.

'Let me see, now. Shoulder to shoulder.' He traced the curve of her shoulder, the bend of her elbow where her gown had fallen away. 'Hip to hip,' he murmured while drawing her close, his hands tugging the spot where the nip of her waist gave way to the curve of her hips. 'Let's see how brilliant we can be.'

As it turned out, they were brilliant all night. And all next morning, too.

Beyond a doubt, Mr and Mrs Marston would be brilliant together for the rest of their lives.

* * * * *

If you enjoyed this story,
be sure to check out these standalone
Historical romances
from Carol Arens

Meeting Her Promised Viscount
The Gentleman's Cinderella Bride
Marriage Charade with the Heir

Or let yourself get swept up in her charming
The Rivenhall Weddings miniseries

Inherited as the Gentleman's Bride
In Search of a Viscountess
A Family for the Reclusive Baron

COMING SOON!

We really hope you enjoyed reading this book.
If you're looking for more romance
be sure to head to the shops when
new books are available on

Thursday 24th October

To see which titles are coming soon, please visit

millsandboon.co.uk/nextmonth

MILLS & BOON

MILLS & BOON®

Coming next month

ONE NIGHT WITH THE DUCHESS
Maggie Weston

'And you're here because…'

She exhaled a deep breath. 'I've come because…'

'Yes?' It was a single word, a simple word, but it left Matthew's lips weighted with anticipation.

'May I ask a favour?'

'You may ask,' he countered, 'but I will most probably refuse.'

'I would like you to bed me.'

Having become somewhat used to people expecting such behaviour from him, Matthew smiled grimly. But, in spite of that, when he said, 'No,' the word left his lips tasting bitter.

*

Isabelle was startled at the abrupt answer, issued from Lord Ashworth with no hint of doubt. 'You're not even going to *think* about it?'

The giant man standing in front of her grinned, his white teeth flashing wolfishly. He ran one large hand through his unstylishly shaggy hair.

'There's no need. I don't *bed* virgins. I don't ruin reputations—'

'That is not what I heard.'

Matthew ignored her comment. 'And I certainly will not be led by the nose into a situation where you could hold any sort of power over me. I'm not the man you're looking for, *Duchess*.'

Isabelle couldn't help the slightly hysterical giggle that worked its way up her throat. 'You… You think that I would trick you into *marriage*?' she asked, somewhat stunned by the notion. 'Have you not been listening to anything I've said?' She waved both hands down towards her heavy black dress. 'I'm in *mourning*. I will be for *years!*' she practically shouted. 'And even if I wasn't, marriage to you is the *last* thing I'd want!'

Because she felt hot and flustered by his looming presence and the entirely inappropriate conversation they were having, she started to pace.

She lowered her voice. 'I'm a *duchess*. I don't need your title. And marrying again before my mourning period is over would cause a scandal that would be completely antagonistic to my main goal—helping Luke.' When he only raised his eyebrows, she continued, 'Moreover, I have no *desire* to get married again.'

'But you're not a duchess—technically. And am I just supposed to trust whatever you say?'

Isabelle turned abruptly to find that he'd closed the space between them, and that instead of looking at his face she was staring at a patch of tanned skin where his collar lay open. She slowly craned her neck back, shifting her eyes away from his chest to his steel gaze.

'Do you honestly believe that I'd be here with any other motive? That I'd want to lose my—' she lowered her voice '—my *maidenhead* to a stranger whose name I picked off a list?'

Lord Ashworth did not try to fight his grin. 'You have a list?'

Continue reading
ONE NIGHT WITH THE DUCHESS
Maggie Weston

Available next month
millsandboon.co.uk

LET'S TALK
Romance

For exclusive extracts, competitions and special offers, find us online:

f MillsandBoon

X @MillsandBoon

◎ @MillsandBoonUK

♪ @MillsandBoonUK

Get in touch on 01413 063 232